John Kenrick

Biographical Memoir of the Late Rev. Charles Wellbeloved

John Kenrick

Biographical Memoir of the Late Rev. Charles Wellbeloved

ISBN/EAN: 9783337016197

Printed in Europe, USA, Canada, Australia, Japan

Cover: Foto ©Raphael Reischuk / pixelio.de

More available books at **www.hansebooks.com**

A BIOGRAPHICAL MEMOIR

REV. CHARLES WELLBELOVED.

BY

JOHN KENRICK, M.A., F.S.A.

Aptissima omnino sunt arma senectutis artes exercitationesque
virtutum, quæ in omni ætate cultæ, quum multum diuque vixeris
mirificos efferunt fructus; non solum quia nunquam deserunt, ne in
extremo quidem tempore ætatis, verum etiam quia conscientia bene
actæ vitæ, multorumque benefactorum recordatio jucundissima est.

CICERO DE SENECTUTE.

LONDON:
EDWARD T. WHITFIELD, 178, STRAND.

1860.

PREFACE.

THE memory of Mr. Wellbeloved has been honoured by various biographical tributes, which, if they have not exhausted the subject, have necessarily anticipated a part of the contents of the present volume. The memoir which occupies three numbers of the Christian Reformer,* in particular, enters fully into the events of his life, and contains a very just and affectionate appreciation of his talents, his virtues, and his public services. Indeed, the writers, having been formerly his pupils, have enjoyed means of describing what he was, in one of his most important relations, which I have not possessed. Yet it seems to be a duty for me, who knew him more intimately than any one now living, to give a picture of his life derived from that intimacy, or from materials not at the command of other biographers.

His life must be written with the disadvantage, that the author is precluded from some sources of interest which are available for the lives of men of humbler station and less eminent attainments. I

* October and November 1858. January 1859.

do not mean from its being destitute of great
events and changes of fortune: they are not to be
looked for in the biography of a pastor, a theologian, and an instructor of youth, sixty-six years
of whose life were spent in the duties of these professions, and in a provincial city. The narrative,
even of a life so uniform and so tranquil, might
have an interest of its own, if means existed for
tracing the earliest influences by which the character
was formed, and its growth and development in
advancing years; and laying open the thoughts
and feelings of the mind, during the most important crises of life. The materials for such a
history have sometimes been found in an auto-
biographical sketch, in a diary, in a copious and
varied correspondence, or in oral communications.
In the present case, all these materials are scanty.
A very brief notice of his school and college life is
all that Mr. Wellbeloved has left; his diaries are
little more than hour-tables of each day's work and
engagements, valuable as evidence of the methodical employment of his time, and the variety of his
occupations, but generally without detail of events,
or expression of sentiment. For the first few years,
after leaving College, he kept up a correspondence
with two or three of his former associates; but his
increasing labours compelled him to lay it aside,
and for many years he wrote hardly any letters
except on business, or briefly to his family in

absence. Writing to his youngest son, then a student at the College of Glasgow, in 1820, he says, "The time of your residence in Glasgow has passed so quickly, and my attention has been, through the whole of it, so incessantly occupied, that I have had little leisure even for letters that I have been obliged to write, and less for those that I felt I could defer from day to day. Letter-writing may be a great amusement to those who have little else to do, and much spare time on their hands, but for one who is writing on very different matters several hours of every day, and who can at no hour say that there is nothing which *demands* his attention, and which *must* be done at that hour, epistolary correspondence is a toil, not a pleasure, and will therefore generally be neglected." Had he laid open his mind in confidential letters, I should have felt myself precluded from using them, by the strong disapprobation which he expressed of the practice of publishing such communications. Nor have I derived much knowledge of his life from his conversation. He seemed to feel that there was something of egotism in speaking of himself, and the more deeply its events interested him, the less was he inclined to make them the subjects of discourse. His biography must, therefore, be chiefly the narrative of his outward life. Such, however, was its manifold activity, its wide-spread influence, its conscientious devotion to the fulfilment of duty, that its history cannot fail to be instructive and encouraging. I have endeavoured to furnish such a history, from the sources which were at my command. The relation in which I stood to him may be thought to have disqualified me for an impartial estimate of his character; but the facts of his life will give a testimony which is above suspicion.

A natural wish has been expressed for the publication of a volume which should contain some of his sermons and other compositions. As regards his sermons, it will be seen that he has left no option to his executor;* nor is there anything in his other MSS. which it would be just to his memory to publish. This circumstance has induced me to make fuller extracts from his publications and speeches than I should otherwise have done. It has occurred to me, however, that a selection might be made from the Reflections contained in his Family Bible, perhaps with some condensation, which would render them more generally known, and more extensively useful; and thus promote the cherished objects of the labour of his life, the due appreciation, intelligent reading and practical application of the Holy Scriptures.

J. K.

York, *Dec.* 1850.

* See p. 161 of this volume.

CONTENTS.

BIOGRAPHICAL MEMOIR

OF THE

REV. CHARLES WELLBELOVED.

CHAPTER I.

CHILDHOOD AND SCHOOL LIFE.

1769—1785.

CHARLES, the only child of John and Elizabeth Wellbeloved (whose maiden name was Plaw), was born April 6, 1769, in Denmark Street, St. Giles's, and baptized at the parish church on the 25th of the same month. The marriage of his parents was not a happy one, and he was removed, when about four years old, to Mortlake. His earliest recollection was of finding himself in the house of his paternal grandfather, situated in a large garden, in which his maternal grandfather had also his residence. His paternal grandfather, whose Christian name he bore, had removed from Cobham in Surrey to Mortlake. He was possessed of a competent property, which ultimately descended to his grandson, and he is styled gentleman, at a time when that title was less indiscriminately bestowed than at present. He appears to have been strongly attached to the child, the care of whom had been cast upon him, and, being himself of a very amiable temper, he easily gained his affection in return. The boy became his companion in his walks and occupations. Though in communion with the Church of England, he was strongly attached to Methodism, and his grandson was taken by him to those early morning services which the founders of Methodism had introduced among their followers, partly to avoid interfering with the hours of church service, partly to give an opportunity to the working classes to join in worship and listen to a sermon before the labours of the day began. If we are to seek for the germ of the habits of after-life in the circumstances of childhood, we might plausibly attribute the practice of early rising, for which Mr. Wellbeloved was so remarkable, to these morning visits to the meetings of the Wesleyans. A safer inference would be that the strong devotional feeling which characterized him through life was cherished by the habits of his grandfather and the religious earnestness and fervour which he would witness among his associates. This was the apostolic age of Wesleyan Methodism, when its preachers were " in perils by their own countrymen, in weariness and painfulness, in watchings often, in labours abundant"; and when the pious and benevolent spirit of its founders had not been narrowed by bigotry* nor debased by worldly ambition. John Wesley was a frequent guest at the house at Mortlake; Mr. Wellbeloved had often heard him preach; he was early familiar with his writings, and in later life used to dwell with pleasure on the circumstance that he had sat on the venerable man's knee and received his blessing. Some of his grandfather's connections belonged to the Calvinistic section of the Methodists, and to one of these his guardianship was entrusted during his minority.

He received the earliest part of his education, according to the custom of the times, when "preparatory schools" were unknown, in a dame-school at Mortlake, from which he was transferred to the charge of the Rev. Mr. Delafosse at Richmond, his grandfather having removed to a house between that place and Mortlake. He always spoke with great respect of his master, though he lamented that the classical instruction of the school was deficient in that careful training in the minutiæ of grammar and prosody which then characterized, almost exclusively, the great schools of England.

* "My brother and I set out upon two principles. 1. None go to heaven without holiness of heart and life. 2. Whoever follows after this is my brother and sister, and mother. And we have not swerved a hair's breadth from either of these to this day."—*John Wesley to Samuel Sparrow, Esq.*, 1773.

It cost him much labour, when he became himself a teacher, to supply this defect in his early education. He was, however, distinguished among his school-fellows, and was noticed for his proficiency by Dr. Demainbray, the astronomer of George the Third's private observatory at Kew. He resided at Richmond, and was a frequent visitor at Mr. Delafosse's school.

The improving life which Mr. Wellbeloved led at Richmond was interrupted, when he was in his fourteenth year, by the death of his grandfather in June, 1782. He was carried off by the epidemic catarrh, which visited England after an interval of half a century, and then first became known by the name of influenza.* By the dispositions of his grandfather's will, his guardianship devolved upon a person of the name of Blackhall, a schoolmaster at Brentford. By him he was removed from Mr. Delafosse's care, and placed at a cheaper but very inferior school at Greenwich, and while he remained there his vacations were spent at his guardian's house. His grandfather had made provision for his being brought up to business, and accordingly, after little more than a year, he was

---

* He was one of the victims of the injudicious lowering treatment then adopted by medical men, and repeated even in our times. Mr. Cappe had nearly lost his life by the bleeding which he underwent when attacked by the influenza in the same year.—*See Mrs. Cappe's Memoirs*, p. 228.

placed in the shop of Messrs. Stock and Cooper,
drapers, of Holborn Hill. The connection was
not satisfactory to either party. Business was
very repugnant to Mr. Wellbeloved's tastes, and
his employers found that his love of reading interfered with that exclusive attention to their concerns which they reasonably required. I doubt if
he was really bound apprentice to Stock and
Cooper. His associate, while in their service, was
Mr. Watson, who afterwards married a daughter
of Mr. Stock, and for many years carried on the
business; and his nephew, Mr. John Watson,
whose name is so well known for many acts of
liberality, informed me that his uncle spoke of Mr.
Wellbeloved as not having been an apprentice, but
coming as an experiment, to see whether the occupation would suit him. It proved utterly uncon-
genial, and he used to say that he learnt nothing
there but how to tie up a parcel, and that he was
glad to escape from it, before he had forgotten all
that he had been taught at Richmond. If he was
only a probationer he would have the less scruple
in showing how much he felt himself to be out of
his place.

CHAPTER II.

COLLEGE LIFE.

1785—1792.

I DO not know when the desire of devoting himself
to the ministry first entered Mr. Wellbeloved's
mind, or what circumstances led to the choice of
Homerton Academy as the place of his education.
His guardian was orthodox, and it must have been
with a view to the ministry among the orthodox
dissenters that he became a student there in 1785;
so that we may conclude him to have no further
deviated from the opinions in which he had been
brought up, than to have ceased to be a Churchman. Homerton Academy was then very different from what it became under the learned pre-
sidency of Dr. Pye Smith; but I believe it was
not inferior in reputation to the other orthodox
dissenting academies in London and the neighbourhood. Dr. Davies was the resident tutor, and
teacher of classics and mathematics; Dr. Fisher,
tutor in divinity; Dr. Mayo, in oratory and elocution. Mr. Wellbeloved was not on the foundation,
but a private pupil of Dr. Davies, and, as such,
enjoyed more independence than the students in

general. Of Dr. Davies individually he spoke
with regard; and it is probable that during the
two years of his residence at the academy, his
time was chiefly devoted to the branches of study
which were under his special direction. But there
were several young men then studying for the
ministry at Homerton, who were far advanced in
their departure from the orthodoxy of their tutors.
The secession of Mr. Lindsey from the establishment, and the opening of the chapel in Essex
Street seven years before, his various defences of
Unitarianism, and, above all, the theological publications of Dr. Priestley, had awakened a spirit of
earnest inquiry into the scriptural evidence of the
Trinity and its dependent dogmas. When the
clergy of the Church of England were so dissatisfied with the doctrines of her articles, as to peti-
tion Parliament for relief from subscription to
them, it is not wonderful that, in a dissenting
academy, heretical opinions should spring up.
Homerton contained at this time several students
of independent spirit and considerable intellectual
ability, who had renounced the orthodox creed,
and subsequently became ministers to Unitarian
congregations—David Jones, David Jardine, William Field, and Thomas Porter. With the two
first of these Mr. Wellbeloved lived in intimate
friendship, and both had great influence in producing the change in his religious opinions which

took place at Homerton. David Jones was the
son of a Welsh landed proprietor, at Bwlch, near
Llandovery, in South Wales, from which circumstance he was led to adopt the signature of " A
Welsh Freeholder " in the defences of Unitarianism against Horsley, then Bishop of St. David's,
which he subsequently published. In a letter to
Mr. Wellbeloved, written several years after his
settlement at York, he speaks of himself as having
been a principal instrument " in bringing you out
of the land of Egyptian bondage;" from which I
conclude that it was to him chiefly that Mr. Wellbeloved's change of opinions was due, as far as it
was at all dependent on personal influences. To
this circumstance I attribute the kindly feeling
which he long retained towards David Jones,
when he had shown himself little worthy of his
esteem. He was compelled to leave Homerton
for his heretical opinions at the close of the first
session which Mr. Wellbeloved spent there ; and
he was one of the students of the New College in
the year which preceded its establishment at Hackney, when the lectures were delivered at Dr. Williams's Library. After finishing his course there,
he became minister of the New Meeting Congregation, Birmingham, then temporarily united, after
the riots, with the Old Meeting Congregation, and
occupying a building in Livery Street. He was a
man of considerable vigour of mind, but of a rest-

less and ambitious temper. Whether the sceptical
spirit of the times had undermined his religious
belief, or he professed scepticism as an excuse for
a conformity to which he was prompted by ambition, I do not know; but when he abandoned the
ministry and entered himself of Caius College,
with a view to taking a degree and being called
to the bar, he justified subscription to the Thirty-
nine Articles, by alleging that all religious opinions
were, in his view, equally uncertain.

David Jardine, Mr. Wellbeloved's other chosen
associate at Homerton, was a man of much purer
and more amiable character. He was the son of
a Welsh dissenting minister of strongly Calvinistic
opinions, a colleague of Dr. Davies in an academical
institution in South Wales. By reading the works
of Dr. Priestley, he had become a Unitarian; and,
as this made him obnoxious to the authorities, he
left the academy and removed to Daventry. After
a short settlement at Warwick, he accepted an invitation to Bath. Mr. Wellbeloved was so much
attached to him, that when he had concluded his
studies at Hackney he meditated a removal to
Bath, in order to live with his friend, a scheme
not carried into effect, owing to the matrimonial
engagements entered into by both of them. Mr.
Jardine died suddenly in 1797, and Mr. Wellbeloved preached a sermon on occasion of his death,
on the blank leaf of which is this emphatic sen-

tence : "A true friend, a firm and zealous defender
of the truth, an able minister of the gospel, a wise
and virtuous man."

Mr. Wellbeloved, not being on the foundation,
could not be summarily dismissed, as David Jones
had been ; but it was intimated to Dr. Davies by
the body which, from their place of meeting in
the Poultry, was called "The King's Head Committee," that his pupil, who was known to be
tainted with the same heresies, could not be permitted to return after the close of the session of
1786–7.* Probably they only anticipated a step
which he would himself have taken, since, besides
David Jones, Jardine, Field, and Porter left Homerton on account of their heresy. His metropolitan education and connections would naturally
incline him to transfer himself to the New College
at Hackney, rather than to Daventry, to which
Jardine, Field, and Porter had removed. He accordingly entered there, in the autumn of 1787, as
a student on his own foundation.

The contrast must have been in every respect
in favour of his new situation. The College was
a spacious and handsome building, surrounded
with pleasure-grounds, and affording ample accom-

---

* From the account now given of Mr. Wellbeloved's connection
with Homerton may be estimated the value of Mr. George Hadfield's
declaration, in the Notes to the Report of the Charity Commissioners,
"that Mr. Wellbeloved was a professed Independent, and was educated by that denomination in their own views of church discipline."

modation for the students, who at Homerton had
been lodged in mean and incommodious apartments, where, if they wished to study in cold
weather, they had to keep up the vital warmth
by putting their feet into a basket filled with hay.
The most eminent men among the dissenting ministers of London were engaged in the different
departments of instruction. Dr. Rees had gained
experience in academical teaching at Hoxton, and
enjoyed a reputation for mathematical and physical
science, which extended beyond the limits of his
own denomination. Dr. Kippis held at least as
high a place in literature, as Dr. Rees in science;
and the other departments were respectably filled,
though by men of less eminence. But the supe-
riority in accommodation or in the means of obtaining knowledge were trifling circumstances,
compared with the intellectual freedom which he
gained at Hackney. Contrasting it with the narrow and inquisitorial spirit of his former place of
education, he must have felt like the prisoner
emerging from his dungeon, when his fetters are
struck off, and he once more enjoys the free light
and air of heaven.

I regard Mr. Wellbeloved's emancipation from
the theological system in which he had been brought
up, as one of the greatest blessings of his life, and
I know that it was so considered by himself. "My
early life," he once said, "was sombre." His mind

was deeply religious, and at the same time exceedingly sensitive, and not without a tinge of melan-
choly.   The gloomy views of Providence, of human
nature, and of human destiny, which the Calvinistic
creed inculcates, could not have been permanently
held by him, without making his religious faith a
burden to his spirit.   His benevolent nature would
have so strongly revolted against a doctrine which
represents a large portion of God's creatures as
condemned to endless and hopeless misery, that
I doubt if it would have been possible for him,
after arriving at the age of reflection, to have
believed in the divine origin of a religion in which
this dogma was supposed to be revealed.   No religious belief could have been a source of support
and consolation to a mind constituted like his,
which represented man as wholly depraved, and
incapable of originating anything good; he was
but too prone to self-depreciation, and such conceptions of his own nature would have been de-
pressing to his moral energies, and fatal to his peace
of mind.

    The first years of the College at Hackney were
the least satisfactory.   The parts of the different
lecturers had not been well cast, and changes were
necessary; the classical department in particular
was feebly administered till Mr. Wakefield came
in 1790.   There was from the first a want of one
presiding mind and one controlling power.   The

maintenance of discipline was divided between the
tutors and the committee, the committee being
composed of men respectable for their character
and social position, but not themselves of academical education, and ignorant of the delicate art of
maintaining authority over those who have been
emancipated from the discipline of a school, and
have not attained to the self-control of manhood.
Hence arose irregularities and breaches of rules,
which seriously impaired the character of the
institution, and were a source of annoyance to
those who were conscientiously devoting their time
to study. Such things form an ingredient in
academical anecdote in all similar institutions, but
at Hackney they proceeded to an unusual length.
The evil was in great measure remedied when Mr.
Belsham took the charge of the College, which,
however, was not till the commencement of the
third year of Mr. Wellbeloved's course. Of the
position among his fellow-students which he had
already attained there is a pleasing proof, in his
being selected to draw up the address which they
presented to Mr. Belsham on his entrance upon his
office. It is expressive of respect for his character
and a determination "to meet the wishes of their
friends, and silence the misrepresentations of their
enemies," by attention to the affectionate advice
which he had given them. The tutor and the
pupil ever entertained a high regard for each

other. Their minds were indeed of different
mould, and in their conclusions on theological and
ethical subjects there was by no means exact
agreement. But both were equally earnest in
their pursuit of truth and sincere in its avowal;
still, with the difference that Mr. Belsham's tone
in the maintenance of his opinions was more bold
and decisive than Mr. Wellbeloved's, who spoke
with diffidence, even when his convictions were
most firmly fixed.

None of his instructors appear to have engaged
more of his affection than Dr. Kippis, whose
character, as drawn by one intimately acquainted
with him, had many points of resemblance to
his own. "His temper," says Mr. Morgan, in
the General Biography, "was mild and gentle,
benevolent and candid; his address and manners
polished, easy, and uncommonly conciliating and
prepossessing." I have heard Mr. Wellbeloved
relate an anecdote very characteristic of both parties. It would hardly be believed, by those who
know the rapidity and ease with which he composed in later life, that composition was at first a
work of extreme labour to him. On one occasion,
when he had an academical exercise to perform,
and had made various attempts without success, he
went in despair to Dr. Kippis, to whom the
department of *Belles Lettres* belonged, and told
him of his difficulties. The Doctor listened com-

placently to his statement, and then, with a
benevolent smile, replied, " Suppose you write on
modesty." He had also a high appreciation of
the character and learning of Mr. Wakefield, who
possessed the talent of communicating to his
pupils his own enthusiasm for the beauties of the
Greek and Latin classics. He has carefully preserved among his papers a Latin theme on the
favourite topic of the day, " De Libertate," with
numerous corrections in the handwriting of Mr.
Wakefield, and one of the treasures of his library
was that gentleman's copy of Maasvicius' Virgil,
with many emendations and notes by him. Dr.
Price had soon . ceased to take any part in the
instructions of the College, but Mr. Wellbeloved
was an attendant on his ministry, certainly at
Hackney, probably also at Newington Green,
and was personally well known to him. An application had been made to Dr. Price, by the guardian
of the late Sir George Cayley, to recommend a private tutor for him, and he suggested the name of
Mr. Wellbeloved. On his declining the office, the
young baronet was placed in the house of Dr.
Price's nephew, Mr. George Cadogan Morgan.
Mr. Wellbeloved had been one of his audience at
the Old Jewry, on the memorable 4th November,
1789, when the preacher's burst of eloquence in
praise of the French Revolution so electrified his
hearers, that some of them with difficulty restrained

themselves from open applause.   His residence
near the metropolis afforded him the opportunity
of witnessing some of the important political proceedings which gave so great an interest to those
times.   He was present in Westminster Hall
during the trial of Warren Hastings; he was in
the gallery of the House of Commons on the
night of March 2, 1790, when ·Mr. Fox, arriving
booted and whip in hand from Newmarket,
delivered his celebrated speech in favour of the
repeal of the Test and Corporation Acts, and he
had kept till his death the number of Woodfall's
Register which contains the report of his speech,
with those of Sir Henry Hoghton, his seconder,
and of Mr. Beaufoy, on the same side, as well as
of Pitt and Burke, in opposition to the motion.

Among his papers is another journal of the
times, the Morning Chronicle of October 19,
1791.   It contains a letter of his to the editor,
signed W. D. (a signature also affixed to a communication which he made to the Monthly
Repository, vol. x. p. 360), consisting of strictures on a letter recently published, in which the
Dissenters were strongly exhorted to refrain from
interfering in politics.   It had been called forth
by the riots at Birmingham, and contained some
illiberal reflections on Dr. Priestley.   The author
of the communication rejects the insidious advice
given to the Dissenters to confine themselves to

the care of their own souls and those of their
flocks, and be content with the form of government under which they lived, and maintains that
the duties of private and public devotion need not
interfere with those of a member of society; that
while they weighed moral evils and sought to
remove them, they might find time to mourn over
the tyranny of governments and seek to remove
political evils. The style has more asperity than
the author's later controversial writings; but the
pamphlet animadverted upon appears to have been
at once arrogant, uncandid, and insidious. The
following are the concluding sentences of Mr.
Wellbeloved's letter:—"Not to leave him discon-
solate, some part of his advice shall be followed.
We will practise our duty as Christians, but we
will never forget that we are likewise called to perform the duties of citizens, though not allowed the
name. We will be mindful of our duty as parents,
and we will teach our children to be good subjects
under good governments. We will not neglect
social religion; and, as far as lies in our power, we
will reform and enlighten mankind. In recovering
them from the tyranny of bad men, as well as of
their own bad passions, we will strive to increase
their happiness. We will preserve alive in our
breasts the piety of our ancestors, but we will not
neglect to cherish their spirit. We will be thankful for religious freedom, but we will never endure

civil bondage." It is intimated that a "Prelate of distinction," no doubt Horsley, was the reputed author of the pamphlet, which was entitled "A Review of the Case of the Protestant Dissenters," and the advice given to them is, at all events, in accordance with his celebrated dictum, "that the people have nothing to do with the laws but to obey them."

Mr. Wellbeloved found many congenial minds among his fellow-students at Hackney. It may be sufficient to mention the names of Kentish, Tayler, Hincks, Joyce, Bostock, Shepherd, Corrie, and A. Aikin, to show how varied and improving was the social intercourse which he enjoyed there. Mr. Arthur Aikin and Mr. Barron of Norwich were his most intimate associates, and scarcely a day passed of which they did not spend a part in each other's rooms. The friendship begun with Mr. Aikin (who did not enter the College till Mr. Wellbeloved's second year), lasted through life. I am tempted to insert here a part of a poetical epistle from him to his friend, in April, 1792, describing the life which they led at College. The taste for natural history, and especially for botany, which accompanied Mr. Wellbeloved through life, was acquired from Mr. Aikin, and kept up by his subsequent intimacy with Mr. Wood, who was a botanist of a high order. The admiration of the poetry of Thomson, shared by the two friends, also remained with him in after years. His childhood had been passed in the neighbourhood of the poet's former residence at Kew, and amidst the scenery which inspired "The Seasons." Their chief charm for him, however, was their truthful picture of natural objects and rural life, and the vein of pious and moral sentiment which runs through them. A pocket edition was his companion in his walks, and when prevented by illness from enjoying the beauties of the outer world, no book of lighter literature was more frequently in his hands.

O Friend beloved! whom late the placid walks
And studious halls of Hackney glad detained;
Though now, far distant on the world's wide scene,
You prove the truth of maxims here imbibed;
And, fired with ardour for the sacred cause
Of Liberty and Virtue, nobly stem
The flood with prejudice and interest charged;
Steal from the bustling cares of life awhile,
And give one hour to friendship and to me.

How Fancy throbs, while Recollection paints
The fleeting forms of bliss we once enjoyed!
And O, how many a pang does thought inflict
That these gay scenes must never more return!
Gay scenes of happiness, a long farewell!
Farewell ye pleasures, ne'er to be renewed!
Yet still will Memory, with officious hand,
Retrace the lines, and with illusion sweet
Recal the calm delights of College ease.

When Morn's first gleams chased off the shades of night,
How oft in rapt attention have we stood,

c 2

Eager to hail the sun's bright orient beams,
Shot from the summit of yon eastern hill,
While every sparkling dewdrop brighter blazed.
As each melodious songster through the copse
Caroll'd more clear, and every opening flower
Gave to the passing gale diviner sweets,
In closer union our enraptured hearts
With friendship's purest influence would expand.

Thus passed our earlier hours; but when the sun
In noontide splendour led the sultry day,
And serious business for awhile gave place
To lighter studies; on the violet bank,
Or careless laid beneath the shady elm,
We gaily urged along the lingering time,
With the rare products of the sportive Muse
That erst, in British or Italian groves,
Awoke sweet echo from her mossy couch.
Thee chief, the pride of Caledonian swains,
Enchanting Thomson, in whose various page
Nature astonished sees her works pourtrayed
With tints as soft, as vivid and as rich
As her own pencil dipt in heavenly dyes.

Nor absent was the rival Mantuan bard,
Who though, like Phœbus, he had power to guide
The epic car, and rein the fiery steeds,
Yet oft in russet garb would deign to tend
The pastoral care, or with his oaten pipe
Would teach the Mincian reeds his Daphnis' name.

But when black clouds and shrilly whistling blasts
Forbade to rove, beside the cheerful fire,
The social glass, gay converse, sprightly books,
Or else backgammon, frighted care away.

Together, too, we climbed the steepy hill
Of Highgate; with botanic sauntering pace
We wander'd devious o'er the heathy bounds
Of Hampstead, on whose topmost ridge arrived *
We breathed free air, and with disdain looked down
On busy London, canopied with smoke,
Nor would have changed our simple heartfelt joy
For all the pompous state the City yields.

These transient dreams of happiness are o'er,
And, lost the dear companion of my youth,
Imagination droops her airy wing.

Mr. Wellbeloved's residence at the College at
Hackney coincided with the æra of the first
enthusiasm with which the friends of liberty
hailed the commencement of the French Revolution. At that time it was viewed with dislike
and apprehension by hardly any, except those who
had no sympathy with the victims of oppression,
or who had a direct interest in the maintenance
of the domestic abuses, the fate of which seemed
prefigured in their downfall in France. It may
easily be supposed that the students were among
the most ardent admirers of Gallic liberty, and in
the exultation to which this feeling gave rise, it
was a difficult task for those, to whom the discipline
of the College was entrusted, to maintain autho-

* To this line Mr. Wellbeloved has added the following reference
to Virg. Æn. i. 423.
"Jamque adscendebant collem, qui plurimus urbi
Imminet, adversasque adspectat desuper arces."

rity and procure obedience, even to the most
reasonable restrictions. It is amusing to read in
the academical correspondence of the day the pro-
testations against the ordinances of the Committee,
and the resolutions to resist their tyranny, couched
in terms as energetic as if all liberty, civil and
religious, were endangered by them. *Ça ira* and
the *Marseilloise* were favourite ditties at the College *symposia*, and kings, priests, and aristocrats,
without much distinction of foreign or domestic,
were the objects of hearty execration. A letter of
one of Mr. Wellbeloved's college friends gives an
account of a social meeting within its walls, at
which an eminent guest was present. "Last Sunday but one, * * * and some others observed that
it be a good opportunity to have a republican
supper, and invite Paine. I left a note for him
accordingly, and when I called in the evening,
Johnson told me that Paine was much pleased
with the invitation, and would wait on us. We
asked George Morgan to meet him, and had the
most glorious republican party that the walls of
the College ever contained. We sat down to
supper, eighteen or nineteen, and were very agreeably disappointed to find Paine as agreeable and
striking in conversation as he is in his writings.
No man, I should think, abounds so much with
anecdotes of Washington, Fayette, Burke, &c., or
has so striking a mode of expression, as this

apostle of liberty. His very countenance points
him out for a great man : for though very weather-
beaten and worse for wear, there is a peculiar
enthusiastic fire in his eyes, especially when he is
pleased with any sentiment in favour of liberty,
which is really wonderful. He breakfasted with
us, and before he went, expressed great satisfaction
at our spirit, and promised to call on us whenever
he came to Hackney. Among other things, he
told us that he had seen a letter to Horne Tooke,
for the Revolution Society, from a club at Sheffield
of 1500 republicans, chiefly manufacturers. Their
method is peculiarly excellent, and upon the true
plan of a national convention. They divide into
fifteen clubs, of 100 each, to discuss popular topics,
and then elect a certain number of members from
each club, to form a general club, for the purpose
of transacting business and comparing their
thoughts. This is, indeed, the bud of a revolution." Another letter from the same correspondent describes a disturbance in the theatre,
occasioned by the call of some of the students for
Ça ira instead of " God save the King." It is, I
believe, not doubtful, that a handbill, circulated at
Birmingham just before that celebration of the
French Revolution, which proved the occasion of
the riots, of such an inflammatory tendency, that
the Dissenters of that town thought it expedient to
treat it as the work of an enemy, and offer a reward

for the discovery of the author, was really written by a young man, fresh from the delivery of a very revolutionary oration at Hackney. The device and motto on the seal of Mr. Wellbeloved's correspondent, a hand with a dagger, the cap of liberty, and "*manus hæc inimica tyrannis*," are characteristic of the times.

It may be said, why record these extravagances, the natural and venial result of the excitement of the æra? Had they been only the ordinary expression of the antagonism of young men to the rules of discipline, and their fervid love of liberty, they would have been unworthy of mention; but the French Revolution is the greatest event since the Reformation, nor can its history be understood, or its effects estimated, unless we know from such facts as these to what a depth it had stirred the heart of England, and especially its influence upon the rising generation. Without adverting to them, the causes of the failure of the College at Hackney cannot be duly apportioned between the errors in economical management, which embarrassed its finances, and the difficulties created by the spirit of the times. This is a matter, indeed, of little interest to the world at large, but of some importance in the history of dissenting academical institutions. The question has often been raised, how far the failure of Hackney was decisive against any attempt to establish a college in the metropolis or its neighbourhood. It is not to be denied that an unfavourable impression had been left on the minds of several of those who had been themselves Hackney students, *e. g.* Mr. Wellbeloved and Mr. Kentish; and that they considered a provincial situation more favourable to diligence in study, economy in expense, and purity of morals. Perhaps they had not separated in their minds the permanent from the temporary elements of the question. At all events, now that the experiment has been resumed, under very different circumstances, we may reasonably hope for a more favourable result.

Another dark cloud which hangs over the memory of Hackney College is the imputation that it was a nursery of infidelity. To those who regard unbelief as in itself a sin, and Unitarianism as its natural parent, it would be useless to offer explanations of the fact that several of those who were educated there as students for the ministry not only abandoned their profession to engage in secular pursuits, but renounced their faith in revelation. But one who considers human nature apart from theological prejudice must be aware, that faith is a state of mind which is affected by other influences than reason and evidence. Were it not so, the strange contrast exhibited by different ages in respect to religious faith would be inexplicable. I can assert, on the authority of

Mr. Wellbeloved, that when he removed to Hackney he was agreeably surprised to find the spirit of his new and heterodox associates more religious than that of Homerton, and he especially mentioned the more decorous performance of domestic worship, and the greater reverence with which the scriptures were treated. There was nothing in the character or sentiments of the teachers at the New College which tended to encourage infidelity among their pupils. Mr. Belsham, Dr. Priestley, Mr. Wakefield, were not only themselves firm believers in revelation, but had all written in defence of its evidences or illustration of its records. Speaking of the imputations cast upon himself, Mr. Belsham says, " In the College I read lectures in defence of the Christian religion, in public I preach in its defence, and take more pains than most of my brethren in explaining the Christian scriptures ; I also lecture the young people of my congregation in defence of the Christian religion, and have been taking a great deal of trouble in answering Mr. Paine's Age of Reason. If, after this, people will not believe that I am a Christian, nothing that I can say or do will convince them of it."* He expressly says, a few years later than the time when Mr. Wellbeloved was at College (1796), " that those of the students who had given up

* " Life by Williams," p. 400.

Christianity were studious and virtuous men;"
and wisely concludes that " to this no remedy
could be applied ; since actions might be restrained,
but thoughts must be left free." When we look
at what had been passing in the world, however,
though we may not discover a remedy, we may
detect the origin of that epidemic renunciation of
Christianity, which affected not only the students
at Hackney, but the youth of England in other
places of education, in the first years of the French
Revolution. Some of the most eminent of those
who had a share, direct or remote, in effecting it,
the grave and laborious Encyclopedistes, the scoffing
Voltaire, the eloquent and impassioned Rousseau,
the calm and philosophic Franklin, were known as
unbelievers, and the admiration excited in the minds
of the young by their services to the cause of
liberty, was extended to their opinions on religion.
The Age of Reason would not have shaken the
faith of so many minds, if it had not proceeded
from the author of Common Sense and the
Rights of Man. It required more discrimi-
nation than can generally be looked for in young
and ardent minds, amidst the general rejoicing at
the downfall of a corrupt establishment of Christianity in France, to avoid transferring to the
religion itself some of the odium justly attaching
to the abuses which it had been made to sanction.
I believe that Mr. Wakefield's book on Public

Worship had an unfavourable effect on the minds
of the young men who were preparing for the
Ministry—not by weakening their faith in Christianity, in which he was himself a firm believer,
but by rendering them dissatisfied with the profession for which they were educating, and preparing
them for its abandonment. It is certain that a
speedy result of its publication was to produce a
remonstrance from some of the students against a
rule of the College, requiring attendance on public
worship, and a bold defence of the remonstrance,
in an oration delivered by a student before the
assembled tutors, committee, and visitors, on one
of the public days.

The great development of deistical opinions
which took place in Europe about this time, and
of which Hackney College only exhibits a specimen, deserves to be considered in a more general
relation than its effects upon a single seminary and
a small religious community. It is a phenomenon
which we shall find repeated periodically since the
Reformation gave freedom to thought, and it seems
a necessary means for the purification of religion
from its corruptions. If we look back upon the
history of religious opinion, we shall find that
such crises have had a double effect. The attacks
of unbelievers have compelled the advocates of
Christianity to consider whether they have not
encumbered themselves with the vindication of

doctrines which are not scriptural,* and thus have given an impulse to scriptural criticism; and they have led them, at the same time, to look to the state of their own defences, to abandon outworks which, having ceased to be available, had virtually become obstructions, and instead of wasting their strength in maintaining these, to concentrate their efforts around the citadel of sacred Truth. The disposition to throw off belief in Christianity which prevailed at the time to which we refer, was not wholly owing to an undiscriminating desire of change; it had a cause, though not a justification, in the unsound nature of some of the evidences which were then urged as proofs of its divine origin. When weak and strong arguments are built together, the weak give way and drag the strong with them.

Mr. Wellbeloved completed his regular college course at Hackney in the summer of 1791. During the vacation of that year, he had paid a visit

* See some admirable observations on the service rendered to Christianity by those who free it from the encumbrance of irrational and unscriptural doctrines, in Paley's dedication of his " Moral and Political Philosophy" to Bishop Law. " Whatever renders religion more rational renders it more credible; and he who by a diligent and faithful examination of the original records dismisses from the system one article which contradicts the apprehension, the experience or the reasoning of mankind, does more towards recommending the belief— and with the belief the influence of Christianity—than can be effected by a thousand contenders for creeds and ordinances of human establishment."

to his friend, Mr. Jardine, at Bath, and they
crossed the Severn together and proceeded to
Bwlch, to the residence of their common friend,
David Jones. It was an expedition on which he
always dwelt with great delight. He had hitherto
seen nature only under the comparatively tame,
though soft and rich, aspect which she presents
in the neighbourhood of London. The journey
was performed on horseback, and through a country where the accommodation of travellers was
indifferently provided for seventy years ago; and
it was consequently diversified with incidents
which fixed its events in the memory. Mr. Wellbeloved was remarkable for what may be called a
topographical memory. He seemed to retain an
accurate picture in his mind of any road that he
had travelled, not merely in its general features,
but in its details, its distances, and its bearings.
In his later years he often spoke of this journey,
and the length of time that had elapsed had produced no diminution in the liveliness of his recollections. The same thing was remarkable in regard
to the topography of London; its highways and
byeways, with which he had become familiar in his
youth, seemed freshly impressed on his memory,
though more than half a century had since elapsed.

The picturesque scenery of Bath, and the pleasant society with which he found Mr. Jardine surrounded, induced him to form the plan before al-

luded to, of living there with his friend, when he should have left Hackney. He returned to the College at the opening of the session in the autumn of 1791, and I believe preached his first sermon at Walthamstow, November 13, 1791. At least, this is the first entry which I find in a record of each Sunday's duty, begun in that year, and carried on regularly till July, 1846. His text was 1 Cor. iii. 9: "We are labourers together with God; ye are God's husbandry, ye are God's building." In thus delaying the exercise of his public functions till after the close of his academical studies (for though residing in the College he was not now a student), he acted on a principle which he would gladly have carried out, when he became the head of a similar institution. He was exceedingly averse to the assumption of the teacher's office by those who were still learners, and reluctantly gave way to the impatience of his pupils and the importunities of ministers or congregations needing supplies.

He had but just established himself at Hackney in the autumn of 1791, when an application was made to him to become assistant to Mr. Cappe, at York. David Jones had recently been chosen minister to the New Meeting congregation at Birmingham, where a son of Mr. Cappe was then residing. Hearing from him of his father's infirm state of health, and of his incapacity to discharge

his duties, he warmly recommended his friend, Mr.
Wellbeloved. The recommendation was forwarded
to York, but in the mean time applications had
been made in two other quarters, and it was not
till these were disposed of that Mr. Jones's suggestion could be entertained. The application was
made through another college friend, Michael Mau-
rice, then settled at Yarmouth, and his account at
once determined Mr. Cappe to invite Mr. Wellbeloved to visit York. His compliance with the
request is contained in a letter to Mr. Cappe, of
January 23, 1792; and on the evening of February 3 he arrived in York, and preached his first
sermons in St. Saviourgate Chapel on the following Sunday, February 5, from Matt. xxvi. 39 and
Acts iv. 19. He had become desirous of settling
with a congregation, in consequence of a matrimonial engagement, formed in the preceding year, with
the eldest daughter of John Kinder, Esq., of Cheap-
side and Stoke Newington; and an invitation to
Salisbury was under his consideration, at the time
when he received the application from York.

CHAPTER III.

LIFE AT YORK, AS MINISTER AND SCHOOLMASTER.

1792—1803.

Mrs. Cappe has recorded in her Memoirs* the impression made by Mr. Wellbeloved, on his first introduction to her husband, and confirmed by all their subsequent intercourse. He, on his part, could not be insensible to the very superior qualities and attainments of Mr. Cappe, and from the commencement of their intercourse to the close of his life, he attached himself to him with veneration and love. Though weakened by an attack of paralysis, which had occurred in the preceding spring, Mr. Cappe still retained his stores of knowledge and powers of conversation, and his noble countenance had been rather improved than impaired by a softened expression, which sickness and grief had given

* "Mr. Wellbeloved was regarded by my husband with an affection truly parental; and became everything to him by his humility, his disinterestedness, his varied talents, his desire of knowledge, especially of religious knowledge, his freedom from prejudice, and his unaffected piety. 'This,' would he often say, 'is the very young man I wanted; he will be eminent in his day.'"—*Memoirs*, p. 256. "He felt for me the affection of a parent," wrote Mr. Wellbeloved on his death, "and received from me in return a filial love."— See *Wood's Sermon on the Death of Mr. Cappe*, p. 23.

D

to it.   He recognized at once in his young assistant
those qualities which as yet had hardly displayed
themselves to the world.   Of these none would
so powerfully recommend him to Mr. Cappe, as his
earnest and serious love of religious truth, and his
attachment to biblical studies.   These had been the
great solace of Mr. Cappe's life ; he had formed to
himself a scheme of scriptural interpretation widely
different from the ordinary theology, and was delighted to find an apt disciple in Mr. Wellbeloved.
I shall have occasion, hereafter, to speak at large
of Mr. Cappe's peculiar system ; at present it is
sufficient to say, that it was fully embraced by Mr.
Wellbeloved, that it was the basis of his exegesis
of the New Testament, and that to the end of his
life his belief in its soundness never altered.   The
very dust of Mr. Cappe's writings was gold in his
estimation.   He taught himself the short-hand
which Mr. Cappe had invented, that he might be
able to read his MSS.   Not long before his death
he had occupied himself in drawing out an elaborate illustration of the explanations of Scripture
terms, which Mr. Cappe had prefixed to his Hymn-
book.   It remains in two small octavo volumes—
at once an evidence of his unaltered convictions,
and a remarkable specimen of his calligraphy, when
considerably more than fourscore years of age.   The
amiable disposition and intelligence of Mrs. Cappe
are too well known to render it necessary to de-

scribe her character. She felt a truly maternal kindness for Mr. Wellbeloved, gave him counsel in all his difficulties, and was especially valuable to him by encouraging him, when his too low estimate of himself would have induced him to despair of success in his undertakings. The whole of Mr. Cappe's family regarded him as a brother. Between the youngest son, Robert, and himself, a friendship was formed, of which Mr. Wellbeloved has left a touching memorial in the sermon which he preached on his early death.

The services of the young minister were very acceptable to the congregation, but it was with some hesitation that he accepted Mr. Cappe's proposal. It was not the small amount of the salary which he could afford to give (£60) which caused the hesitation, but some of the congregation wished that after Mr. Cappe's death two ministers should be appointed. It was an unreasonable proposal, for the whole income amounted only to £180, and certainly the duty was not greater than one minister could well perform. On receiving an assurance, however, from the principal members, that, as far as depended on them, he might reckon on the sole succession, he determined to fix himself at York, and declined the invitation to Salisbury. One of the very few memorials which he has left of his own feelings and motives is a paper drawn up at this

time, and containing a statement of the reasons
which decided him to remain at York :—

" I do, indeed," he says, " earnestly desire to stay ; it appears from the character of the congregation that they have
no one who would exert himself, and to do this is my first
wish and chief intention.   It is the hope that in time I may
do some good—may in some measure serve what I consider
the cause of truth and the interests of virtue, which keeps
me here.   I am not vain ; I know the difficulty attending
the spread of rational religion, in a place where the establishment is so flourishing as it is here ; and I know how poorly
I am armed for the field ; but I am determined to try to
effect something, and perhaps I may.   Should I go, some
one may succeed me who would be dispirited and sit down,
without making any exertion.   The cause of what I deem
truth does weigh with me much more than any other consideration.   If I stay it will be my first object to explain the
Scriptures of the New Testament.   I shall endeavour, as soon
as my stay is determined, to know Mr. Cappe's mind upon
this subject, and if he has no objection, I shall begin upon
something immediately, only by explaining obscure passages
as they occur in the reading of the day, and not with the
regularity which I should do after his death."

The practice which he proposes was well adapted
quietly to substitute more correct interpretations
of scripture for those from which false doctrinal inferences had been drawn.   The method of exposition
was adopted by my father, under similar circumstances at Exeter, where a considerable part of his
congregation, at the time when his own sentiments
changed, were not Unitarians.

So zealously did he apply himself to his new
duties, that I find a memorandum of his having
commenced a Sunday-school on the 18th of March
1792, only six weeks after his coming to York; and
in a sermon preached in July of the same year, he
announces a plan of instructing the young people
of his congregation, from the age of fifteen to
twenty, after the afternoon service. He was much
gratified by a request from the servants of the congregation, that they might receive some special religious instruction. For some time the whole duty
devolved upon him, for Mr. Cappe never preached
after he came to York, though he long flattered himself with the hope of resuming his pulpit duties, and
used to say to his assistant, at the close of the service, "I hope, sir, to be able to preach next Sunday."
In the latter part of 1792, however, he was joined
by his friend Arthur Aikin, who lived with him in
lodgings, and occasionally preached for him, especially during the visits which he paid to London
in the year and a half which elapsed before his marriage, in July, 1793. There was, at this time, perfect sympathy between them in religion and politics;
similarity of tastes in literature, and in the pursuits
of natural history; with sufficient diversity of temperament, to make each useful in counteracting the
bias of his friend's character. He remained in York
till after Mr. Wellbeloved's marriage, but removed
in the latter part of that year to Shrewsbury, as

afternoon preacher with the Rev. John Rowe.
I will make an extract from a letter of his, preserved by Mr. Wellbeloved, in illustration of what
I have said of their respective characters. It was
written in December, 1793 :—

" It really grieves me exceedingly that you are dissatisfied
with your situation ; and the more so, as I fear you have
good reason. I am, however, glad to find that your Sunday-
school flourishes so well, and I confess I cannot help hazard-
ing a prophecy, that you will not be finally unsuccessful.
Allowing that those of your congregation, who are arrived
at manhood are impenetrable, they must shortly quit the stage
and make room for their successors, who are receiving the
benefit of your instructions, and in whom alone you must
expect to find the good effects of your labour. It is upon the
young and the young only, as Dr. Priestley has more than
once observed, that we can expect to make any lasting and
important impression. I shall almost as soon expect to root
the Wrekin from its base, as to overthrow habits which have
been implanted in youth and confirmed in maturer years.
So, my dear friend, have a little patience. Your situation is
now at the worst; it will every year be meliorating and improving, and I anticipate the period when you will have a
very respectable congregation, with the additional satisfaction of being able to say, ' This is all my own doing : these
are the fruits of many an anxious day of incessant labour,
of patient continuance in admonishing and instructing.' If
I could wish to alter anything in you, it would be that diffidence in your own abilities, which prompts you to give up
a pursuit as beyond your power, before you have really
made a fair trial. Such a disposition is, I know, in a good
measure constitutional ; and most heartily thankful am I
that my failing is on the other side. For, however liable a

sanguine temper may be to momentary disappointments, yet, under the full persuasion that all things are working together for good, it can never be long dejected, even at the failure of its most favourite schemes."

Lest a sentence in the preceding extract should be misunderstood, I should observe that it was not from fickleness of temper, or want of perseverance, or dread of labour, that Mr. Wellbeloved ever gave up an undertaking in which he had embarked, for no one could work more steadily or perseveringly than he did, in the face of obstacles and discouragements; but, as his correspondent observes, he had too low an opinion of his own ability. In the early years of his manhood, indeed, he formed various schemes of a literary kind, which were either given up after a short time, or never advanced beyond the embryo state; but this was owing partly to the increased calls of duty, partly to his being unable to satisfy himself with anything less than a perfect work. To plan in early life, what exceeds all human powers of execution, is a mark of an ardent mind, intent on great and useful aims. One of his plans was the publication of some popular illustrations of natural history, respecting which he had a correspondence with the celebrated wood-engraver, Bewick of Newcastle. It was abandoned as being too expensive for the purpose which Mr. Wellbeloved had in view. Another scheme, in which he was to

have been assisted by David Jones, was the periodical publication of a condensed account of recent
voyages and travels. In the year 1794 a local
periodical publication in 12mo was begun at York,
entitled the Yorkshire Repository. It had a predecessor in a Yorkshire Magazine, whose course began
and ended in the year 1788. The Repository was
designed to contain moral essays, criticisms, scientific
communications, and reviews of books, along with
mathematical problems, rebuses, charades, enigmas,
and answers to them. These last have the character
of mediocrity, which generally belongs to such publications, but the work was to include a semi-annual
review of the literature of the year, theology,
morals, ecclesiastical history, civil history, topography, travels, biography, and heraldry, being included in the first number, which was also the last.
Mr. Wellbeloved had become acquainted, soon after
his settlement in York, with Mr. Wilson, the printer,
a churchman, but a liberal politician, who was one of
the publishers of the Repository, and was no doubt
engaged by him to become a contributor to it. Under the signature of Erastus (a translation of his own
name), he discusses the question whether $\theta\eta\rho\iota\omega\mu\alpha\chi\epsilon\omega$
(1 Cor. xv. 37) is to be understood of a real or a
figurative combat with wild beasts, and decides for
the latter sense. In a second paper on Rev. ii. 17,
the words, "I will give him a white stone, and in
the stone a name written, which no man knoweth

saving he who receiveth it," are thus explained, that
no one can know the value of the rights and privileges of the gospel but those who embrace it; and
that this value consisted in the safety and protection
to which the faithful followers of Jesus would be
entitled, in that time of tribulation and destruction
to all unbelievers and faithless Christians, which was
coming on with the desolation of Judæa. It appears
from this explanation that the author had adopted
Mr. Cappe's view of the meaning of salvation in the
New Testament, and its connection with faith. I
find him in this year recommending to his friend,
Arthur Aikin, the work of Nisbett, whose views
very nearly coincided with Mr. Cappe's. The
Review department comprehends notices of all the
principal theological publications of the half-year.
Among them is Dr. Priestley's farewell discourse
at Hackney. Of this the Reviewer says, " The
calmness and serenity with which he reflects upon
his past sufferings and contemplates his change of
situation; the philosophical and Christian reflections upon the opposition he has endured, and the
odium to which a large class of men in this
country are subject; the manner in which he takes
leave of his congregation, to which he was strongly
attached, and the style in which he addresses those
whom he supposes to have come thither for no
good motive, must certainly place him in a point
of view in which the eye of prejudice is unaccus-

tomed to consider him. The appendix contains some honourable testimonies of esteem and affection from his congregation, his catechumens, the Unitarian Society, and the Dissenters at Birmingham. We call ourselves neither the friends nor the enemies of this eminent exile, but as the friends of science we deplore his departure." In a review of Dr. Priestley's sermon on the Fast Day, "The present State of Europe compared with the ancient Prophecies," strong dissent is intimated from the author's application of them. Mr. Wellbeloved had already renounced the notion that the Scriptures contain prophecies of modern history, and referred those of the Apocalypse to events impending, or supposed to be impending, in the Jewish state and the Roman Empire.

After giving an account of Newcome's Historical View of English Biblical Translations, and the works of Symonds and Roberts on a kindred subject, the Reviewer proceeds:—"They will, we hope, promote the great design which some of the most pious and learned men of our country have long been labouring to accomplish. There is now before the public a large mass of evidence to prove the necessity of a new version of the Bible, and we cannot suffer ourselves to imagine, that the fashionable fear of innovation will long oppose itself to a reform which the times seem to render necessary." Many changes of fashion have taken place since 1794, but none in the fear of innovation in religion, and the event which Mr. Wellbeloved then thought near at hand, seems, after the lapse of three quarters of a century, as far off as ever.

The following are his remarks on "Paine's Age of Reason:"—

"The celebrated author of The Rights of Man has given to the world his sentiments on the important subject of Revelation in a work entitled The Age of Reason, a work so replete with false reasoning, unfounded assertion, and shameless abuse, as to produce no just cause of alarm in the mind of the friends of Revelation, but, on the contrary, to excite the warmest hopes that it will eventually serve the cause which it is designed to overthrow. Mr. Paine has in most places mistaken the nature of Revelation. Whatever may become of those doctrines, generally, indeed, considered as those of Christianity, upon which he has lavished his unfeeling wit and indecent ridicule, Christianity itself stands upon a rock of evidence which no efforts of Mr. Paine's can shake. Those who find the articles of their creed here rudely attacked may perhaps do well to consider, whether the existence of that creed is not a cause of this abuse of Revelation. We wish not to discourage any one from giving his thoughts to the public, whatever they may be, persuaded that truth will in the end prevail over error, and that her empire is accelerated by every discussion; but we do wish to discourage every man from obtruding himself on public notice, on subjects which he does not understand. And we are sure that it can do no honour to Mr. Paine, nor any service to his cause, to avow his contempt for learning, when writing on a subject which involves much knowledge of ancient times and languages."

What caused the early failure of the Yorkshire Repository I do not know; such provincial publications have usually been short-lived; but the liberal tone of the passages I have extracted would not increase its chance of success in the Yorkshire of 1794.

Various circumstances combined to render Mr. Wellbeloved doubtful whether York should be the permanent scene of his ministry. The first years of a young minister's life are usually years of painful trial, at least to minds constituted like his. Enthusiastic hopes of the results of his labours have to be toned down by experience. No lectures on preaching or pastoral duty, which he may have heard at College, can have taught him beforehand how his own flock will require to be addressed, or prepared him to meet their special wants. The labour of composition, where the whole duty rests on one, becomes exhausting, and the necessary variety of topics difficult to be attained. To these causes which tend to produce a collapse of zeal, some special ones were added. The congregation at York comprised a few families connected with the gentry of the county. Alarm from the progress of the French Revolution, which had passed into its Jacobinical type, tended to alienate persons of this class from dissent, as being in their view associated with disaffection. Mr. Wellbeloved's political opinions, which were not concealed by him, were sufficiently strong to excite his own astonishment in

later years, and I find from some gently-worded
cautions of Mr. Cappe's, that his venerable friend
was not without apprehension of the effect which
might be produced by his unreserved expression of
them.   Those who, from any cause, have been in
meditation of flight from a dissenting congregation,
frequently lay hold of a change of ministers, as a
convenient opportunity for withdrawing, without
proclaiming the abandonment of their principles.
The congregation were not wholly Unitarians.   Mr.
Cappe had long been so in the strictest sense, but
the strain of his preaching had been wholly practical and devotional, and neither his opinions respecting the person of Christ, nor his peculiar mode of
interpreting Scripture, had been brought forward in
his public services.   Mr. Wellbeloved was little disposed to controversial preaching, but he had been
trained in a different school from Mr. Cappe, a pupil
of Doddridge, and spoke more openly on points of
doctrine.   On the second Sunday after his settlement at York, he preached a sermon from Micah
vi. 6, 7, on the cover of which (the sermon itself
has been destroyed) is a memorandum, " This discourse furnished a disaffected member of the congregation with a pretext for withdrawing himself."
The subject of the sermon was Superstition, and it
may be easily imagined that it might afford a colour-
able plea for defection, to one who was looking for
it.   Another member left the chapel, because in two

sermons, preached in 1794, on the character of
Judas Iscariot, the preacher had adopted the opinion of Macknight, that he was rather an ambitious
than a treacherous man, who had not betrayed
his Master, but placed him in peril, that he might
compel him to exert his miraculous power for the
establishment of the expected kingdom. Whatever
may be thought of the soundness of the criticism,
it is evident that there must have been a foregone
determination to leave the Dissenters, in the mind
of one who could allege such a reason for his change.
These things, though they caused pain at the time,
produced no lasting effect on Mr. Wellbeloved's
mind, for his services were warmly approved by the
great majority of the congregation. But the prospect of an increasing family, and the probability
that he might yet remain for several years in the
position of an assistant minister, rendered it necessary for him either to seek a more remunerative
situation, or to add to his income by tuition. He
chose the latter, and in the year following his marriage received his first pupils, the eldest * and second sons of the late Sir William Strickland, of
Boynton. Mrs. Cappe was connected, through her
mother, with this and some other families of importance in the county of York, and her influence,

* The present baronet, Sir George Strickland, member for Yorkshire, in the Parliament which passed the Reform Bill, and for
Preston in several successive Parliaments.

joined to the character which Mr. Wellbeloved speedily established for learning and skill in tuition, procured him pupils. To accommodate boarders* he removed, in 1796, to a larger house at the end of Gilligate, and in 1799 purchased the house in Monkgate, in which the remainder of his life was spent. Before he took the decisive step of enlarging his plan at York, he had meditated a removal to Palgrave, in 1795, to succeed Dr. Philipps, who had recently announced his intention of resigning the school at Palgrave, and the pulpit at Diss. The school had enjoyed a high reputation under Mr. Barbauld, and the situation was supposed by Mr. Wellbeloved's friends to offer advantages much superior to his prospects at York. He accordingly visited Palgrave, and might have been elected by the trustees, had he not found that the prospect of pupils was very uncertain,† and that the school could hardly be made profitable, except by means repugnant to his feelings. Mr. J. W. Robberds, in his Life of William Taylor of Norwich, has preserved the letter of recommendation of Mr. Well-

* The first pupil whom he received into his house was a son of Mr. George Russell of Birmingham, and elder brother of the gentleman to whom we owe the establishment of the Ministers' Benevolent Society.

† It may amuse the collectors of comparative statistics to be informed that in a paper which Mr. Wellbeloved drew up, comparing the probable expenditure of York and Palgrave, the wages of three servants (two maids and a boy) at the former place are set down together at twelve guineas.

beloved, addressed to him, as one of the trustees, by Mr. Barbauld. It is so appropriate and just, that it deserves a place in this Memoir :—

"He whom I am thus convinced I may recommend without partiality to him, with credit to myself, and with justice to the institution, has, I am told, been already mentioned to the Trustees. His name is Wellbeloved. He is a Dissenting minister, and has preached for some time at York, where he now is. He was brought up at the New College at Hackney. Both Mr. Belsham and Mr. Wakefield, who were his tutors, will, I doubt not, if applied to, give him the character of a diligent student and good scholar, and this, were Dr. Kippis still alive, would, I am sure, from what I have lately heard him say, have been confirmed by him. As to sweetness of temper, gentleness of manners, and propriety of conduct, every one acquainted with him will readily allow they all belong to him. Of his modesty and integrity I have this opinion, that did he not think himself equal to the task, he would not come forth as a candidate, and that were he not in reality fully equal to it, he would be the very last person to imagine that he was. I would further observe, that he is an early riser, has formed a habit of close application, and possesses a solid and well-cultivated understanding. Tuition is not an art to which he is a stranger; he has now a few pupils, and he takes pleasure in instilling knowledge into the youthful mind. As a minister, his good sense and moderation, together with his seriousness and desire of being useful, would, I dare say, render him very acceptable to the congregation."

His thoughts turned also to Norwich, where his college friend, Mr. Barron, was settled, and which had at this time the attractions of an excellent literary society and a flourishing Unitarian congregation; but he found that there was little chance of establishing a school there. Dr. Enfield, who had tried the experiment, had only two pupils from the county and one from the city.

A higher sphere of employment in the work of education seemed to be opened to him by the proposal to remove to Manchester, and to succeed Dr. Barnes, as theological tutor in the College, which had been established there ten years before, after the dissolution of Warrington. This proposal was not declined without long and anxious deliberation. In November, 1797, Mr. Robinson of Manchester and the Rev. Wm. Wood of Leeds had visited York on the part of the College Committee, to express their wish to him that he should undertake the office. A formal invitation was sent by Dr. Percival in the following month. In his first deliberations he was much influenced by the accounts which his friends in London had received through the late Lewis Loyd, who had been himself at once a student and assistant classical tutor in the Manchester College, of the relaxed discipline of the institution. He determined, however, to visit Manchester himself, which he did in the winter of 1797, and had an interview with Dr. Barnes and some of the leading supporters of the College. Dr. Barnes, though not disposed to look favourably on a successor of Unitarian opinions,

E

satisfied him that the reports of insubordination and misconduct were at least exaggerated, and inquiries in other quarters concurred in the same result. Mr. Wellbeloved was much pleased with the reception which he met with in Manchester; but there were several circumstances which made him hesitate about accepting the invitation. There was no permanent fund, and only a small subscription list. The salary of the Divinity tutor was a hundred guineas, with a house free of rent and taxes, and liberty to take such fees as he might fix from lay-students attending his classes, and to receive boarders, for whom only thirty guineas a session had been paid. What weighed most unfavourably upon his mind was the conviction that the College was injudiciously placed in Manchester itself, and that while it remained there the proper maintenance of discipline was impossible. From Manchester he proceeded to London. His friends were generally indisposed to his removal. Mr. Belsham, who had himself declined a similar invitation, and had been consulted by letter by Mr. Wellbeloved, sums up, not very encouragingly, the arguments for and against his acceptance. "You must not exchange your present situation for that of a tutor, under the expectation of having your mind more at ease. If you undertake the office with a view to make a better provision for your family it is well. If

with a probable prospect of more extensive usefulness, better still; and these motives will invigorate
and support your mind under the difficulties, disappointments, and mortifications you will have to
encounter. * * * I think the difficulties attending
such a situation are so great, that nothing but a
clear conviction of having acted from the best
principles in accepting the office will support the
mind under them; but this testimony will carry a
man through everything." Before leaving London,
however, he wrote to Mr. Robinson, authorizing him
to say that "the choice of a theological professor
was made." This was considered as a virtual
acceptance of the office, though not an official
communication to Dr. Percival. What other circumstances had produced a change in his views
after his return to York I do not know; but the
parents of some of his pupils whom he had hoped to
take with him had declined to send them to Manchester, and others who had promised him pupils
withdrew the promise. When, in the beginning
of February, 1798, he finally declined the invitation, the following resolution was sent to him
by Dr. Percival:—"Rev. Sir,—The Special Committee of the New College, now assembled, have
received your letter with much surprise and disappointment. They wish you all prosperity in
your undertaking, and will proceed without further
delay to the nomination of another gentleman to

fill the vacant chair of Theology. Signed, THO. PERCIVAL, Chairman." The tone of this letter, though softened by a friendly communication from Mr. Robinson, gave Mr. Wellbeloved much pain. He had informed Mr. Robinson of the change in his determination, and of its reason; but that gentleman had not intimated it to the Committee, on whom, therefore, it came entirely by surprise. Throughout life, Mr. Wellbeloved, when conscious only of honourable purposes, used less caution in his communications than those who make Prudence their chief divinity. In reference to an affair in which kindly feeling had placed him in a position of some embarrassment, he wrote some years afterwards, "Wisdom must generally be very dearly purchased; it is too precious an article to be bought cheap." The vacant offices were filled up by the appointment of the Rev. George Walker, the Rev. Charles Sanders, and Mr. John Dalton, and the Institution was carried on for five years longer.

From this time till 1803, Mr. Wellbeloved devoted himself to the care of his school and his congregation. Mr. Cappe died at the close of 1800, and he was unanimously chosen as his sole successor. The following letter was addressed by him to the people whose pastoral charge he was about to undertake :—

"I return you, my Christian friends, my sincere and

grateful thanks for the flattering testimony of your regard which I have so lately received, in being chosen to the important office of your minister. It is a matter of peculiar satisfaction to me that we are not strangers to each other, but that we have the experience of eight years to regulate our mutual expectations, and to prevent any pain which might arise from disappointment. That I should serve you in the honourable station in which Providence has placed me, with the ability that distinguished the services of my much-loved and venerated friend, your late faithful and affectionate pastor, is more than I can promise or than you will expect. Some portion of his spirit will, I hope, rest upon me, and enable me to discharge the important duties of the station I am called to fill, so as to promote our mutual and lasting benefit.

"This, our more intimate connection, commences at a period distinguished by the most awful events, and such as loudly call upon us to pay the most serious attention to our conduct in our respective stations. May I so preach, and you so hear, that under all the changes of these eventful times we may be consoled with the testimony of a good conscience, and prepared not only to do, but to suffer, the whole will of God. In the hope that the relation we sustain to each other may contribute to this important end, I beg leave to subscribe myself,

" Your faithful friend and servant,

" C. WELLBELOVED."

He addressed his people for the first time from the pulpit, as their pastor, January 18, 1801, from 2 Cor. i. 24—"Not that we have dominion over your faith, but are helpers of your joy." Having disclaimed all right to dictate a creed to them, he proceeds to show what is the Christian teacher's duty, in reference to the religious opinions of his hearers :—

"The Christian teacher may, and ought, on all proper occasions, to propose to his hearers those doctrines which he regards as of divine origin and of practical importance; but having proposed them, with the diffidence which becomes a fallible being, he must leave them to be examined, and not insist upon their being implicitly received. If his views differ from the views of those to whom he addresses himself, he is not to be censured for proposing them; nor is he to indulge the expectation that his views will produce universal conviction. As he should have liberty to speak, his audience should have liberty to hear. What he deems important truth, his conscience will compel him to unfold: he can do no more without infringing on the right of private judgment, which he has exercised for himself, and which he should therefore freely allow to others. Though he claim no dominion over the faith of his hearers, he will sometimes find himself compelled to treat upon subjects of religious controversy. He should not make these the constant, or even the frequent, topics of his instruction; but occasionally he must, in obedience to the dictates of conscience, warn his hearers of error, and confirm them in the truth. In what state, my friends, is the Christian world around us? Are they professing that faith which was delivered by Christ and his Apostles? or, on the contrary, are not the original truths of the gospel defaced by the most absurd and dangerous inventions of man? In the mass of error which prevails, are not the doctrines which the Apostles preached confounded and almost lost? Are not the principles of the popular creeds and articles and confessions at variance with the best feelings of the human heart, and, if acted upon, highly detrimental to human happiness and virtue? By their prevalence, is not the faith of many, even in the glorious privileges and hopes of the gospel, destroyed, and infidelity enabled to boast of victories over uninformed minds? Do not these corrupt principles throw obstacles in the way of the philosopher, and afford the pretender to wisdom too fair a pretence for pouring ridicule upon the Christian Scriptures? How, then, can the Christian teacher, who has any zeal for the interests of truth or the success of the gospel, maintain a constant silence upon subjects of such moment? My friends, I doubt not this will appear to you, as it does to me, a matter too important to be neglected by any one who is desirous of discharging the duties of the station which I now fill. To make the pulpit the scene for angry declamation and abuse of those who maintain not the same opinions as we hold sacred, is to violate the plainest injunctions both of reason and Scripture; to injure, not to serve, the interests of truth. But a fair and dispassionate statement of the arguments on which our faith is founded, will both confirm us in our belief in revelation, and increase the influence of our principles upon our temper and conduct.

"The Christian teacher who exercises his ministry among those who dissent from the established Church, should occasionally exhibit the principles on which this separation is justified. We should have some more solid reason to allege for our assembling here than the example of our fathers, or the custom of our education. The dissenting teacher should endeavour to confirm his hearers in the profession of their religious liberty. Our characters have been unjustly aspersed, our principles wilfully misrepresented, our conduct cruelly vilified. Every means has been taken to render us suspected by our fellow-citizens, to prevent those who approved our sentiments from joining us, and to withdraw from us the inexperienced, or those of any consequence in the world. Our name is cast out as evil; persons of weak

minds have been terrified into desertion of the cause which
they had espoused; and the votaries of interest, fashion,
or ambition, affect to despise the appellation which they
once bore. It will, then, be my duty occasionally to call
the attention, of my younger hearers especially, to the
grounds of our separation from the established Church,
to confirm them in their principles as dissenters, and to
strengthen their adherence to the cause of religious liberty.
You will justly expect this from the character which I sustain; and, by the grace of God, I will endeavour to fulfil
this injunction of duty.

"It belongs also to the Christian teacher, at all times, to
direct the frequent attention of his hearers to the evidences
of divine revelation. Those who call themselves by the
name of Christ should be able to give some reason of the
hope that is in them. But at a time when infidelity is so
prevalent, and the efforts of unbelievers to shake the con-
stancy of Christians so zealous; when imposing arguments
and insinuating ridicule are levelled against our faith; when
the youthful mind is tempted to aspire after manly independence of character, by rejecting all religious sentiments;
when persons of every age, and of both sexes, are ambitious
of the appellation of *free-thinkers*, it is the duty of the
Christian teacher to stand forward in the defence of the
principles thus madly assailed. This is an object which
demands the steady efforts of wisdom and of zeal. I feel
what I think true candour towards those who do not embrace
the Gospel; unbelievers are not necessarily, as some repre-
sent them, men of depraved minds and vicious habits. But
I must confess it appears to me that they are in a state of
considerable danger, and that the most exemplary among
them have less virtue, and certainly less happiness, than
Christianity would have imparted to them. Firmly believing in the Gospel, and not without experience of its excellent effects, I shall feel it my duty, as it has long been my

practice, to illustrate the evidence upon which it rests, and
to fortify the minds of the inexperienced against the attacks
to which they will be exposed on their entering into the
world.

"But my most frequent and most earnest endeavours will
be used to render you perfect in every good work. It is of
importance that our faith should be firmly established, but
still more important that it should be manifested by our
works. Over your faith I shall never claim any dominion ;
but as the helper of your joy, encouraging you to all that
will impart true peace now, and ensure the rewards which
the Judge of all will bestow, I shall, by the blessing of God,
zealously and constantly stand forward. May this blessing
give success to all my labours which have this great end in
view, and may He grant, that when the period of my service
here comes to a close, and both you and I shall be called to
give an account of the deeds done in the body, we may meet
in that blessed state where our faith shall be realized and
our happiness be unalloyed and eternal ! "

How energetically he had laboured to counteract
the prevailing tendency of the times is evinced by
his having preached in 1794–5 a series of seven
sermons, on the Unreasonableness of Infidelity.
Besides this, the illustration of the evidences of
Revelation, and the removal of the objections of
unbelievers, formed a very frequent incidental topic
in discourses not directly bearing on this subject.

Few of Mr. Wellbeloved's pupils while he was a
schoolmaster are now living, and I have not found
among his papers any detail of his course and mode
of instruction, nor have I been able to procure such
a statement from any survivor of them. I can

describe it, therefore, only from incidental information derived from himself, or from some of his
pupils whom I have personally known. As their
number was small, he was able to carry on their
whole literary and scientific education by himself.
He was enabled, by the same circumstance, to
substitute vigilant superintendance and the influence of kindness, example, and precept, for
those harsher modes of. discipline which were
commonly employed in schools. His own training
had been one of mechanical routine ; he made it
his aim to call out the intelligence of his pupils ;
to make them understand, as well as remember.
In his biography of his friend Mr. Wood, he has
described the mode in which he carried on the
instruction of his female pupils, and I have no
doubt, from the unreserved communication which
took place between them, that Mr. Wellbeloved
adopted his plans, as far as they were applicable,
in the education of boys. He was the companion
of his pupils in their amusements and in their
walks, which were made the means of instruction
in natural history, as well as of placing the teacher
on that footing of confidential intercourse with his
scholars, which is at once an incentive to diligence,
and a preservative of correct moral feeling and
conduct. No person very distinguished in after
life proceeded from his school, but as far as I have
been able to trace their course, they have filled

their stations honourably and usefully, and I have
never known one who did not speak with respect
and affectionate gratitude of his master. Several
of them, whom circumstances allowed to maintain
subsequent intercourse with him, became in manhood his attached friends. One pleasing testimony
to the moral influence of his example was publicly
given by his pupil, a clergyman of the established
Church, the Rev. William Fenton, founder of the
Doncaster School for the Deaf and Dumb, who,
in a speech made at a meeting in York, in 1833,
attributed his own zeal for philanthropic objects
to Mr. Wellbeloved's instructions and example,
when he lived under his roof.

In the year 1802, Mr. Wellbeloved added to
his various occupations that of a literary critic.
Messrs. Longman and Rees had projected the plan
of an Annual Review, which should give an
account of all the English works published within
the year, and as many of the foreign publications as
space permitted. It was to perform the same
office for literature as the Annual Register had
long done for history, and to have nearly the same
form. The editorship having been given to Mr.
Arthur Aikin, who had now settled in London,
and devoted himself to literary and scientific occupations, his friend at York naturally occurred to
him as one well fitted to undertake the department
of Theology and Metaphysics, for which " a man

of moderation and learning" was required, and Mr. Wellbeloved accepted the offer, which promised a fair remuneration for his labour,* and gave him the opportunity of becoming acquainted with all the literature of the year relating to the subjects in which he was most interested. The chief business of the critic, according to the old idea of reviewing, which The Edinburgh was soon to put out of fashion, was to give a fair analysis of every important work. Mr. Wellbeloved would more readily engage in the undertaking, as several of his friends were to bear a part in it, among the rest Mr. Wood, to whom Natural History was assigned. In the letter containing an account of his coadjutors, Mr. Aikin mentions Dr. Yellowly, and his own brother Charles, for the various branches of medicine; William Taylor of Norwich, for politics, history, and German literature; Frend for mathematics; Carr for legal works; and Mrs. Barbauld for the leading articles in poetry and belles lettres. How far these arrangements were permanently carried out, except as regards Mr. Wellbeloved and Mr. Wood, I do not know. The hope of engaging Mr. Porson for classics was not realized, and his place was taken by Mr. Dewhurst. Mrs. Barbauld contributed to the first

---

* As a contribution to the History of Prices, I may mention that Messrs. Longman and Co. paid their labourers seven guineas and a-half per sheet.

volume the review of Chateaubriand's Genie du
Christianisme and of the second volume of Miss
Baillie's Plays; but with her known distaste for
compulsory labour, she was not likely to work long
in such a literary treadmill.   In sending Mr. Wellbeloved a parcel of fifty-five theological works, the
editor says, "these are, I imagine, a full half of
the books which will fall to your share."   He
furnished to the first volume about eighty-six
pages of print; a MS. which would have occupied
another sheet and a half having been lost in trans-
mission.   Some of the articles, therefore, in the
latter part, were supplied by other coadjutors.
The review of the labours of the Baptist Missionary Society was written by Robert Southey, who
was a large contributor in various departments.*
Mr. Wellbeloved's part includes reviews of Cappe's
Critical Dissertations, and Nisbett's treatises on the
subject of the Second Coming of Christ, Marsh's
translation of Michaelis, and some pamphlets occasioned by his theory of the origin of the three first
Gospels, Paley's Natural Theology, Maltby's Illustrations of the Truth of the Christian Religion,
Fuller's Calvinistic and Socinian Systems Compared,
Porteus's Lectures on the Gospel of St. Matthew,
Burder's Oriental Customs, Lindsey's Conversations
on the Divine Government, Zollikofer's Sermons,

* See his Life, by the Rev. C. C. Southey, vol. ii. pp. 250, 294.

and some pamphlets on the Calvinistic or non-Cal-
vinistic character of the Articles of the Church of
England. It is to be feared that a review of a year's
productions in theological literature, at the present
day, would not furnish so rich a list of original and
valuable works. It must have been a pleasant, as
well as an improving, labour to analyze and judge
them, and this duty has been carefully and candidly performed by Mr. Wellbeloved ; but it was
impossible, with such a host of authors waiting
for review, to dwell elaborately on even the most
important. I infer that the tone of his articles
was thought by the editor too indulgent, as I find
him suggesting, after the publication of the first
volume, that though he had abandoned flagellation
in the case of his pupils, a smart touch of the
scourge might do good to some flagrant offenders.
It was very foreign to Mr. Wellbeloved's nature to
inflict pain, even on the worst of literary sinners,
but the following article on Simeon's Five Hundred Skeletons of Sermons, vol. ii. pp. 1 and 2,
will show that he could effectively administer the
corrective of playful satire :—

" More than three hundred of these skeletons have been
sent into the world already, and, to the great annoyance of
the nervous and the timid, have, we fear, been obtruded
into our pulpits. Skeletons are, to most persons, frightful
and disgusting objects ; and however artfully they may be

adorned, present a loathsome appearance. No art or device of man can ever effectually conceal them. Who will not be able to detect the artificial eye, or the false and painted cheek? Who will fail to discover the borrowed muscular appearance of the limb, or the wiry joint? Can anything less than a miracle cause the dry bones to live? But to be serious. We cannot express too strongly our disapprobation of the skeleton helps to composition, which Mr. Simeon has *prepared* for our younger divines. The eloquence of the English pulpit has long been defective, and if the publication now before us should come into general use, it will be utterly destroyed. Our sermons will lose every portion, even of the excellence they now possess; they will be destitute of vigour of thought, as well as elegance of language, and a cold, dry, uninteresting style will usurp the place of even that little energy by which the majority of our pulpit compositions is now distinguished."

The Annual Review, though its first volume had a considerable sale, seems never to have been popular. A volume in royal 8vo, in double columns, and consisting of 968 pages, might be useful as a book of reference on the shelves of a library, but was appalling from its bulk, and it came too late for the class of readers who take up a review, in order to keep themselves in the current of literary history. An attempt was made to remedy this evil by publication in weekly parts, but without success. It was an inherent inconvenience in the plan, that the obligation to notice all the publications of the year, however briefly some of them might be despatched, curtailed the space which might have been allotted to works of high merit. The edge of public curiosity had been taken off by the monthly publications (quarterlies, in those days, there were none), before the Annual made its appearance. The publication was irregular. The editor was not a man of business habits; the publishers complained that the contributors were not punctual; the contributors alleged that they were allowed too little time for their work. "I judge with you," writes Mr. Wood to Mr. Wellbeloved, "that our learned lords and masters, thinking it to be as much a mechanical business, and quite as easy, to write as to print a book; sensible, also, that as it is generally much less profitable it ought to take up proportionally less time, and, perhaps, not considering that we are but young in the book-making business, have most unconscionably hurried us, and poured in upon us more matter than we can *read* with sufficient attention, to say nothing of digesting, arranging, and other processes of that kind, which were formerly thought of some consequence in the craft and mystery of authorship. Bad as my task is, I find yours is worse. I have only thirty-two vols. and one pamphlet! I believe it will be best to make ourselves easy, and say to Messrs. Longman and Rees, as the convict on his way to the

gallows said to the mob, 'Gentlemen, you may
hurry as you please, but depend upon it, nothing
can be done till we are ready.'"

Notwithstanding the great increase in his labours produced by the removal of the College
from Manchester to York, Mr. Wellbeloved continued his contributions to the theological department of the Annual Review till its close. Mr.
Aikin resigned the editorship after publishing the
sixth volume, and the seventh was undertaken by
the Rev. Thos. Rees. The publication was rather
suddenly dropped, when he had already finished
some articles for an eighth. It must not be supposed, however, that all the theological reviews
were contributed by him. Some few were supplied by the editor, some by Mr. Dewhurst; but
all the more elaborate ones were from Mr. Wellbeloved's pen. By a mistake of the publishers,
some works designed for him in the volume for
1806 were sent to Mr. Wm. Taylor, and reviewed
by him. The articles on Methodism and Missions,
in the two first volumes, are by Southey. The
review of Middleton on the Greek article, in vol.
vii., is also by another writer, I believe Mr. (Dr.)
Jones, author of a Greek Grammar and Lexicon,
and of the Illustrations of the Four Gospels,
reviewed by Mr. Wellbeloved, with discriminating
praise and censure, in the same volume.

Mr. Wellbeloved had already, on more than one

F

occasion, appeared before the public as an author. Dr. Horsley's outrageous attack upon the Unitarians, in a letter written to the clergy of the diocese of St. David's, calling upon them publicly to recommend the case of the French priests, compelled to emigrate by the Revolution, had not been forgotten by him. The same prelate had betrayed his bias towards popery by recently declaring in the House of Lords, that "if there was any defect in the ecclesiastical establishment of this country, it was in the want of religious forms to arrest the attention and seize on the imagination of the people." Mr. Wellbeloved availed himself, in 1799, of a custom, then frequent among Dissenters, the celebration of the fifth of November as a providential deliverance from popery, to vindicate Unitarians from the reflections of the bishop, expressed in the following words:—

"You will remind them" (your respective congregations) "that the persons for whom we, in the name of God, implore aid, however they may differ from us in certain points of doctrine, discipline, and external rites, are, nevertheless, our brethren, members of Christ, heirs of the promises; adhering, indeed, to the communion of the Church of Rome, in which they have been educated, but more endeared to us by the example they exhibit of patient suffering for conscience' sake, than estranged by what we deem their errors and corruptions. More near and dear to us, in truth, by far than some, who, affecting to be called our Protestant brethren, have no other title to the name of Protestants than a Jew or a Pagan, who, not being a Christian, is, for that reason only, not a papist; persons who, professing to receive our Lord as a teacher, as the very Mahometans receive him, call in question, however,—what is not called in question by the Mahometans,—the infallibility of his doctrine; and under the mask of an affected zeal for civil and religious liberty, are endeavouring to propagate in this country those very notions of the sovereignty of the people, the rights of man, and an unlimited right of private judgment, in opposition to ecclesiastical discipline,—those treasonable and atheistical notions which, in France, have wrought the total subversion of the civil and ecclesiastical constitution, the confusion of all rights, the abolition of all property, the extinction of all religion, and the loss of all liberty to the individual, except that of blaspheming God and reviling kings."

This passage was written, as will be evident from its allusions, several years before; but Mr. Wellbeloved justifies himself for bringing it before his congregation, by observing, that such sentiments were still held of the faith and practice of Unitarians. There is no reason to believe that the Bishop of Rochester would have retracted or modified what the Bishop of St. David's had said. Appealing to his text, "By their fruits ye shall know them," he claims for the principles of Unitarianism a tendency to produce a character wholly unlike the bishop's description. To the objection which might be made to his argument, he replies :—

"It militates in no respect against our principles, that

there are those amongst us who profess them without feeling their influence. Many amongst us are persons of an inquisitive turn of mind, who, from indifferent churchmen, have become, through the force of truth, Unitarians, and have brought their indifference with them. They have embraced this doctrine as they would any speculative truth; and having never been in the habit of reducing their faith to practice, they continue what they were — men of the world. Others are Unitarians because their fathers were so before them; the word of truth in them, not having any deeper root, is easily choked by the cares and riches and pleasures of this life, and so bringeth no fruit to perfection: so it is in all other denominations of Christians. But we can reckon those, and many of them too, who, having received the doctrine in an honest and good mind from conviction, not only of its truth, but of its superior practical tendency, keep it and bring forth fruit with perseverance.

"The Bishop of Rochester will not allow us so much of Christianity as the Mahometans possess; and another equally uncandid and more popular writer, calls Unitarianism, in a manner somewhat canting and vulgar, '*the halfway house to Deism,*' by which he means infidelity.

"In the earliest, the apostolic age of the Gospel, that man was a Christian, who believed in his heart that Jesus was the Christ, and confessed his faith openly to the glory of God the Father. Whatever, therefore, modern teachers of the Gospel may assert concerning us, we have the testimony of the Apostles in our favour, and in this testimony we have reason to rejoice. We believe with our whole hearts that Jesus is the Christ, and we are not backward to profess our faith with all boldness and zeal; with more zeal and boldness, indeed, than some who will not allow us the honourable name of Christians. That some have gone out from us cannot be denied; that Unitarians have become unbelievers, is a fact too notorious to be disputed; but what

sect is there from which, of late, there have not been numerous similar defections? The charge lies against all
parties, and, consequently, has no force as applied to us
alone. We are as far, and, as it appears to me, much
farther removed from infidelity than they who profess a
corrupt Christianity; and it can only be owing to that infatuation which God is now permitting to operate upon the
minds of men, in order eventually to produce some important change in the religious world, that any who have once
enjoyed the light of the primitive Christian doctrine should
choose to wander in the oppressive gloom of infidelity and
atheism. This infatuation has seized men indiscriminately,
and all the different sects of Christianity have to lament its
diffusion."

The author repels, with great energy, the slander
that the Unitarians were partizans of anarchical
principles.

" I must detain you a few moments longer, while I
endeavour to refute a more insidious, and an equally unfounded charge. We are classed with levellers and regicides,
blasphemers of God and revilers of kings—madly bent
upon the destruction of regular government—ready to
become plunderers of the property of others, and secretly
endeavouring to bring upon our country all those evils
which have desolated a neighbouring nation. Good God!
to what will not religious bigotry impel men! Have Unitarians then alone no interest in the peace and prosperity of
their country? Have they no property to lose? Have
they not among their number manufacturers and merchants
of the first name and credit, whose whole substance depends
upon the preservation of public tranquillity and subordination, and who have, therefore, as powerful motives to
support the constitution of this country as any one who sits

upon the episcopal bench? In our sentiments respecting the person of Christ, what is there which necessarily leads us to adopt political opinions, or to engage in political practices, hostile to the peace and welfare of our country? In any other article of our religious faith, what is there that perverts our understanding, and corrupts our hearts, so much as to cause us to prefer violence, tumult, and rapine, to the enjoyment of personal liberty and security, and the unmolested possession of our property? Nothing, surely, in the eyes of the sober-minded and candid. No article in our religious faith produces that depravity which rejoices in the sufferings attending all political convulsions; nor are we of that needy class which subsists upon the spoils of others. Those who have avowed principles at all tending to anarchy, have been neither Unitarians nor Churchmen; they have been persons of no religion, removed from the influence of that doctrine which breathes good-will to all, and instructs us to live peaceably with all men.

"We may have intemperate men amongst us, and their language may, in many instances, have been misapplied and misunderstood; so it has happened to other religious denominations. We may have had, and still may have, amongst us those, who in their closets have conceived that the most perfect theoretical form of government is the Republican:— the Church of England has, in her own bosom, persons of exactly the same description. It cannot be decided, from the speculative principles, even of such persons, what their political conduct, when tried, would prove. But whatever may be the speculations of a few individuals amongst them, as a body I feel no hesitation in asserting that they are firmly attached to that form of government, under which this nation has been so long prosperous and happy. And should occasion require it, notwithstanding the unjust suspicions of many of their countrymen, they will be found as ready as any other class of the community in giving it effect, and in warding off the evils of anarchy and levelling principles. Protestant Dissenters have served their country in times of great necessity and danger, and all denominations of them are ready to serve it again. Whatever the uncandid may say to the contrary, I am well assured that they are not the persons who would invite an enemy to destroy the liberties of Englishmen, or assist the invader in the execution of his nefarious purposes. They will defend, when called to it, that government which their ancestors contributed so greatly to establish, and under which, though they do not enjoy all the privileges they desire, nor all to which they think themselves entitled, they do yet enjoy enough to attach them to its interests.

" The sentiments they entertain concerning the nature of the Christian Church can have no effect whatever upon their political principles and conduct. In separating the Ecclesiastical from the Civil Constitution, they do no more than others, not Unitarians, have done also; although they regard the alliance between Church and State as unscriptural and unfriendly to the true interests of the Gospel, the Constitution, consisting of King, Lords, and Commons, may, and does, appear to them wise and beneficial.

" Such, my friends, is the defence we honestly set up; and in the judgement of the impartial it will have due weight. Upon the minds of those who are predetermined to condemn us, who have none of that ' charity which is kind, which doth not behave itself unseemly, which thinketh no evil;' neither this, nor any other attempt to justify ourselves, can produce the desired effect. In regard to such persons, we must pray ' that it would please God to forgive our enemies, persecutors, and slanderers, and to turn their hearts,' while we console ourselves with the testimony of a good conscience."

This spirited vindication of their faith and principles made Mr. Wellbeloved extensively known
to the Unitarian body in other parts of England,
who, from the remoteness of his situation, and the
narrow sphere of his duties, had previously been
strangers to his abilities and attainments. My
first acquaintance with the name, which was afterwards to be so familiar to me, was made in copying
the book-lists of the Western Unitarian Society, of
which my father was Secretary, and which had
placed his sermon in their Catalogue.

The extracts from this sermon show, among
other things, the effect which the events of the
closing years of the eighteenth century had produced in changing political feeling.   The sympathy
which the friends of liberty had felt for the French
Revolution, and even for the French Republic, had
given place to disgust at the crimes by which the
cause of freedom had been sullied, and dread of
the military ambition which had succeeded to the
patriotic ardour with which invasion had been
repelled.   This change is still more strongly
marked in the next sermon which Mr. Wellbeloved
printed, preached on occasion of the day of national
humiliation, October 19, 1803, and published "to
testify his attachment to the civil constitution
under which he lives, and to aid the virtuous
exertions of those who are so zealously offering

themselves in its defence." The peace of Amiens,* which had been employed by the Chief Consul of France in extending his dominion and preparing the means of executing the ulterior schemes of his ambition, had been broken in the preceding spring, under circumstances which had roused the spirit of the nation, and even those who admitted that France might have the advantage in an argument founded on the letter of treaties, could not deny that the whole course of her proceedings had been a violation of their spirit.

Mr. Wellbeloved took for his text Isaiah's prophecy of the destruction of Sennacherib.

"It is a subject at all times of pleasing and useful reflection, but possessing a more than common interest at the present crisis, when the enslaver of Europe is preparing to descend upon the shores of our native island, and menacing us with a vengeance that shall find no parallel in the history of former periods."

Having detailed the events of Sennacherib's invasion, his insatiable ambition, his insidious promises, and arrogant threats, the preacher proceeds :—

* On occasion of the announcement of peace in 1801, Mr. Wellbeloved writes to Mr. Wood. "What say you to a trip next summer to Paris? I should like exceedingly to be one of a party with you. By some means or other I will, if not absolutely impossible, see that wonderful deposit of curiosities, dead and living, animate and inanimate, in the course of next year." It was found, I suppose, impossible, and Mr. Wellbeloved never crossed the Channel.

" Can anything more strongly resemble the character
and conduct of the present ruler of France ?   Has not the
historian of the house of Judah delineated, as by the pen
of prophecy, the boastful conqueror of this western world,
the ambitious invader of the rights and liberties of Europe?
How long have his emissaries been reviling that happy constitution under which Britons have lived and flourished, and
endeavouring, but in vain, to weaken the attachment of the
people to that family who have occupied the throne of these
islands with credit to themselves, and advantage to the
people, in times both of public danger and of public tranquillity !   How loudly and incessantly does the usurper
make his boast of the peoples of Europe who have submitted to the resistless, all-conquering arms of the great
nation, or of those whom, by deceit, no less than force, he
has reduced to become his tributaries and vassals !   In
what insulting terms has he not spoken of our national
character, and what contempt does he not even still affect to
pour upon the energetic means by which we are preparing to
repel his plundering bands !   By assuming in the different
nations through which he has carried his arms, the religious
character by which those nations are distinguished, march-
ing in Italy under the banner of the cross, and in the east
of the crescent, he has shown his utter contempt of all
religion, and degraded it by rendering it subservient to the
cause of lawless power and cruel tyranny.   And now, having
thus openly despised and ridiculed the God of truth, he
dares to call himself his appointed minister, chosen and
commissioned to deal the vengeance of Heaven upon a
nation which he hesitates not to assert has long been a
curse to Europe and the world.   He, too, like his predecessor of Assyria, with no less art than falsehood, has
attempted in every country to persuade the inferior orders of
society that they are not the objects of his anger, nor will
be the sufferers from his success.   He comes, he would fain

have them believe, to lighten and remove their burdens, to procure for them the blessings of real liberty and lasting peace; not considering the lesson which the subjugated nations of Europe are now reading to us, nor the bitterness of the complaint which they are daily uttering. 'His little finger is thicker than our former ruler's loins. If we have before been chastised with scourges, we are now chastised with scorpions.'"

In the following animated passage the preacher expresses the grounds of his hope that the ruler of France might meet with the same discomfiture which attended the expedition of Sennacherib.

"The war is a defensive war. Upon its issue depends not the possession of a few islands on a distant ocean, or of rich provinces in a distant continent, but our existence as that free people who have been long the admiration of the world. However trivial the pretext for entering upon the war may have been, the cause for which it is carried on is momentous—no less than the preservation of our liberties and our lives. We are fighting for the shade of our own oaks and the streams from our own springs. We are now called to defend our rightful monarch from degradation and insult; our princes, our nobles, and our senators from poverty and exile; our wives and daughters from the brutal violence of a lawless soldiery; our fathers and sons from slavery and death. When we think over the magnitude and extent of the misery with which we are threatened, instead of despondency, why feel we not confidence? The proud Assyrian led in vain his locust troops to pollute and destroy the little hill of Zion: the Persian despot, having marched in eastern pomp, at the head of the whole force of his empire, to insult and overthrow the venerable seat of ancient liberty, returned a miserable fugitive, unpitied and

alone, through those very provinces which were lately not
sufficient to supply the luxuries of his table. Wo, ourselves,
in later times, were discomfited, when we unjustly attempted
to prevent the independence of our powerful and distant
colonies, and to fill our treasury on the banks of the Thames,
with the profits of the industrious settler on the shores of
the Ohio. Even those who are now threatening to be the
invaders were not suffered to fall before the numerous and
well-disciplined forces that were on their march to dictate to
them the government they should form, and the laws they
should obey; why, then, may we not humbly trust in the
same beneficent Providence, to baffle and bring to nought
those counsels and those attempts which would deprive us
of our dearest privileges; violate our most sacred rights;
rob us of our most valued possessions and reduce us to
slavery, misery, and ruin?"

The result of a successful invasion by France
would be, that—

" Those wise and salutary laws, which have received the
sanction of ages, and under which we and our fathers have
lived in security and freedom, would give place to a code
formed by some ephemeral legislator, subversive of all our
former habits, and liable to perpetual and vexatious change,
according to the caprice or interest of successive tyrants.
The religion for which our ancestors fought valiantly in the
field, and bled undauntedly on the scaffold, would yield to
one more favourable to despotic power; the stately temples
in which our mitred prelates give borrowed dignity and splendour to the Protestant faith, would once more resound with
invocations to saints, angels, and the Mother of God; while
our more humble buildings would be either wantonly insult-
ed, closed against our entrance, or compelled to echo only
the praises of tyranny and the eulogies of the oppressor. A

power already too mighty for the repose of Europe, would be enlarged beyond all calculation; an ambition which grasps at extended dominion, would suffer itself to be limited by no bounds. Our navy, which now rides, the defence of the oppressed and the protection of the weak, would insult every shore, and convey the ministers of destruction from one end of the world to another. The levities and vices of the conquerors would be widely diffused; injury felt on one side, and injustice committed on the other, would raise and cherish the worst of passions. When we contemplate this probable result of the success of our inveterate foe, may we not without presumption, encouraged by the perfections of the great Ruler of nations, hope that our country is not destined to yield to the prowess of invading Gaul? The interests of the world are involved in the issue of this awful contest; and we have reason to believe that the Ruler of the world will not permit these interests to be the sport of ambition and of tyranny."

I have quoted more freely from these early publications of Mr. Wellbeloved, because from the length of time that has elapsed they can have been seen only by a few of the present generation. They appear to me to prove that had he enjoyed more leisure, and been excited, by a wider sphere of ministerial duty, to cultivate the art of pulpit oratory, he would have obtained high distinction as a preacher.

To the period of his life preceding the removal of Manchester College to York, belongs also the publication of his Devotional Exercises for young persons, of which the first edition appeared in

1801. Both as a parent and an instructor of
youth, he had felt the want of a work which should
inculcate religious principles, and lay the foundation of rational piety. I am not aware that any
manual existed, composed on a similar plan to his,
and combining a form of devotion for every morning and evening of the week, with appropriate reflections; and had such forms existed, proceeding
from an orthodox pen, they would of course contain sentiments and phrases, the use of which a Unitarian parent could not sanction. His aim was to
produce a work which, while it provided a variety
of moral and pious sentiment, should comprehend
only those grand principles in which all Christians
are agreed, and contain nothing which should be
obnoxious to any particular sect of Christians. In
this the author succeeded so well, that his work
found its way into the hands of many young people
belonging to the Established Church. I find, indeed, his friend, Lindley Murray, objecting to Christ
being said to be " distinguished above all the creatures of God." If he had given more weight to
the words of St. Paul, who calls him (Col. i. 15)
" the first born of every creature," than to those
of the Athanasian creed, which declares the Son to
be uncreate, he would hardly have raised the objection, but finding the expression to be a stumb-
ling block to the orthodox, Mr. Wellbeloved omitted
it in his subsequent editions. None of the author's

works had so gratifying a success as this.   Seven
editions of it were called for, between 1801 and
1826; to the fifth edition, published in 1811, considerable additions were made.   An eighth edition
was published in 1832. It was reprinted and largely
circulated in America, and during the first quarter of
the present century there were few families in the
author's own communion, in which it was not used
in the religious training of the rising generation. I
have never heard it spoken of without gratitude for
the early sentiments of piety which it inspired, and
the lessons of wisdom inculcated by the reflections.
A second week of prayers and reflections, which had
been promised in the preface to the first edition,
was appended to the seventh, and an advertisement
announced, as preparing for publication, An Introduction to the Holy Scriptures, designed for the
Use of Young Persons. The long delay in the
publication of the second week will not surprise
any one who considers the author's various and
pressing engagements.   The Introduction would
have taken the form of a series of Letters to his
second daughter, written during her recovery from
a dangerous illness, but it had not been completed
at the time of her death, and was never resumed
after that event.

He had at one time contemplated the introduction of a Liturgy into the public worship of his
congregation, and had composed some forms which

he communicated to Mr. Wood, when he was en
gaged in preparing a Liturgy for the Mill Hill Chapel.
They were not, however, suited to Mr. Wood's plan,
and Mr. Wellbeloved abandoned the idea of introducing a Liturgy into his own chapel.* His recorded opinions on this subject are not favourable
to its use. In his Life of Mr. Wood (p. 92), he
says, " Let Liturgies be drawn up with ever so
much caution, they will unavoidably partake of the
nature of a confession of faith, and may be felt as
a painful restraint by those who succeed the original composer; and on the other hand, prejudices in
the breasts of some of the worshippers, not wholly
subdued, may break forth; objections, founded upon
better grounds, may be felt by others; or even the
caprice of some who are by no means whatever to be
satisfied, may soon render it necessary, in order to
preserve the peace and union of a society of Christians, who acknowledge no human authority in
their worship of God, to withdraw the most perfect
forms that can be composed." His own congregation had certainly no reason to regret the want
of a Liturgy while he conducted their devotions.

He had not long been settled in York when
he manifested that desire for public usefulness,
which was one of the great characteristics of

---

* See his Address to a class of Divinity Students, annexed to his
Sermon, preached June 24, 1810, p. 57. It appears that he had
begun to print his Liturgy.

his life. The York Subscription Library has grown out of a Book Society, which he instituted, in conjunction with some of his friends, and of which, for a time, he managed all the concerns. The parties with whom it originated were either Dissenters, Quakers, or liberal Churchmen, and as a natural consequence the plan was denounced, by Tories and High Churchmen, as dangerous to existing institutions. This opposition of the most influential classes in York prevented any great increase of its numbers for several years. At length, when its value was acknowledged, and it had escaped the danger of their opposition, it was exposed to an opposite danger from their patronage. They endeavoured to possess themselves of its management, with a view to the exclusion of all works but those which favoured their own opinions. Happily they were defeated by the constitution which the founders had given to the society. In Birmingham and Leeds, by a system of packing committees, men of liberal sentiments were gradually excluded from all share in the management of libraries which they had founded; Mr. Wellbeloved and his friends, anticipating this danger, had vested the choice of books, not in a select committes, but in an open meeting of the members. Inconvenience has no doubt occasionally arisen from the exercise of this function by so numerous, so fluctuating, and so miscellaneous a body; but on a

G

balance of advantage and disadvantage the wisdom
of the founders has been justified by the result.
The society celebrated its jubilee in April, 1844,
and Mr. Wellbeloved was requested to address the
members on that occasion, and gave an interesting
history of its origin and growth. He was then the
sole survivor of the founders.

No public institution, whether of a literary, scientific, or philanthropic character, was set on foot in
York, which did not receive his active support.
Though he lived so much among books and in the
past, the present interests of his fellow-creatures
were never neglected by him. He was qualified
for the effective discharge of public business by his
methodical habits, his clear and calm judgment,
and the candour which, springing from an unfeigned humility, made him ready to defer to the suggestions of others, where no important principle was
concerned. His attention had been early directed
to the imperfections in the English poor-law system, and particularly to the management of poor-
houses. I find him, in 1802, in correspondence
with Mr. Wilberforce, respecting some papers on
the management of the poor-house in Hamburgh,
drawn up by Mr. Voght, who, in consequence of
his exertions in that city, had been invited to Vi-
enna by the Emperor, with a view of establishing a
plan for the abolition of mendicity, the promotion
of industry, and the improvement of the condition

of the lower orders, on the principles of the Hamburgh Reform. Mr. Wellbeloved was desirous of translating these papers of Mr. Voght, and publishing them along with a pamphlet by the same author, in order to induce the people of York to form a similar institution. Mr. Wilberforce, however, had placed them previously in the hands of a professional translator, and much delay occurred in obtaining them from him. The scheme was never carried out, whether from this cause or the new engagements into which Mr. Wellbeloved was about to enter, I do not know.

CHAPTER IV.

LIFE AS THEOLOGICAL TUTOR AND PRINCIPAL IN
MANCHESTER COLLEGE.

1803—1840.

Sect. 1. 1803—1810.

A CRISIS had once more occurred in the affairs of
Manchester New College, and the Rev. George
Walker, who had been compelled for the last two
years to sustain the whole duty of tuition, had
announced his intention of resigning his office at
Midsummer, 1803. A variety of opinions was
manifested among the supporters of the College.
Some, disheartened by repeated failures, were inclined to abandon the Institution altogether. Mr.
Walker himself favoured the plan of its removal
to Halifax, in order that Mr. Jones, the author of
the work mentioned in p. 65, might be placed at
the head of it. Mr. Belsham strongly recommended Birmingham, where Mr. Kentish was
already settled and my father had accepted an
invitation to settle, with a view to their dividing
its duties between them. The Halifax scheme
met with no patron; my father's subsequent determination to remain at Exeter rendered a removal

to Birmingham impracticable,* and the Trustees, at a general meeting, held March 25, 1803, unanimously adopted the proposal of the Committee, that it should be removed to York, and placed under the superintendence of Mr. Wellbeloved. Mr. Wood, who well knew the qualifications of his friend, was strenuous in urging him to accept the invitation, as he had been in pressing the removal upon the Trustees. After an interview with Mr. Wood † he no longer hesitated, and on the 11th of April signified his ready acceptance of the office conferred upon him. In September of that year, accordingly, Manchester College was removed to York. It opened with four divinity and four lay students, besides whom he was completing the education of three youths who had been his scholars.

---

* On my father's death in August, 1804, Mr. Wellbeloved declined a proposal to be his successor at Exeter.

† Their meeting took place at Tadcaster. "It may illustrate the habits and the manners of the men and the times to mention, that when Mr. Wellbeloved desired a consultation with Mr. Wood, beyond what the means of written communication afforded, their habit was to fix a meeting for the first leisure day, at some point between York and Leeds,—Thorp-Arch, Tadcaster, Bramham Moor, Wetherby, or Aberford. Here each repaired on horseback in the morning. Whichever arrived first ordered dinner at some later hour. They walked an hour or two, dined, and at the end of the day returned to their respective homes."—*Christian Reformer*, N. S., vol. xiv. p. 684. The meeting at Borrowby, and visit to Hartlepool and Helmsley, mentioned in the same passage, took place in 1794, when Mr. Wood was in his fiftieth, and Mr. Wellbeloved had just entered his twenty-sixth year.

After accepting the office of Theological Tutor, his first care was to obtain the services of a colleague in the classical and mathematical department. The first application was made to Mr. Lant Carpenter, who, after finishing his studies at Glasgow, had recently settled at Liverpool as Librarian to the Athenæum. His subsequent success as an instructor of youth makes it not doubtful, that had he accepted the office, Mr. Wellbeloved would have found in him a most efficient colleague. He visited Liverpool for the purpose of a personal interview, but, after a period of anxious deliberation and consultation with friends, which lasted six weeks, Mr. Carpenter finally determined to remain at Liverpool. As his decision was not made known till the commencement of the session, Mr. Wellbeloved had for some weeks to carry on the whole business of the College. We cannot wonder, therefore, at the joy with which, in a letter to Mr. Wood (Nov. 26, 1803), beginning Εὕρηκα, Εὕρηκα, he announces that a load of care had been taken from his mind by his having secured the assistance of Mr. Hugh Kerr of Glasgow College, who had been recommended by Professor Young. He did not, however, enter on his duties till February, 1804. Although a member of the Scottish Church, and strongly attached to its doctrines, his amiable temper made him a very agreeable colleague. Before accepting the invitation he had inquired whether

there were any restrictions on the religious sentiments of the assistant tutor. Mr. Wellbeloved
replies, " Respecting his religious opinions, neither
the Trustees nor myself make any inquiry. You
are informed, no doubt, that I am, in the strictest
sense of the word, a Unitarian, and all that I
should expect from a colleague who is engaged as
Classical Tutor is what his own good sense would
point out as proper; that if he should have occasion to illustrate philologically any passage in the
Scriptures, he would carefully avoid dogmatic
theology." Mr. Kerr was an effective teacher in
his department of classics and mathematics, and,
notwithstanding some external disadvantages, he
secured the regard and respect of his pupils. He
left York in 1807, and, on the recommendation of
Professor Young, became first of all a literary
amanuensis to Dr. Charles Burney, and afterwards
an assistant in his school at Greenwich. His place
was supplied by the Rev. Theophilus Browne, who
had been educated at Cambridge, but seceded from
the Church of England, and became the minister of
a Unitarian congregation at Warminster. He removed to Norwich, and became minister of the
Octagon Chapel there in 1809.

The first years of his official life were years not
only of great anxiety to Mr. Wellbeloved, but of
severe and overpowering labour. He was new to
the duty of governing young men, and at first felt

painfully the different relation in which he stood
to them and to the pupils in his school.   He had
to arrange plans of study, to devise laws, and to
prepare lectures on a variety of subjects.   As he
could accommodate only a small number of the
students in his own house, he had to provide
lodgings for them, and the maintenance of discipline, always a matter of difficulty, was rendered
much more difficult by their being thus removed
from his immediate superintendence.   Allowance
was not always made by parents for the occupations
with which he was overwhelmed, and which prevented him from filling up their sons' time so fully
as they wished.   It was evident that a third tutor
was required, but as yet the finances of the College
were inadequate to his support.   When it was
removed from Manchester, the whole of the permanent income (£141) was not enough to pay the
salary of two tutors (£100 * a year to each), and
though the subscription list, which in 1803 had
only amounted to £148, had increased in 1806 to
£218, it was impossible without a large increase to
engage the services of another tutor, and at the

* From a note to the Treasurer of the College it appears, that
among his memoranda of the arrangements for the removal of the
College to Manchester, Mr. W. had omitted to note what his own
salary was to be. The terms for lay students were fixed at eighty
guineas per session, which then began on the first Thursday in
September (afterwards changed to the third), and closed the last
Thursday in June.

same time grant exhibitions to students, and meet the other necessary expenses of the Institution. Mr. Wellbeloved had a serious illness in April, 1807, and it will not appear wonderful that his health should have given way under such labours as he describes in the following letter to the Chairman of the College Committee in May of that year :—

"In consequence of the wish you expressed when I had the pleasure of meeting you at Leeds, and our conversation turned upon the necessity of providing, if possible, a third tutor, I beg leave to communicate by you to the Trustees, at their annual meeting, the plan of study which I wish to pursue, but which cannot be carried completely into effect without further assistance.

"During the three first years all the students are expected to read—
The higher Greek and Roman Classics.

Mathematics and Natural Philosophy, the whole of the course pursued at Cambridge (beginning with Euclid and the elements of Algebra), including Mechanics, Hydrostatics, Pneumatics, Optics, Astronomy, ending with Sir Isaac Newton's Principia.
Experimental Philosophy, Chemistry,* &c.
A course of History, ancient and modern.
Natural History.
The Philosophy of the Human Mind, including Logic.
Universal Grammar,
Oratory and Criticism, and other branches of the Belles Lettres.

* To lessen in some degree Mr. Wellbeloved's labours the Trustees voted a sum of twenty guineas for a course of lectures on Experimental Philosophy and Chemistry, but it does not appear that this plan was carried out.

Moral Philosophy and Jurisprudence, with a View of the
English Government.

DIVINITY STUDENTS.

The Evidences of Natural and Revealed Religion.
Hebrew. — Hebrew Poetry from Lowth's Prælections,
Chaldee.

FOURTH YEAR, FOR DIVINITY STUDENTS ONLY.
The Old Testament, critically read.
The Septuagint.
The Antiquities of Josephus.
Syriac.
Analysis of Sermons.

FIFTH YEAR.
The New Testament, critically read.
The Jewish War of Josephus.
Ecclesiastical History.
Lectures on Pastoral Duties.
Composition of Sermons.

"Such is the plan which, with the approbation of Mr. Wood,
Mr. Turner, and others, I have laid down, and to this plan
(in a very imperfect manner I confess) I have hitherto adhered.
It is certainly extensive, but not more than so than the present state of knowledge appears to me to require in an Institution designed to afford the means of a liberal education.
It is not, I own, *absolutely necessary* that a young man,
intended for a dissenting minister, should be instructed in
every subject mentioned in the above plan, but it is desirable. If our ministers be thus educated, they will be well
qualified for the discharge of their important duties, and able
instructors of youth.

"A plan much less extensive might be adopted, but the
present state of the Dissenters, and the liberal contributions

to the support of the Academy, appear to me to demand as complete a course as can be arranged. I hope the Trustees will see this in the same light.

"To carry such plan into effect no reasonable exertion on my part shall be wanting—none hitherto has been wanting. But no one is fully equal to what has fallen to my share. Mr. Kerr has confined himself (and he has been fully employed) to the mathematics and classics: upon every other subject I have attempted to lecture. I have, therefore, seldom delivered less than four, generally five lectures a day, each lecture occupying an hour. It is to be recollected that the preparation for most of the lectures cannot be made in so short a time as is occupied in their delivery. The labour, therefore, which I have undergone, since the Academy was removed to York, has been greater than is consistent with other duties incumbent upon me as a minister and as the father of a numerous family, and also with a regard to my health. The inclosed course of study must be very considerably curtailed, or another tutor must be provided, who shall take those branches which are not particularly connected with theology; to which I wish almost exclusively to apply myself."

Mr. Wellbeloved speaks lightly of the illness which had been caused by his exertions, but it had been of a very serious kind, and had produced great alarm among his friends and family connections. It recurred several times during the course of his life, under similar circumstances. In 1809 he was again so much indisposed as to be forbidden to write for a considerable time, and three months' residence at Filey were necessary to restore his strength, which had been so much impaired that he had been unable to give his lectures at their usual length. The strain of such labours as he describes in a letter to Mr. Wood (December, 1809), could not but be injurious to his health: —"Some work is always pressing to be done, and that work so various as greatly to distract my attention, and yet so urgent, that it cannot be postponed. I envy the Scotch professors, who have only one object to attend to, one branch of knowledge to teach, and who can therefore bend the whole force of their minds to one point, and find leisure to make themselves complete masters of the subject before them; who have not to go from Virgil and Tacitus to theology, from theology to ancient history, from ancient history to modern, from that to Hebrew, from that to Greek grammar, and from that to ethics, and then to theology again; and so on without intermission; and after five days' fagging in this distracted manner, to sit down to sermon-writing." Mental exertion and anxiety aggravated a constitutional tendency to dyspepsia and an irregular action of the heart, which seemed to indicate a fixed disease of that organ. This happily proved not to be the case, but the effects were distressing, and it was very difficult for him to free his mind, when they recurred, from the apprehension of immediate danger. Mrs. Cappe, who had witnessed the severity of his labours, and their effects upon his health, addressed a letter to Mr. Turner of Newcastle, in which, after stating her views of the importance of the maintenance of the College, and the risk of Mr. Wellbeloved's health giving way, if such heavy duties continued to be thrown upon him, she strongly urged him to use the influence which his name and station gave him, to obtain such an increase of subscriptions as would justify the Trustees in appointing a third tutor. Mr. Turner was his personal friend, and warmly interested in academical education. The Monthly Repository of 1807 contains the first of a long series of reports furnished by him of the annual examination, and he avails himself of the opportunity to urge the desirableness of completing the course of education by the appointment of a third tutor. This object, however, was not attained till the sessions of 1809 and 1810. In the former of these years, Mr. Browne having resigned, Mr. Wm. Turner, who had finished his theological studies at the College, and spent a session at Edinburgh, was appointed tutor in mathematics and philosophy, Mr. James Yates relieving Mr. Wellbeloved of some of the duties of the classical department. At the commencement of the session of 1810, I undertook that department, to which history, ancient and modern, with literature and composition, were added, and Mr. Wellbeloved's wish was realized, of being able to devote himself entirely to theology. He lectured henceforth ordinarily only four days in the week, reserving Wednesday for his private studies, and Saturday for preparation for Sunday's duties.

From 1803 to 1811, as there were no separate buildings allotted to the College, the students were lodged either in Mr. Wellbeloved's own house, which, however, could accommodate only a small part of them, or in lodgings in the neighbourhood. Meals were taken in his house, and lectures delivered in a room which had been built contiguously to his former school-room, now appropriated to the library, which had been removed from Warrington to Manchester, and from Manchester to York. The inconvenience of this plan was not felt while the number of students was small, but became very perceptible as it increased. Yet, notwithstanding the encroachment made upon the privacy of his family, I believe that, after the two first years were past, he felt himself more at ease, and enjoyed more the relation between himself and his pupils, than at any subsequent period. Meeting at meal-times without the restraints of the class-room, and in numbers not exceeding those of a large family, there was an opportunity for familiar conversation, especially in the evening, and the cultivation of a feeling of personal friendship, such as was scarcely possible under the system subsequently introduced, and with increased numbers. When I mention the names of Madge, Hunter, Astley, Robberds, William Turner, Yates, and Hincks, among those who were students in this first stage of the College, it will be readily understood that the pleasant and improving intercourse of the tutor and his pupils would produce the affection and esteem which prevailed between them throughout after-life.

In the spring of 1808, Mr. Wood, who had been Mr. Wellbeloved's friend since his first settlement in Yorkshire, and had of late years been brought into more intimate relations with him by the share which he had taken in the removal of the College to York, and by his office of visitor, was seized with a disorder which terminated fatally in the course of a few days. His loss was, in some respects, to Mr. Wellbeloved irreparable. They had lived in that perfect unison of convictions, sentiments, and pursuits, which Cicero pronounces to be the essence of friendship, in the passage which he has prefixed to his Memoir: " Recordatione nostræ amicitiæ sic fruor, ut beate vixisse videar, quia cum Scipione vixerim ; quocum mihi id fuit, in quo est omnis vis amicitiæ, voluntatum, studiorum, sententiarum summa consensio." With him he had discussed the College laws and course of studies ; he had looked to him for advice and assistance in the various difficulties which arose in the first years after its establishment at York ;

his last act, before the illness of which he died, was to write a letter in answer to one which Mr. Wellbeloved had addressed to him, respecting a serious infraction of College discipline. He had the painful duty of preaching his funeral sermon, and a few months later published an extended Memoir of him. At the time of life which Mr. Wellbeloved had reached, the loss of such a friend is seldom repaired; in his case it certainly was not.

Mr. Wood's second son, George William, was appointed to the treasurership of the College, soon after his father's death. He inherited, along with his zeal for its interests, his regard and affection for its theological professor. Throughout the long series of years to which their official connection extended, no cause of dissension ever arose between them. Mr. Wellbeloved relied on his judgment and principle, and was much guided by his opinions; and Mr. Wood, in their intercourse, always observed the deference due to Mr. Wellbeloved's age and character. In all the arrangements of the College, he watched carefully over his interests, which would have suffered had it been left to himself to urge their claim; his sympathy was ready and warm in all that affected his happiness, and especially in those domestic afflictions which befell him a few years later. His management of the finances of the College was farsighted, cautious, and yet bold and liberal. He had seen the weakness of academical institutions which depended wholly on the fluctuating source of annual subscriptions; and while he made every exertion to increase the subscription list, he gradually built up a permanent fund, as a resource in any temporary diminution of support, and an assurance of stability to the public.

One of the first measures of Mr. Wood's administration was to carry out Mr. Wellbeloved's strong wish that a proper building should be provided for the domestic accommodation of the students. With the feeling which then prevailed respecting the control and supervision of young men in their academical years, it was not likely that the public would long be satisfied that divinity students, and still less that lay-students, should reside in lodgings. Yet it was impossible that Mr. Wellbeloved's house should receive any additional numbers; indeed, as his family grew up, it was a great inconvenience that any part of it should be so occupied. Some influential supporters of the College had announced their determination not to send their sons as lay-students till a building for their residence should be provided. It fortunately happened that a property composed of several tenements, nearly opposite to Mr. Wellbeloved's house, was on sale at this time, and it was purchased in the beginning of 1811. The alterations necessary to adapt them to their new destination

were scarcely completed at the commencement of
the session in the autumn of that year, when they
were occupied by the students. Mr. Turner and
myself, as assistant tutors, took up our residence
in the College, the management of the domestic
establishment remaining wholly with Mr. Wellbeloved. The buildings were old, and made no pre-
tensions to a collegiate character, but they answered
their purpose well; and their division into separate
houses was, on the whole, more favourable to order
and tranquillity than if all had been collected in
one large and symmetrical edifice. Humble as the
College was, I believe many will bear testimony that
within its walls they gathered the best fruits of academical education—sound knowledge, the free intercourse of mind with mind, recollections of innocent
pleasures and manly recreations, virtuous and life-
long friendships. It must be admitted that some
inconvenience resulted from the domestic establishment not being under that constant supervision
which it would have received had Mr. and Mrs.
Wellbeloved resided in the College. The servants
were not under the control of the assistant tutors;
and even if no just grounds of dissatisfaction had
existed on the part of the students, it was almost
inevitable that they should think their comforts
were not sufficiently cared for. Their complaints
were a source of uneasiness to one of Mr. Wellbeloved's sensitive mind; and other unsatisfactory con-

sequences gradually developed themselves, which, in 1819, led to a change of system.

Relieved from the extraneous duties which had been thrown upon him, in the early years of the College, he was enabled to devote his time more entirely to the proper work of the theological department. Not having been his pupil, I cannot describe, from my own knowledge, his mode of teaching; and there remains little among his papers from which light can be obtained. His lectures were seldom written out at length, and he read copious extracts. His course was substantially the same as is detailed in his letter to Mr. Robinson, p. 89. Should this volume be taken up by a stranger to the Manchester College, he will probably be surprised that systematic theology has no place in the scheme. Judging from the analogy of other theological seminaries, he will naturally expect to find that the religious opinions of the Professor were required to be in strict conformity with those of the supporters of the institution, and that to propound and enforce these opinions was his office. Education among the English Presbyterian Dissenters had long been freed from the shackles of a doctrinal subscription; the student was received upon satisfactory testimony of his unblameable character, his aptitude for the ministry, and his determination to devote himself to it. And ample references had been given to authors, on both

sides of all the disputed questions in theology in
the course of the student's reading.   But a certain
system had been usually set forth and fortified by
proofs; deviations and objections being treated only
incidentally. Such is the form of Doddridge's Lectures, which was long the text-book in those dissenting academies which were presided over by his
pupils and their successors. Dr. John Taylor, the
first Divinity Professor in the Warrington Academy,
composed a Scheme of Scripture Divinity, which he
made the text-book of his academical instructions,
and presented to his pupils, not indeed as an authoritative standard of faith, but as embodying the
result of his own most careful study of the Scriptures.*   Mr. Belsham made use of Doddridge as a
general text-book; but when he came to treat of the
Trinity, the Deity, and Pre-existence of Christ, he
collected together the comments of orthodox and
heterodox divines on the passages on which the con-

---

* To prevent it being thought that he meant to impose a creed,
he prefaced his Lectures with a solemn exhortation to the student to
give no weight to his opinions, except so far as they should be supported by his own examination of the Scriptures. This exhortation
is published in the preface to his Scheme of Scripture Divinity, and
was adopted by Mr. Wellbeloved as introductory to his own lectures.
(See Christian Reformer, Vol. xiv. p. 633, where will be found a
sketch of his lectures on Theology). According to Dr. Taylor's idea,
it was as much the duty of a Professor of theology to propound to
his pupils what he believed to be the true doctrine of Scripture, as
of a Professor of chemistry or physics, to teach what he believed to
be the truths of these sciences, leaving it, however, to his auditors to
adopt, modify, or reject them.

troversy turns, leaving the student to form his own
conclusions by a comparison of them. In deviating
from these plans of his predecessors, and making
his theological lectures critical and philological, not
dogmatic, Mr. Wellbeloved was influenced in some
degree by a tract by the Rev. John Simpson, of
Bath, in which the author recommends this mode
of studying theology.* It approved itself also to
his judgment, as the only method by which the
teacher could be strictly impartial; since if he teaches
a system of divinity, or even proposes authorita-
tively his own interpretation of texts, he creates a
bias in the student's mind. In the sciences which
are taught by propounding a system, as psychology
and ethics, I have observed that with a change in
the opinions of the teacher, those of the pupils
begin to run as strongly and exclusively in the new
direction as they had done before in its opposite.
It was also far more in harmony with the modesty

---

* See his Essay on the Impropriety of the Usual Mode of Teaching
Theology, London, 1803, 12mo., pp. 17. In this brief, but very valuable pamphlet, the author strongly points out the unsoundness of the
dogmatic method, "which makes the theological system the interpre-
ter of Scripture, instead of allowing Scripture to be the test of the
idea of Christianity," and recommends the historical as the only proper one. The strictly historical method was so far departed from by
Mr. Wellbeloved, that the Evidences of Revelation, being introduced
in the third year of the course, preceded the regular study of the
Scriptures which began in the fourth. This was necessary in order
that the lay-students, whose curriculum extended only to three years
and was often contracted to two, might partake in this important part
of religious instruction.

and candour which were so characteristic of Mr.
Wellbeloved's mind, not to take on himself the decision of questions, respecting which men of the
greatest eminence were divided. Some of those who
studied theology in this manner, under him, have
indeed felt that it left them in a painful state of
doubt at the end of their course, and that they had
to commence their duties as Christian ministers,
without definite conceptions of the system of Christian truth.   The effect, however, is probably in
great measure owing to the circumstance, that in
.the New Testament itself no system is promulgated, and that the reader has to collect its doctrines, and weave them together for himself, as
they have been strewn by the wayside in our
Lord's biographies, and the discourses and letters
of his Apostles.   The prevailing sentiment among
Mr. Wellbeloved's pupils has been that of gratitude, for the entire freedom of judgment which
his mode of teaching allowed them.

There was another reason which, I believe, induced him to abstain from proposing any interpretations with the sanction of his own authority, or stating his own opinions in a systematic
form.   He was well aware that his interpretations
of some portions of the New Testament not only
differed widely from those commonly current, but
were viewed with apprehension even by many of
the supporters of the College, and it would have

been very injurious to its interests, that he should be supposed to use the influence of his office to make converts among his pupils. This seems the most suitable place for a statement of those opinions, which have been specially connected with the name of Mr. Cappe.

It is mentioned in his biography that, when a student at Northampton, he had entertained doubts of the truths of Christianity, and had subjected its evidences to a most rigid scrutiny. Whether, even then, he had shadowed out to himself the mode of interpretation which he afterwards elaborated into a system, we are not told; but it was his firm conviction, in which Mr. Wellbeloved shared, that only by such means could the Gospel be defended against the objections of unbelievers. The most marked peculiarity of this system, though not its germ,* was the interpretation given to that passage in the Gospel of St. Matthew (xxv. v. 31–46), in which the second coming of our Lord appears to be connected, on the one hand with the destruction of Jerusalem, on the other hand with a general judgment and retribution. The passage had been a serious difficulty to enlightened expositors, and a handle to the enemies of Revelation. If a second coming of Christ in the clouds of Heaven, to judge the world,

* According to the preface to Mr. Cappe's Dissertations, which was written by Mr. Wellbeloved, his system originated in an endeavour to fix the Scripture meaning of the terms, Kingdom of Heaven, Kingdom of God, Kingdom of Christ.

to bring the present system of things to an end, and make an eternal separation between the righteous and the wicked, had been really predicted, as an event to be witnessed by the generation in which . our Saviour lived (Matt. xvi. 28), it would be difficult to escape the edge of Mr. Gibbon's sarcasm, who, in assigning the secondary causes of the rapid diffusion of the Gospel says, " In the primitive church the influence of truth was very powerfully strengthened by an opinion, which, however it may deserve respect for its usefulness and antiquity, has not been found agreeable to experience. It was," he says, " universally believed, that the end of the world and the kingdom of Heaven were at hand. The near approach of this wonderful event had been predicted by the Apostles ; the tradition of it was preserved by their earliest disciples, and those who understood, in their literal sense, the discourses of Christ himself were obliged to expect the second and glorious coming of the Son of Man in the clouds before that generation was totally extinguished which had beheld his humble condition upon earth. The revolution of seventeen centuries, however, has taught us not to press too closely the mysterious language of prophecy and revelation." Grotius, in his treatise, *De Veritate Christianæ Religionis,** had admitted that the Apostles enter-

* Lib. ii. § 6. Nisbett's Scripture Doctrine concerning the Coming of Christ, V. i. p. 5.

tained this persuasion, and that the error had been
permitted for the sake of its useful results, and a
similar admission had been made by Lowth, the
father of the Bishop of London, and by Dr. Edwards,
in a sermon preached before the University of Cambridge. The majority of interpreters admitted, what
could not indeed be well denied, that the predictions in Mark and Luke referred to the destruction
of Jerusalem, but thought that in Matthew predictions of the end of the world and the general
judgment were mixed together : the nearer event
being, in our Lord's mind, a type of the more remote. In opposition to these views, Dr. Hammond,
in his Commentary, had suggested that the whole
of the prophecy had reference solely to the destruction of Jerusalem ; and the same view had
been maintained even more broadly by Mr. Nisbett,
a Kentish clergyman, in his " Attempt to illustrate Various Passages in the New Testament,"
published in 1787.* Hammond's Commentary was

---

* Ambigua sunt Christi responsa quorum nonnulla apprime convenient excidio Judæorum ; nonnulla videntur aptius describere
mundi ipsius consummationem. Mihi magis adridet ejus (Hammondi)
sententia, quæ tamen potest aliquatenus cum altera conciliari ; si
Judæorum excidium habeatur quasi imago quædam consummationis
mundi. Cleric. ad Hammond. Matth. xxiv. 3. Even Hammond
seems to have felt the difficulty of referring Matth. xxv. 32 to the
destruction of Jerusalem, as he says in his paraphrase, " Universus
Judæorum populus, credentes non credentes, *et omnes homines quot-
quot unquam mortalem vitam in his terris egerint*, quibus omnibus
talentum concreditum est a Deo, ab Angelis ut rationem reddant
coram illo congregabuntur."

no doubt well known to Mr. Cappe, but his opinions were definitely formed long before the appearance of Nisbett's work. In his view, the end of the *world* (συντελεία τοῦ αἰῶνος) was only the end of the age, the Jewish dispensation, brought to a close by the destruction of Jerusalem; the coming of the Son of Man in the clouds of Heaven was only this signal manifestation of divine power, confirming the truth of his predictions; the darkening of the sun, the shaking of the powers of the heavens, were a symbolical description of great political revolutions; the angels who gather the elect, are the preachers of the Gospel, who gathered believers into the church; the salvation promised to faith was the safety enjoyed by those who, believing the predictions of Christ, separated from Judaism and escaped the destruction which fell on its obstinate adherents; the goats and the sheep were respectively the unbelievers and the believers; the everlasting punishment (κόλασις αἰώνιος) of the one, the everlasting life (ζωὴ αἰώνιος) of the other, were the respective states of suffering or happiness which resulted from unbelief or belief, in the αἰών, the age or dispensation of Christianity, which succeeded to the abolished system of Judaism. The Apostles did not misunderstand their Master's meaning; but when they speak of his coming, always refer to the destruction of Jerusalem, and its effects on these two classes of persons.

In the application of Scriptural language, commonly understood to refer to a future life and general judgment, to the destruction of Jerusalem, and its effects as regarded unbelievers and Christians, Mr. Cappe, however, went far beyond Hammond and Nisbett. Thus, John v. 28, "Marvel not at this; for the hour is coming in the which all that are in their graves shall hear the voice of the Son of Man, and shall come forth, they that have done good unto the resurrection of life, and they that have done evil unto the resurrection of condemnation," is paraphrased by him, "The time is at no great distance, when all who are *now* in their graves, who at present sit in darkness and the shadow of death, shall hear the voice of the Son of God summoning them to judgment, and shall come forth out of their present state of darkness and ignorance, to a new state of mind, to a resurrection which, to those who have been obedient to the calls of Providence, shall issue in the preservation of their lives, amidst the calamities which will overwhelm their country; to those who have refused to hearken to them, shall issue in their condemnation," Diss. vol. i. p. 325. In John vi. 40, "And this is the will of Him that sent me, that every one who seeth the Son and believeth on him may have everlasting life, and I will raise him up at the last day," the concluding words are rendered, "and that I should exalt him hereafter."

In St. Paul's address to the Thessalonians (1. iv.
13), " I would not have you be ignorant, brethren,
concerning them which are asleep, that ye sorrow not
even as others which have no hope;" those who are
asleep are explained by Mr. Cappe to be those who
are not yet awakened to receive Jesus and his
Gospel; and the declaration that " we who are
alive and remain unto the coming of the Lord
shall not prevent those who are asleep " is said to
mean, that " we who are already Christians, waiting
for His coming, shall not, in respect of any
pleasures or benefits to be derived from His actual
presence, or any personal communication with
Him, be beforehand with those who are yet un-
awakened, if in the end they be brought to the
acknowledgment of the truth," vol. i. p. 263. There
are other points in which Mr. Cappe differed
widely from commentators in general, as in referring the petitions of the Lord's Prayer and the
precepts of the Sermon on the Mount, exclusively
to the Apostles, and considering the Kingdom of
Heaven or Kingdom of Christ to be his dispensation
of miraculous powers to his disciples, beginning with
the day of Pentecost and ending with the destruction of Jerusalem.   The *repentance* which the
Baptist preached was, according to Mr. Cappe, only
a change of mind (μετάνοια) from worldly to spiritual
conceptions of the Kingdom of Heaven.

Mr. Cappe, and Mr Wellbeloved after him,

rejecting the common interpretation of the passages
supposed to refer to a general resurrection and day
of judgment, believed that the state of reward and
punishment began to each individual at his death
—a belief which involves that of an immaterial
principle in man. A hearer of Mr. Wellbeloved
could hardly fail to observe, that he carefully
avoided the usual phraseology, and instead of it
employed that of a "future retributory scene."
He regarded the Resurrection not as an example
of the future life which awaits all mankind
(in which view the analogy must be acknowledged to be very imperfect), but as a miracle, confirming the truth of our Saviour's teaching, which
everywhere assumes the doctrine of a future life of
retribution, though it does not teach it in most of
the passages which have been supposed to bear
this meaning. His conception of Revelation
generally was, that it did not so much bring new
truths to light, as confirm them by miracles; or, as
he sometimes expressed it, "Christianity is a re-
publication of the law of nature with miraculous
sanctions." It is not my purpose to examine the
soundness of these interpretations; but the circumstance of their being adopted, as I believe
they were in all leading points by Mr. Wellbeloved, is too important to be passed over in his
biography. The knowledge that they were regarded by many as detracting from the interest of

the New Testament writings, by referring to an
event of comparatively little importance, passages
which had been considered among the most
precious in the Christian Scriptures, could not fail to
give him uneasiness; for while some only expressed
a candid dissent, others gave utterance to strong disapprobation. It produced a degree of reserve on
his part in respect to this portion of his theological
system, especially in his lectures. I believe that
at one period he was accustomed to present his
views more freely, and that they were the subject
of discussion between him and his pupils; but he
found the inconvenience of such a practice, and
afterwards abstained from it. He probably felt
that a want of readiness in colloquial argument
prevented him from doing justice to his own cause.
He wished also to avoid every appearance of
employing personal influence to bias his pupils in
favour of his opinions,* and though willing that
his own should be freely canvassed, his reverence
for Mr. Cappe made it painful to him to hear his
criticisms assailed by those who could not possess

* In his speech at Manchester, on the Commemoration of the
Fiftieth Anniversary of the foundation of the College, he said, speaking
of the impartiality which he had always endeavoured to preserve, "It
is pretty well known that I entertain some opinions which I believe
are not usually entertained by persons professing Unitarian principles. How is it that, in the course of the thirty-three years that I
have held my present office, not any of the young men, who have
been educated under me, have left the College professing these peculiar opinions, if I had not been impartial?"

his knowledge or maturity of judgment. His convictions remained unchanged. When I presented him with a copy of a Sermon preached before the Unitarian Association in 1826, observing the motto—

Tarda venit dictis difficilisque fides
At certe credemur ait;*

he said, "That is my motto in regard to what some people call my crotchets." Many years before, he had written it in the blank leaf of one of Nisbett's volumes. And to a considerable extent it has proved true. Modern criticism would probably pronounce that Hammond, and Nisbett, and Cappe were right, in maintaining that the whole passage in Matthew was spoken with reference to the destruction of Jerusalem, whatever difficulty there may be in discovering in the historical event a complete correspondence with all the descriptive circumstances of the prediction. Criticism, however, cannot admit the principle that there *must* be such a correspondence, and that the interpretation which establishes it must be true.†

---

* Ovid Fasti, iii. 350.

† A recent commentator evidently supposes that in the minds of the Apostles, if not of our Saviour himself, his second coming involved both the destruction of Jerusalem and the general judgment of the living and the dead. See Jowett, Epistles of St. Paul, on Ἡμέρα Κυρίου, 1 Thess. v. 2, and the Essay on Belief in the Coming of Christ. vol. i. p. 108. This supposition would certainly not have been admitted either by Mr. Cappe or Mr. Wellbeloved.

I much regret that Mr. Wellbeloved has left no detailed exposition of Mr. Cappe's system, as it appears that he had once the intention of doing. A lady, who had been for some months a hearer of his at York (Mrs. C. Heyes), had strongly urged him to publish such a connected view, and had obtained a promise that at some time or other he would undertake it. At her death, in 1844, her will was found to contain a clause bequeathing £300, three per cent. Consols, to the Rev. Charles Wellbeloved, of York, on condition of his publishing "a work in the preparation of which he has been for some time past engaged, in illustration of the views entertained of the Christian scheme by the late excellent and Rev. Newcome Cappe, of York, provided that it should be published in the author's lifetime, and within ten years after the death of the testatrix." Mr. Wellbeloved resumed the work, but abandoned it after the affliction which befell him in the year 1846, and has left nothing bearing on the subject, except those illustrations of the Index of Scripture Terms in Mr. Cappe's Hymn-book, to which I have before referred.

I believe that in other instances, as well as in reference to the passages commonly understood of a general judgment, Mr. Wellbeloved adopted Mr. Cappe's criticisms, though different from those of commentators generally, as in the interpretation of the Proem to St. John's Gospel and Philipp. ii. 6. The Temptation Mr. Cappe regarded as neither a visionary scene, nor a real narrative, but a figurative description of temptations really occurring to our Lord, as he wandered exhausted in the Desert, or crossed a lofty mountain on the way from Jordan to Jerusalem, or looked down from the pinnacles of the Temple on the courts crowded with worshippers below; the intervention of an evil spirit being merely the form in which Jewish ideas respecting the origin of temptation clothed themselves. With Mr. Cappe and Mr. Wood, Mr. Wellbeloved regarded miracles as the effect of the *immediate* energy of God, and the person by whom they are said to have been wrought as merely prompted by a supernatural impulse to *predict* the effect which followed.[*]

It naturally devolved on Mr. Wellbeloved to take the principal part in administering the discipline of the College. To reprove was always to him an unpleasant duty, even when lighter infringements of rules were to be animadverted upon, and it became most painful when graver delinquencies required more serious rebuke, and the infliction of severer and extreme penalties. It might truly be said of him, as of Dr. Law, when

* Memoirs of Mr. Wood, pp. 37, 32.

master of Peterhouse, that when he had occasion
to censure, he often suffered more than the party
censured. But whatever effort it cost him (and
only those who were associated with him could
judge what the effort was), he did not shrink from
it when demanded by the duty of his office, though
he never felt that office more onerous, or was more
disposed to resign it, than when such occasions
occurred. It was hardly to be expected that all
those on whom these censures fell should, at least
at the time, admit their justice; but they must
have felt that they were dictated by a sincere
regard to their welfare, and they were never
aggravated by unnecessary harshness of tone or
manner. Such unpleasant feelings were rare, and,
where they existed, they generally vanished before
the final separation between the tutor and his pupil.
He has preserved numerous letters, written by
those who were leaving the College, in which
their gratitude and esteem are most warmly expressed. The authors of the following letters will,
I am sure, excuse my quoting them, in the belief
that the years which have elapsed since they were
written have produced no change in the feelings
which they express. Apologizing for not having
written sooner, Dr. Hutton says :—

"I can sincerely assure you that my silence is not in-
compatible with the most strong and grateful sense of all
your kindness, and of the many benefits for which I was

most deeply indebted to you. I am not capable, I trust, of ever forgetting the many happy, and, I think I can safely say, not altogether unprofitable days (certainly some of the most profitable of my life), which I passed under your truly kind care. All my adopting mothers* are dear to their unworthy son, and shall be remembered by me to my latest day with fond and filial affection, but especially my last, for to her I think that I owe the most. To the three years which I spent at York, weak and relaxed as I know my exertions were, I can say, with truth, I feel myself more indebted than to any preceding period, perhaps of double the length; and surely I have reason to think of my York Alma Mater, and of the highly-respected friends who preside over her interests, with gratitude and affection. I sincerely hope and believe that I do.

" I remain, with much respect,

"Dear Sir,

" Your very affectionate and obliged

"friend and pupil,

"Jos. HUTTON."

Mr. J. J. Tayler thus expresses himself, in a letter dated July 3, 1820, after thanking Mr. Wellbeloved for the pleasure and benefit he had derived from his instructions :—

"I have now lived four years at York, and I do not hesitate to call them the happiest and most profitable of my life; and though now, when I have bid a last farewell to its quiet and studious retreat (for it was so, at least, to me), I leave it with views and destination somewhat dif-

---

* The writer had been previously an alumnus of Trinity College, Dublin, and Glasgow College.

ferent from those with which I entered it ; * though one of
the most pleasing and virtuous friendships which it was
ever my happiness to form, and from which I anticipated a
long and improving intercourse, an animating participation
of kindly affections and liberal views—rational discussion
and useful learning,—though this delightful connection has
been prematurely dissolved, yet I hope and trust the love of
intellectual improvement, the thirst for moral and religious
truth, and the desire of honourable usefulness which was
kindled in me by this happy disposition of circumstances,
will not be so soon extinguished, nor expire but with my life ;
and that, though now I can do little more than make verbal
professions, yet I may be permitted to show their sincerity,
by a life, if not wholly and exclusively, yet regularly and
steadily, consecrated to the prosecution of the same studies,
the conscientious maintenance of the same principles, and
the enjoyment of the same pure and rational pleasures, for
which I conceived my first, or nearly my first, fondness at
York."

It is to be regretted that no record remains of
the addresses which he occasionally delivered on
Sunday evenings to the assembled students. They
were full of wise and affectionate advice, extending
beyond academic life to the principles and duties
of that period of independent action on which
they were soon to enter. The students of the
session 1809–10 requested him to publish a sermon preached in St. Saviourgate Chapel on the
Sunday preceding its close, and he complied with

* Alluding to an intention which the writer had once formed of
joining the profession of medicine to that of a minister.

their request.   It was entitled "Objects of Pursuit proper to Young Persons who have received a Liberal Education."

One use which Mr. Wellbeloved made of the lightening of his burdens by the appointment of a third tutor, was to engage in the publication of a family Bible.   I believe that he had for many years contemplated the publication of a new translation of the Scriptures, with notes, and had communicated his plans to Mr. Kentish and Dr. Carpenter, whom he desired to engage as his coadjutors, in 1813.   To this he seems to refer when, in his Memoir of Mr. Wood,* speaking of his arrangement of the Old Testament, he says, "One differing in several respects from it, the writer knows, by experience, may be formed.   In what his plan differs from that of his venerated friend cannot here be stated; he looks forward to a time when it may be in his power to lay before the public the result of his own investigations."   That time, however, might have been indefinitely postponed, but for a proposition made to him by Mr. David Eaton, in the spring of 1814.

Eaton, who was a Scotchman by birth, had settled as a shoemaker at York, and had become well known to Mr. Wellbeloved, in consequence of his having been a principal instrument in form-

* P. 49.

ing, chiefly among his brother workmen, a small
society of Baptists, who, by the examination of
the Scriptures, had become Unitarians. He had
published, in 1799, an account of this change,
and the steps by which it had been brought about,
in a book entitled "Narrative of the Proceedings
of the Society of Baptists in York, in relinquishing
the popular Systems of Religion from the Study
of the Scriptures." The Rev. Mr. Graham, a
popular and much-respected leader of the Evangelical party in York, in his "Defence of Scripture
Doctrines," intimated his conviction that the author and his friends must have derived their
opinions from Unitarian books, and not, as he
professed, from the study of the Scriptures alone;
and in conversation, though not in print, he gave
to Mr. Wellbeloved the credit of having had a
large share in the production to which Eaton's
name was attached. In a correspondence which
ensued, Mr. Wellbeloved distinctly disclaims having
had any share in the work beyond making a few
grammatical corrections, or having guided Eaton
in the course of his theological inquiries, by putting
Unitarian books into his hands or recommending
them to him. And he thus speaks of the author:
—"They only who know nothing of the author,
but that he is an uneducated shoemaker, will be
surprised at this. His natural talents are of a
superior kind, and he has employed every hour he

could spare from the labours of his occupation to improve them by reading and reflection. Many of his friends have pursued a similar method, and rendered themselves well informed upon every subject of theology, and exhibit a curious and interesting chapter in the history of the human mind." Mr. Graham could not, of course, withhold his assent from Mr. Wellbeloved's disclaimer, but he did not abandon the belief that Eaton must have consulted Unitarian writers, or at all events have had a knowledge of Unitarian sentiments, before he began his theological inquiries. Eaton, indeed, had not asserted that he and his friends had never read Unitarian books; he expressly says (p. 84), "Though we have seen what both sides have to say, yet we wish to observe that our minds were nearly made up, by attending to the Scriptures alone, before we had read any of their works." *

The little Baptist Church, which Eaton and his friends had founded, after they had been successively members of the Church of England, Methodists, Huntingtonians, and Calvinistic Independents, subsisted for many years in York, and extended its operation to the neighbourhood. The Unitarian congregation at Welburn owes its origin to them. They subsequently acquired a chapel of their own, where Mr. Wellbeloved occasionally

* See also Eaton's letter in Monthly Repository, vol. xx. p. 479.

preached, and the students frequently. Some of the elder members kept aloof from his place of worship, deeming any kind of religious communion with those who had not undergone adult baptism to be unlawful; but gradually this prejudice wore out, and when their chapel was swept away in the construction of the new market-place, the dissolution of the church added several intelligent and valuable members to his congregation.

David Eaton had left York in 1802, and settled for a short time at Billericay in Essex, as minister of a Baptist congregation. Ultimately he removed to London as a dealer in old books, and occupied the shop (187, High Holborn) in which Marsom and Vidler had carried on the bookselling business.* Soon after his settlement he had taken a leading part in the establishment of the Unitarian Fund in 1806, which had for a principal object the promotion of Unitarianism by means of popular preaching.† His zeal and activity had given him,

---

* Bookselling was not the only branch of productive industry which he carried on. Writing to Mr. Wellbeloved in 1828 he says, " I am obliged to make what I can by my pen, which is chiefly employed in the service of University men in the sermon way. I made 30l. by a learned doctor last year. I wrote also an assize sermon, for which I received 3l., besides a political pamphlet of thirty or forty pages, for a reverend doctor for 6l. More than all, I have nearly finished lithographing twenty-five original sermons, chiefly for the service of the same learned body."

† He had communicated his ideas on this subject to the world, in a letter to the Universal Theological Magazine, then edited by Mr. Vidler. See vol. iv. p. 127.

notwithstanding his deficiency in education and in manners, considerable influence among a portion of the Unitarians of London, and his own want of learning did not prevent his appreciating the learning of Mr. Wellbeloved and correctly estimating the benefit which might result to the cause of truth, if it could be employed in some popular theological work. The plan which he proposed to him had been prepared in conjunction with Mr. Stower, the printer, who was originally intended to have been a partner in the undertaking. The first suggestion was made to Mr. Wellbeloved in a letter from Eaton of March 14, 1814, and it comprehended a reprint of the authorized version, with marginal corrections, and notes designed chiefly for the unlearned, with copious moral and religious reflections. The whole was to be comprised in two volumes 4to. I am confirmed in the opinion that Mr. Wellbeloved must long have contemplated such a work, by the readiness with which he accepted the proposal to become the editor. In May of the same year the prospectus, which had been submitted to Mr. Kentish and Dr. Carpenter, appeared. Eaton's original plan had been so far modified that the authorized version was made the basis, but corrections of readings or renderings were to be introduced into it, instead of being merely indicated in the notes; and three volumes, instead of two, were announced as the probable

extent of the work.   It was arranged between the
editor and the publisher that it should be their
joint property, the outlay being supplied wholly by
the publisher.   Eaton's means were slender, but he
calculated that the sale of one part would provide
the means of paying for another.

It has been imputed to the Unitarian body that
this work did not receive that support from them
to which it was entitled.   I find, indeed, from
Eaton's correspondence, that some who were expected to become subscribers declined to give their
names till they saw a specimen of the work, and
that others were deterred by its magnitude and the
time that its execution would probably occupy.
But, on the whole, I do not consider the imputation
just.   A list is before me of 621 names of subscribers, while Eaton's calculation was that 500
would be sufficient to cover the cost of publication.
Mr. Wellbeloved's friends, knowing Eaton's want
of capital, of business habits and business connections, were very averse to his engaging in a
work to which so - much of his time must be
devoted, with no other publisher.   At their suggestion he proposed to Eaton that he should
associate with himself one of the great publishing
houses.   To this Eaton somewhat indignantly
replied, that alone he had devised the plan, and
that he could not fairly be expected to share the
benefit with another. He knew well that nothing but

the lion's share would satisfy a powerful coadjutor. How, indeed, could it be expected that the *magnates* of the Row, if they chose to have anything to do with a work proceeding from a Dissenter and a Unitarian, would unite their names on a title-page with one who was not of *the trade*, and who kept a little second-hand book-shop in Holborn? There was at this time no Unitarian publisher, holding the place that Johnson had held, whose position among the booksellers gave respectability to the heterodox theology which issued from his shop. Irrespectively of profit, Eaton had a pride in the undertaking, which he thought would not only be the great work of Mr. Wellbeloved, but reflect glory on the author of the scheme. As far as I can judge, he honourably fulfilled all his engagements, and was willing to incur expense beyond what had been stipulated, when Mr. Wellbeloved wished to enlarge the plan. The actual sale was indeed smaller from the first than the subscription list had promised; but there is nothing of which it is more true that "singula anni prædantur euntes" than a subscription list; and five years had elapsed before the first part appeared. It was not till September, 1817, that a portion of it was submitted to Mr. Kentish, on whose critical judgment the author greatly relied, and through whose hands every part of the translation passed. Instead of the Pentateuch, which it was expected that the first part would contain, the subscribers were disappointed to receive, when it was published in 1819, only the book of Genesis; and some intimated to the publisher that they should discontinue their subscription, as there was no probability that a work on so large a scale, so slowly brought out, would be finished in the author's lifetime; while others alleged the same reason for keeping back their names. The Pentateuch was not completed till 1825.

That the delay and irregularity of publication were fatal to its success there can be no doubt. The delay arose in the first instance from the announcement of the scheme before sufficient preparation had been made. The time necessary for its execution had not been calculated. Such a calculation it was impossible for Mr. Wellbeloved himself to make beforehand. Two most important elements in it were uncertain—what time it would require to bring his labour to that state of perfection in which he could be satisfied to offer it to the public; and what time could be spared for this object, from a life almost every hour of which was already occupied. I do not think it would be an exaggeration to say that, in order to execute such a work as the author's sense of duty demanded, and to bring it out with the regularity which the publisher and the subscribers looked for, he should have been free from all other duties but those of his pastoral office. So far was this from being the case, that during the session of College he could command only one day in the week for undivided attention to it, except when assistance from one of his colleagues enabled him to dispense with his usual preparation for Sunday, and devote Saturday to the Bible. It was not a work to be executed by mechanical compilation. The text was first to be settled by a careful comparison of critical authorities; the translation and the notes to be then anxiously weighed; and even the part which might seem most easy of execution, the practical reflections, often caused a delay, when all the rest was ready for the printer. Mr. Wellbeloved had by this time become much engaged in the management of public business in York; his health was by no means firm, and had recently suffered from a very severe illness;* and the leisure of the vacation, which should have been devoted to strengthening it, was much curtailed by his occupations. The combination of these circumstances rendered delay unavoidable; yet some of them could not in any way

* In the Monthly Repository for September, 1822, p. 546, he notices the complaints which had been made, and says, "When I published the Second Part of my Family Bible, I expressed my hope that the Third Part, which was to complete the Pentateuch, would appear in the course of the last year. I was proceeding to realize that hope, and had printed the Book of Numbers, when I was attacked, now more than twelve months ago, by very severe illness, which compelled me to lay the work aside and, till nearly the present moment, has rendered me incapable of resuming it."

be altered; nor others, unless it had been by his renouncing all share in engagements not strictly professional. The imperfections of the business arrangements would alone have been destructive to the success of the work. Its distribution was very irregular. It does not appear to have been clearly settled which of the subscribers were to be supplied from York, and which from London. Beyond a notice in the Monthly Repository, that subscribers might obtain their copies on application to D. Eaton, no intimation was given that a part was published; and this notice many of them never saw. Except in very few instances, there was, no one who undertook to receive the copies and distribute them in his own locality; and the many complaints of country subscribers, that they could not get their copies through their booksellers, excite a suspicion that the *collectors* of the great London houses, as Eaton's shop did not lie in their usual beat, neglected the orders of their correspondents. No notice was taken of the work in the literary journals. Thus everything conspired to prevent the sale, notwithstanding the favourable opinion which competent judges passed upon it, and the account exhibits a larger number left on hand of each successive part. The complaints of the publisher, who laid the whole blame on the author's delay, and expressed himself in bitter, and often harsh and disrespectful language, must have been very painful to Mr. Wellbeloved; and had he not loved his work for its own sake, he would certainly have renounced it. Eaton died in 1829, and his business was carried on by his widow till 1835. The last (9th) part was published in 1838 at Mr. Wellbeloved's expense. The first volume, called Part I., contains the Pentateuch; the second, called Part III., Job, the Psalms, Proverbs, Ecclesiastes, and Solomon's Song. To complete the history of this "illfated work," as its author was accustomed to call it, a large portion of the impression of the first eight parts was sold, without his knowledge or concurrence, to pay arrears of warehouse rent.

Instead of sharing the surprise expressed by his publisher and subscribers at its slow execution, the reader of his life is more likely to enquire, how he contrived to carry on at once so many occupations? For, besides all his official duties, there were few weeks in which he had not to attend meetings of the various public bodies on whose committees he had been placed. An hour and a half was devoted to exercise in company with his wife, and afterwards with his invalid daughter; and politics and modern literature were not altogether neglected. One great secret of his being able to do so much was, that he rose early, in winter lighting his own fire; so that when he made his appearance at morning prayers, with his Hebrew Bible in his hand, to follow the lesson from the Old Testament,

and note the changes or remarks which suggested
themselves, he had already enjoyed three hours of
quiet study.   The employment of his time was
methodized, and he had that instinctive sagacity
which saw at once the right mode of setting to
work on whatever was to be accomplished, and
prevented time being wasted on fruitless ex-
periments.

It may, perhaps, be thought that a plan, com-
prehending at once the settlement of the text, a
corrected version, notes critical and explanatory,
and practical reflections, aimed at too much.   But
if it had been less comprehensive, it could not have
been undertaken at all.   It was to be a Family
Bible; and had it promised only a revised text
with notes, it would never have obtained sufficient
patronage to authorize its publication.   Those who
are familiar with the habits of Presbyterian dissenters towards the close of the last century and
the beginning of the present, will remember, that
the custom of reading, at family worship, morning
or evening, a portion of the Scriptures, accompanied by the notes and reflections of Doddridge or
Orton, or of Matthew Henry himself, was not ex-
tinct.   But the style of even the most modern of
these was unsuitable to the altered taste of the
age, and the religious system of the authors had
been abandoned or modified.   There was, therefore, a general desire among us for a work which

should embrace the same objects, but be unobjectionable in point of doctrine; and Mr. Wellbeloved's project was welcomed, as promising to supply a want which now, probably, is not equally felt. The urgent claims of business and gaiety had not then so completely absorbed the leisure of both morning and evening, as to leave no room for family devotion and scripture reading; the general prevalence of afternoon services in our chapels at that time, afforded the head of a household the opportunity, at least on the Sunday evening, of assembling his children and servants for these purposes. Many, therefore, who would have been indifferent to a corrected text and a new translation, were pleased with the idea of possessing a work for practical religious use. There can be no question that, in embracing so much, the risk was incurred that the undertaking might be left unfinished; and this is to be regretted, as having limited the benefits of the author's labours. As regards his reputation, it was better that it should remain, finished in execution, though incomplete in extent, than that it should have been hurried on by a rapid and superficial treatment.

For the general character of this, the chief literary labour of Mr. Wellbeloved's life, I would refer the reader to the fair and comprehensive criticism upon it given in the Christian Reformer, vol. xv. 36. In the years which elapsed between his first

K

publication of the Pentateuch, and his final revision of his translation, Hebrew criticism had
made great progress, and its principles had become less arbitrary. The character of the Sama-
ritan Pentateuch, and its authority, in comparison
with the Hebrew text, had been better ascertained;
and, generally speaking, the tendency of criticism
had been to discourage conjecture, to exalt the
authority of the Hebrew MSS., and, in philology,
to abandon those interpretations of words which
had been deduced from the cognate dialects, and
make the Hebrew its own standard. Mr. Wellbeloved's correct taste always repelled him from the
style of Geddes's translation; but when he undertook the publication of his Bible, he was more
disposed to defer to him as a critic than in later
years.

Devoted as he was to biblical studies, and deeply
impressed with the value of the sacred writings, it
was natural that he should hail the formation of
the Bible Society, though well aware of the imperfections of the common version, and the im-
possibility that the Scriptures should be everywhere understood, if read in that version "without
note or comment." But he rejoiced in the catholic
spirit by which its founders appeared to be animated, and spoke eloquently in its behalf at a
meeting held in York in 1815. He was at first
a member of its committee, and one of his family

acted for many years as secretary to the Ladies'
Bible Society. Gradually, however, the unsec-
tarian spirit in which it had been founded suffered a change. There was not, indeed, in York,
as in some places, an attempt to exclude Unitarians from the committee, but it was evident that
their presence was unwelcome, and he ceased to
attend the meetings. In 1835 he finally withdrew, one of the speakers at the annual meeting
having asserted, without contradiction from those
in authority, that the Society was Trinitarian. In
a letter replying to Mr. Wellbeloved's announcement of his withdrawal, the treasurer expresses his
regret, acknowledging him to have been one of the
original founders and most zealous advocates of the
Society, disclaiming at the same time for himself
the sentiment complained of.

The health of Mr. Wellbeloved's family, as well
as his own, made it necessary for him to spend a
considerable part of his vacation on the coast of
Yorkshire; and Filey, then a mere fishing village,
was recommended to him as a quiet retreat, and an
interesting spot for the naturalist. If a more in-
land situation was deemed desirable, he resorted to
Helmsley, a small town in the Vale of Pickering,
which combined many objects to gratify the tastes
of a cultivated mind. The neighbourhood was

rich in botanical productions; the mansion of
Duncombe Park contained some choice specimens
of painting and sculpture; and within the grounds
stood the ruins of the ancient castle, and of the
Cistercian Abbey of Rievaulx, the most beautiful, in the union of scenery and architecture, of
all the monastic remains of Yorkshire. He seldom undertook more distant journeys. One exception I remember with peculiar pleasure, when
he accompanied me on a visit to my native place.
We met at Birmingham in July, 1813, and proceeded through Bewdley and the ancient domain
of the Mortimers, to Ludlow, where his friend
Arthur Aikin and his sister were staying. Mr.
Aikin had begun the study of the natural history
of Shropshire during his residence at Shrewsbury;
he had been an early cultivator of the then infant
science of geology, and had visited the county
several years in succession, in order to collect
materials for a geological map. We could not,
therefore, have had a better guide to every object
of interest in the neighbourhood. We visited with
him the castle of Ludlow, where the room is still
pointed out, in which Comus was first acted by the
daughter and sons of the Earl of Bridgewater,
who, as Lord Warden of the Welsh Marches, kept
his court here; and the remains of the other castles
and castellated houses, with which this border-land
abounds. From the eminences in the neighbour-

hood, Yeo Edge and the Titterstone hills, we had views stretching far and wide over the beautiful scenery of Shropshire and the adjacent counties, to the Wrekin and Caer Caradoc, Snowdon and Cader Idris, the mountains of Radnorshire, Brecknockshire, and Monmouthshire, with the nearer Malvern Hills. We visited also Downton Castle, a beautiful domain, in which Mr. Payne Knight had exemplified the principles of picturesque gardening and architecture, which his work on Taste lays down. Everything conspired to heighten our enjoyment; the weather was bright, with occasional showers and passing clouds; every spot we visited was replete with historical interest and natural beauty. The renewed society of his friend, from whom he had been separated for many years without any diminution of affection, and the animated conversation of his sister, gave him recollections of the four days spent at Ludlow, which never seemed to fade; and when recalled, at however remote a period, he dwelt upon them with delight.

Our journey lay through several towns and cities, containing remains of ecclesiastical architecture—Tewkesbury, Gloucester, Bristol, Glastonbury, and Wells; and to visit and study these was a leading object with Mr. Wellbeloved. The love of antiquities had been formed since his settlement in York. There was little to inspire it in London, where the traces of Roman and even mediæval times have been buried beneath the accumulation of ages, destroyed by fire, or swept away by modern improvements; nor was the spirit of the period in which his youthful tastes were formed, likely to produce reverence for the aristocratic and ecclesiastical institutions with which mediæval buildings are associated. But the sight of York Minster seems to have made him an antiquary; for in the first letter which he wrote from York, he speaks of it with an admiration, which was only strengthened by longer contemplation and more minute study. In the year 1804 he had published a guide to the Minster, which shows how thoroughly he appreciated its beauties, and how accurately he discriminated the styles and ages of its different parts. Such critical knowledge was then rare, and we seldom visited a cathedral in which he had not occasion to call in question the traditionary lore of the vergers. Some of them were inclined to do battle on behalf of their legends, but the majority received the correction of them with deference, and were evidently impressed with the belief, that the visitor who displayed so much knowledge must be himself a dignitary of some cathedral. He has noted the verger at Gloucester, as one superior to his class. He had some characteristic anecdotes of George III., whom he had accompanied round the church, when he visited it from Cheltenham. On being

told that the pillars of the nave were Saxon (Saxon
and Norman were not discriminated in those days),
the king observed, "If they are, they will be found
to be three times as high as their circumference."
"I measured them," said the verger, "the very
next morning, and I found they were between
twenty and twenty-one feet in circumference and
sixty feet high;" and his reverence for royalty
seemed to have been not a little increased by this
proof of his sovereign's sagacity. Dean Tucker,
who was in attendance upon the king, observed,
that some persons found fault with the massiveness
of the pillars. "They are wrong, they are wrong,"
said the king; "what would they expect or have?
The persons who built these pillars built them according to the fashion of the times; they knew no
other form of pillars, and they show the architecture of the times." Observing the paltry and
barbarous screen which good Bishop Martin Benson erected, he spoke of it in terms of severe
reprobation. "Benson! a good man and a good
bishop,* but no taste; but he is not so much to
blame as the architect, who ought to have known
his business better. It was no fault in the bishop
to be ignorant of architecture, but it was in the
person whom he employed. Who was the man?"
"Kent, may it please your majesty." "Kent was

* "Manners with candour are to Benson given."
                    Pope. *Epilogue to the Satires.*

a fool." Our visits were very unlike those usually paid to such places. At Gloucester we were four hours in the cathedral; at Wells, the verger left us in the building after morning service, and we remained till it was opened again for evening prayers. One circumstance had cast a gloom over the latter part of our journey—the absence of any tidings from his home, owing to the letters which had been directed to him at Bath having been sent back into Yorkshire by mistake.* The unhappiness which this caused him for several days can be only estimated by the depth of his domestic affections, and his proneness to be

> " over-exquisite,
> To cast the fashion of uncertain evils."

After visiting all the points of interest in the neighbourhood of Exeter as far as Torquay, and making a short excursion to Plymouth, Mr. Wellbeloved returned by Bridport, Salisbury, Stonehenge, Warminster, Bath, Bristol, and Birmingham to York. He had been absent seven weeks and two days. In concluding his journal, one of the very few which he kept, or has preserved, he says, — "In this tour I have experienced much

---

* The Rev. Dr. *Waddilove*, Dean of Ripon, had been sojourning at Bath, and the postmaster, concluding that Mr. Wellbeloved's letters were meant for him, had despatched them to Ripon. They were not recovered till he visited Bath a second time, on his journey home.

pleasure, and I hope I have derived some improvement; and for the comfort and protection enjoyed in it, and a safe and happy return, my thanks are due to a kind and ever-watchful Providence." It had not only introduced him to a part of the kingdom with which he was previously unacquainted, but had made him known to a large number of persons of the same religious persuasion. Everywhere his pulpit-services had been highly acceptable, and his visit did much to strengthen the College in public estimation. He paid one other visit to Devonshire, accompanying my wife and myself to the romantic coast of Lynmouth and Ilfracombe, after the meeting of the British Association in Bristol in 1836.

It was soon after his return from this journey into the west that Mr. Wellbeloved was led to take a part of the management of the York Lunatic Asylum. This institution had been established in 1772, primarily for the reception of parish paupers and other indigent persons afflicted with lunacy, by a general subscription of the county, and the building was opened in 1777. In process of time, however, it was so far diverted from its original purpose, that the physician who was at the head of the establishment derived a large emolument from the wealthy patients who were confined in it, while the comfort and due treatment of the poorer classes of the

inmates were shamefully neglected. Instances of
neglect and cruelty were believed to be frequent,
and with good reason, as was subsequently shown.
The York Asylum was not, perhaps, worse in these
respects than other establishments of the same
kind, but there had sprung up near it an institution of similar object, the Friends' Retreat,* the
humane and successful management of which, as
exhibited in the publication of Mr. Samuel Tuke,
provoked a comparison greatly to the disadvantage
of the Asylum. What had been long suspected
was brought to light, in the close of the year
1813. A case of flagrant neglect and ill-usage
of a patient came under the notice of an energetic and independent magistrate, the late Godfrey
Higgins, of Skellow Grange, near Doncaster, who
insisted on its investigation by the court of governors. Strong interests were leagued in the
endeavour to suppress the truth. The physician
was connected with the gentry of the county, a
circumstance nowhere more potent than in Yorkshire ; he had many friends among the governors
resident in the city ; every officer whose character
was implicated, from the physician himself to the
lowest of the servants, was ready to declare that
the charges were false ; and the quarterly court,

---

* Mr. Wellbeloved's friend, Dr. Robert Cappe, had been physician
to the Retreat, and in his Sermon on his death he speaks with high
praise of the treatment of the insane adopted there.

held December 2, 1813, satisfied with this evidence, passed a resolution declaring them to be so. The public did not share in this satisfaction, and thirteen gentlemen, of whom Mr. Wellbeloved was one, became donors of twenty pounds each, in order to qualify themselves to act as governors at the adjourned meeting of the quarterly court, held December 10. They were of course charged with caballing to obtain a majority, and carry their motion for a committee of inquiry by surprise; but they were fully justified by the result of the inquiry, which showed gross inhumanity and dishonesty on the part of the keepers, and a system of management radically bad. The occurrence of a fire in a wing of the Asylum, on the 28th of the same month, in which two of the patients at least lost their lives, owing to the absence of the attendants, filled up the measure of public indignation, and called the attention of the whole country to the necessity of a thorough reform in the system of lunatic asylums, which has been since carried out by legislative enactments. From this time Mr. Wellbeloved took a very active part in the management of the Asylum. His benevolence led him to feel a lively interest in those who were suffering from this grievous affliction; he was convinced of the power of gentleness and kindness to remove what severity only tended to aggravate. He felt none of that undefinable terror of the

insane which affects many persons of stronger
nerves and greater physical courage, but mixed
freely and fearlessly among them. His voice and
manner were peculiarly suited to soothe a troubled
mind and win confidence, and his sagacity pointed
out to him how their delusions were most effectually to be dealt with. For twenty years he filled
the office of chairman of the committee, and when
he resigned it in 1850, he received the cordial
thanks of that body for the "great and eminent
services which he had rendered to the institution."*

SECTION 2.   1819—1840.

The arrangements which were made in 1810 and
1811 had proved so far successful, that the support
given to the College, and the numbers of the students, had steadily increased. But this increase
of numbers made more sensible the difficulty of
proper management, without the actual residence
of the head of the establishment. The difficulty

---

* In the year 1815, an accident happened which Mr. Wellbeloved
has recorded in a note to the diary of Sunday duty to which I have
referred, p. 31: "The service was interrupted this day, almost
immediately after I had entered the pulpit, by a full of several portions of the ceiling. The greater part fell upon the reading desk,
and in all probability my life must have been lost, if I had not left
the desk sooner than usual. This day, therefore, is to be remembered by me with gratitude to the Preserver of Life." He preached,
on the re-opening of the chapel, from the text, Acts xvii. 28: "In
him we live and move and have our being."

was increased by the marriage of my colleague, and his consequent removal to a separate residence; and my position, when thus left alone, was so unsatisfactory, that I made known my intention to resign my office at the end of the session 1818–19. Ultimately it was settled that Mr. and Mrs. Turner should remove into the College, and undertake the domestic management, such pecuniary arrangements being made with Mr. Wellbeloved, as seemed likely to secure him an equal remuneration, with less responsibility and care. I went to Germany for a twelvemonth, my place as classical tutor being partly supplied by my friend Mr. J. J. Tayler, who was then finishing his divinity course. I returned to my post in 1820, and in the following year entered into a relation which united me more closely than ever to Mr. Wellbeloved. In the meantime, a domestic affliction had befallen him, the first of a series of losses by which his patience and resignation were most severely tried. His second son had devoted himself to the ministry, and after receiving an excellent classical education in Mr. Cogan's school, had been for three years a student in the College, where he had gained great distinction, and had just received the prize for Greek composition, offered for several years by a friend to the College, under the name of Euelpis. Knowing how much his father desired for him an opportunity of becoming thoroughly acquainted with German, I offered to take him with me, and we left England in July, 1819. We designed to pass the winter in Göttingen, but had established ourselves previously for a few weeks in the pleasant residence of Homburg, near Frankfort-on-the-Maine. In the end of the month of September, when we were preparing for a short tour previous to settling at Göttingen, he was attacked by a nervous fever, which became typhus, and carried him off in the course of a fortnight. From my own knowledge, I can fully confirm the character given of him by his fellow-student, Mr. Tayler, who describes him as "gifted by nature with superior talents, and furnished by education with the amplest means for their development; possessing a thoroughly warm, benevolent, and guileless heart, joined with a rectitude and purity of feeling, which guided him aright even in his gayest and most thoughtless hours."*

* Monthly Repository, xiv. 704. Our amiable princess Elizabeth, who was married to the Hereditary Prince of Hesse Homburg, had been greatly interested by my companion, and when she left Homburg on a visit to her sister, the Queen of Wurtemburg, during his illness, she desired me to inform her of its issue. In showing us her apartments in the castle, she had pointed out to us a copy of a volume of sermons by the Rev. George Carr, Episcopal Minister of Edinburgh, which had been a great favourite with her father. The king had marked many passages with his pencil, and often read in it to the queen. Mr. Carr was, like his successor Alison, a tasteful expounder of the morality and the evidences of the Gospel, and the marked passages were all of this practical character. Mr. Carr's name is connected with the story of the attempted alienation of the

By the warm eulogy of a friend may, in some
degree, be measured what he was to his own
kindred, and what was the grief of his parents,
in this sudden blighting of their fairest hopes.
It was the cherished thought of his father that
his son would pursue the line of his own favourite
studies, and carry out the work which he might be
compelled to leave unfinished. He has written in
the margin of his diary, "O spes meæ inanes!
Ergo omnis mea cura ad alienos spectat." Sorrow
pressed heavily on every member of the family,
but his mother, I think, never recovered the blow.
Her health had been feeble from an early period of
her married life, and its cares and anxieties had
exceeded the common standard. Anxiety about
the health of her husband had recently been added.
The death of Mrs. Cappe, in the summer of 1821,
had agitated him more than an event so much in
the course of nature might have been expected to
do; but it had been sudden; it had called upon him
for additional exertion, at a time when his strength
and spirits had been impaired; it had prevented
his usual relaxation at the sea-side; and it deprived
him of a friend, whose cheerful views of life, and
firm faith in Providence, banished doubt and de-

estate of the Offley family. See a pamphlet by Mr. Hunter, who
has stripped off some of the fabulous additions to the story made by
the author of Tremaine, and placed the conduct of Mr. Carr in a
less reprehensible point of view.

spondency from the minds of those who came within her influence. The illness to which he alludes in his letter to the Monthly Repository (see p. 125) had been so alarming, that he had gone to London in the winter succeeding her death to consult Dr. Birkbeck, and had been warned that some relaxation of the severe labour which he had imposed upon himself was absolutely necessary. He accordingly spent part of the vacation at Redcar.

Another and still heavier affliction than that from which he was recovering, overtook him in the winter of the following year, in the death of his wife, with whom he had lived in the most perfect harmony for nearly thirty years, and who had borne him nine children, of whom seven survived her. She was a woman of very amiable disposition, of cultivated mind and polished manners, devoted to her children and beloved by them, and well fitted, by an even, calm, and yet cheerful temperament, to be a helpmate to a husband more susceptible of fluctuation of spirits, more liable to be disturbed by passing events. The sorrow which her loss occasioned was too deep and too sacred to be dwelt upon; it may be conceived by one who reads his own reflections upon the narrative contained in the 23rd chapter of Genesis: "They who know what it is to be deprived by death of a valued friend and companion, may in part be able to sympathize with the venerable patriarch; but they only who have lost their partner in the joys and sorrows of life can fully comprehend the distress of those moments, when he sat weeping at the door of the tent, and closed the mouth of the sepulchre of Macpelah."

It was, upon the whole, a fortunate circumstance that at this time he had been drawn into a theological controversy, which necessarily gave a new direction to his thoughts, and the demands of which were too urgent to allow of delay. I allude to his Letters to Archdeacon Wrangham. Captain Thrush, a naval officer, had printed, in the summer of 1821, a letter to the inhabitants of the parish in which he lived, containing a statement of the reasons which had induced him to discontinue his attendance on the services of the Established Church; and in doing so, in order to justify himself in the eyes of his neighbours, had urged his objections to the doctrines which are embodied in them. The letter had been communicated to Mr. Wellbeloved in MS. by Captain Thrush's friend, the Rev. Benjamin Evans of Stockton. He warmly advised its publication, and thus began, as he expresses himself in his Memoir, "a friendship on which the writer looks back as one of the most pleasing circumstances of his life." As this letter had been extensively circulated in the neighbourhood of Captain Thrush's residence in the North

L

Riding, the Rev. Francis Wrangham, who had just been appointed to the Archdeaconry of Cleveland, thought himself called upon to notice it in his primary visitation charge, delivered in July, 1821. He did so in the following terms :—

" It is not for our national Establishment alone, essential as we affirm that Establishment to be to the continuance of a sober and truly evangelical faith amongst us, that we must now, one and all, exert· ourselves.   The contest is no longer on the subject of this or that various reading, the interpretation of half a dozen disputed texts, or even the genuineness of one or more entire chapters of the sacred volume.   The boldness, no doubt, which garbles, and the ignorance which mistranslates, should have their severe and sufficient reprehension.   And I am concerned to state, that, in some parts of this archdeaconry, opinions of the character alluded to have been gratuitously forced into vulgar circulation, which (from whatever motive they have emanated) may require to be examined and exploded in a future charge.   For surely next—at whatever width of interval—next to the Deist stands the Socinian ; next to him who impugns the inspiration of the Gospel, he who denies the divinity of its first Promulgator."

Captain Thrush, not daunted by the threatened explosion, published, in the end of 1821, a letter to the Archdeacon of Cleveland, to which he sub-joined a reprint of some remarks on the Athanasian Creed by a lady (supposed to be the celebrated Mrs. Carter), and of his own letter to the inhabitants of Filiskirk.   The Archdeacon redeemed his pledge by a charge delivered the following summer, which was printed by the particular desire of the clergy, and to which an Appendix and Notes of forty-three pages were annexed, in confutation of Captain Thrush's letters and for the overthrow of his system. His language was that of a man who had no doubt of annihilating his opponents.

" As to the sect at large, I trust that I have, in the following notes, without much parade of ' ponderous erudition,' vindicated my censure—not unadvisedly issued—of ' the boldness that garbles and the ignorance (to use the mildest phrase) that mistranslates.' This has already been often proved before. But although crushed wherever they have sprung up, ' they rise again, with twenty mortal murthers on their heads.' Their skill, indeed, in arguing must be owned, if it be any test of it that, like the poet's village schoolmaster, ' e'en though vanquished, they can argue still.' After

> Ruin upon ruin, rout on rout,
> Confusion worse confounded—

new generations rush presumptuously forward ; and from the rags and tatters, the miserable remnants of former frays, vamp up new dresses of heretical patchwork,

> ——— refusing
> *Right* reason for their law, and for their king,
> Messiah."

The Appendix is written throughout in the same strain of boastfulness and bad taste :—

" Why am I to be harassed with the squabbles of South and Sherlock, or to be called upon to digest the nauseating

crambe recocta of Lindsey and Priestley, and Cogan and
Carpenter, and Belsham and Capt. Gifford, R.N. ?   These
may all be securely consigned to their respective antagonists.
Their lances are shivered.

> Postquam arma DEI ad Volcania ventum
> Mortalis mucro, glacies ceu futilis, ictu
> Dissiluit."—P. 86.

Captain Thrush, finding, as he told Mr. Wellbeloved, that the battle, in the language of the
profession which he had not yet renounced, now
required heavier metal than he carried, called on
him to take his place; and he, feeling that he was
" set for the defence of the Gospel," responded to
the call.   He was personally acquainted with
Mr. Wrangham, at whose church of Hunmanby
he had sometimes attended when staying at Filey,
and had heard him edify his people with the sermons of the "pious Dr. Watts."   They had met
at the table of Sir George Cayley, to whom Mr.
Wrangham was related by marriage; their intercourse had been pleasant, and they had this at
least in common, that both were of the Whig
school in politics.   In character no two men could
well be more unlike.   The Archdeacon had been
distinguished as a scholar at the University, and
had obtained the more questionable honour of
winning Seatonian prizes; he had a tenacious and
ready memory, a self-possessed address, and, with
the polish of a gentleman, not a little of the pride

of an academic and a churchman, to whom, as a
matter of course, a Unitarian Dissenter was at
once a sciolist and a schismatic.* I have no doubt
that Mr. Wellbeloved's unassuming manner, his
unwillingness to engage in colloquial disputation,
and his proneness to conceal rather than display
his stores of knowledge, had produced in the
Archdeacon's mind a very false idea of his powers,
and that when he heard that he was preparing for
a conflict, he was confident, like the Philistine
champion, that he should speedily "give his flesh
unto the fowls of the air and the beasts of the
field." Probably this opinion was general; for the
Archbishop had called Mr. Wrangham "the ornament of his diocese;" he was spoken of as "a
Colossus of literature;" and, till enlightened by
the result, the world usually gives its confidence to
those who show confidence in themselves.

The publication of Mr. Wellbeloved's reply was
delayed for several months by the loss of his wife,
but it made its appearance in the course of 1823 ;†

---

* "It is against that school, as I will term it, of sciolism and
schism, that I lift my hand."—Appendix, p. 23.

† "These Letters were on the point of being put to press, when a
very heavy domestic calamity interrupted the writer's pursuits, and
deprived him both of the power and the inclination to attend to anything unconnected with the awful dispensation of Providence by
which his faith and fortitude have been most severely exercised."

$$\text{Τί γὰρ ἀνδρὶ κακὸν μεῖζον, ἁμαρτεῖν}$$
$$\text{Πιστῆς ἀλόχου;}$$

Letters, 2nd Ed. p. 2.

and in the appendix to his third charge, delivered in August of that year, the Archdeacon animadverted upon it. Mr. Wellbeloved replied in three additional letters, published in 1824; and there the controversy ended.* He had not thought it necessary to notice, except in passing, a letter addressed to Archdeacon Wrangham, in vindication of the Athanasian Creed, by the Rev. James Richardson, one of the vicars-choral of York Minster; or the three letters addressed to "Mr. C. Wellbeloved, Tutor of the Unitarian College, York," by the Rev. John Oxlee. A single quotation from the latter work will justify him, I think, in the eyes of the reader, for this neglect :—

"Thus you perceive, sir, to what a pitch of folly, ignominy, and crime, that spirit of sectarism of which you are the sworn advocate has reduced the Christian world; and if you retain within you a single spark of honest and manly pride, you will either make an effort successfully to repel those charges, or else candidly confess that, like the spots in the panther's skin, they are inherent in the very composition, and inseparable from the character, of the Christian Dissenter."

* A second edition of these first Letters was published in 1823. A few strong expressions of censure directed against Bishops Horsley and Magee were modified in this edition, but I do not find that the author had occasion to alter or suppress any statement or criticism contained in the first edition. He had indeed been misinformed in regard to the supposed omission of the Athanasian Creed at York Minster, mentioned in the note on p. 47 of the second series.

The publication of these letters gained for Mr. Wellbeloved a foremost place among the defenders of the Unitarian cause, his zeal for which had been called in question by some, in consequence of his rarely introducing controversial subjects into his preaching; his determination, as a teacher of theology, not to make himself the advocate of any system of dogma; and his reluctance to countenance among his pupils the premature display of their doctrinal opinions.* He had vindicated the names most honoured among them from the sarcasms and groundless accusations of Mr. Wrangham; he had shown how shallow was his knowledge of biblical criticism, amidst all his pomp and prodigality of learned quotation, and had demonstrated the injustice of either classing Unitarian Christians with Deists, or imputing to their princi-

* He always resisted the application of the name Unitarian to the chapel in which he preached, giving it the designation affixed to it by its founders, Presbyterian. In reference to the coldness with which some zealous Unitarians viewed the College, he wrote in 1809, "I was told in London that some persons would not subscribe to us, because they thought the academy not strictly Unitarian; they feared I would not teach Unitarianism. I said I considered their censure the highest praise. I do not and I will not teach Unitarianism, or any -ism but Christianity. I will endeavour to show the students how to study the Scriptures, and if they find Unitarianism there, well; if Arianism, well; if Trinitarianism, well: only let them find something for themselves; let it not be found for them by their tutor." "Wisdom is justified of her children." When the Hewley case was brought forward, Mr. Wellbeloved was able truly to allege, that his chapel was not a Unitarian chapel, nor the college a Unitarian college.

ples any necessary tendency to produce unbelief. He had retorted the charge of sciolism upon his antagonist, by proving that he had copied and aggravated the mistakes of his predecessors. He had shown a perfect mastery of the weapons of controversy, close reasoning, and terseness of style, relieved with such a sprinkling of good-humoured raillery as is necessary to keep up the attention of the reader, and enliven a subject not in itself particularly interesting.

On a theological question it is almost impossible to select judges, whom one side or the other may not challenge for unindifferency. The nearest approach to impartiality may perhaps be found in those who, without sharing the religious opinions of Mr. Wellbeloved, judged the controversy on the ground of evidence, argument, and temper alone. It must therefore have been particularly gratifying to him to know, that in the opinion of such men as Professor Smyth, Sir James Mackintosh, Mr. Hallam, and the Rev. Sydney Smith, he had been completely successful. Sydney Smith expressed his judgment in a characteristic way :—" If I had a cause to gain, I would fee Mr. Wellbeloved to plead for me, and double fee Mr. Wrangham to plead against me."*   Lord Chancellor

* Not less characteristic is the following letter from the Rev. William Shepherd, though he cannot be reckoned among the *indifferent* judges :—" I cannot resist the impulse which I feel to thank

Brougham, in the argument on the exceptions taken to the defendants' answers to interrogatories in the Hewley case, thus expressed his opinion of the disputants :—

" Mr. Wellbeloved's learning is of a kind which it is rare to meet with in any church, either within the pale of our church or out of the pale. And when I say *within* the pale of the Church of England, I say it with the deepest veneration for the learning of that most eminently-lettered hierarchy, and for the purpose of bestowing a still higher panegyric on the learning of Mr. Wellbeloved, when I say that he has in controversy conflicted with some of the most learned members of the Church and overthrown them, as far as mere learning goes. I speak not of doctrine, but as far as learning goes he has signally and triumphantly defeated them, by mere force of superior endowments; and the more I doubt his being in the right, the more I am bound to say that his great learning prevailed over his antagonists, notwithstanding they were in the right. But I must add, what in my eyes is a far higher praise, that the controversy was carried on without the least deviation from

you for the pleasure which I have received from the perusal of your second series of letters to Archdeacon Wrangham. I think you have blown this dilettante theologian completely out of the water; and if he has any sensibility and any grace, he will be ashamed of having committed himself as he has done. He is evidently a very minor dealer in second-hand goods. He keeps what in London is called a marine store-shop; and dealers and chapmen of this species are perpetual objects of the vigilance of the police, as being gifted with more dexterity than honesty. You have brought the culprit before the bar of public opinion, and have effected his conviction. The queries with which you close your pamphlet fall about his ears like a hail-storm, and I opine he will defer answering them *ad Græcas calendas*. They should be published substantively by the Unitarian Tract Society."

the rules of humanity, piety, and charity, exhibiting to the
controversial world an example of which their whole history
shows polemics stand so greatly in need,—that learning,
sincerity, and zeal may well be united with the most entire
forbearance and meekness."

The emphatic protest of the learned Lord against
being supposed to think Mr. Wellbeloved in the
right in point of doctrine, gives the greater weight
to his judgment respecting his success in the argument. The discussion had been much read by the
lawyers, whose judgment upon it Lord Brougham
represents; and among the Archdeacon's clerical
brethren the opinion was freely expressed, that he
had sadly committed himself. The controversy
produced a temporary alienation between the parties, but they had met and shaken hands before
Mr. Wrangham's death. The only circumstance
which can excite regret, in looking back on this
affair, is, that the leisure of several months was
absorbed by it, and the appearance of the promised
part of the Bible consequently retarded.

Notwithstanding the prominent part which Mr.
Wellbeloved took as an advocate of Unitarianism,
he lived on terms of friendly intercourse with several
of the clergy of the Established Church, among
whom the amiable and accomplished Archdeacon
Eyre may be particularly mentioned. He was so far
from courting the society of men who were placed
above himself in social rank, that he rather shrank

from it; but there was no constraint, no want of
self-respect or self-possession, in his intercourse with
them. Benevolence and modesty combined in his
character to give him that true politeness which is
the outward expression of these qualities of the
heart; and his quick perception of proprieties prevented him from feeling embarrassment, in any
society into which he might be thrown. Among
the clergy of the Establishment with whom he
associated on a friendly footing was the Rev.
Sydney Smith, who, when he first came to reside in
Yorkshire, took up his abode at Heslington, near
York. Though Mr. Wellbeloved's finer sensibility
and more correct taste may have interfered with his
relish for a humour pushed sometimes to the verge
of levity, he thoroughly appreciated his unrivalled
talent of conversation, and admired the intrepidity
with which, in opposition to his worldly interests,
he combatted every form of intolerance and injustice. When he was preparing his well-known
article on Dissenting Marriages, in the Edinburgh
Review, he applied to Mr. Wellbeloved for materials, and sent him the following acknowledgment
of the offer of some books upon the subject :—

"DEAR SIR,—I shall be much obliged to you for the
loan of the publications you allude to, or any other that
may have since occurred to you: they will, I dare say, do
very well for a peg, and in addition I have no doubt they
will contain a full, sensible, and reasonable view of the case.

I have, and can have, no other motive for meddling with this matter, than the detestation I have for anything like persecution in religious opinions. And it is gross persecution to say to any man, 'Your only method of getting married shall be by listening to, repeating, and appearing to acquiesce in, doctrines, which in your conscience you do not believe to be scriptural.' I write this to you in confidence, though I should not, on proper occasions, object to preaching it at the Market Cross: indeed I have done so before now.   " Yours, dear Sir, very truly,
                                        "SYDNEY SMITH."

The following playful note refers to the missionary preaching of the students at Welburn and Barton in the neighbourhood of Foston :—

" Your Unitarian preachers have stolen away four of my congregation, who had withstood Ranters and Methodists. I shall make reprisals, and open a chapel near the College ; but it shall be a generous and polite warfare—such as is the duty, not the disgrace of a Christian divine."

Mr. Wellbeloved replied by expressing his satisfaction at the announcement, as it would give him the pleasure of seeing Mr. Smith more frequently than he had done lately. Sydney Smith was a great patron of the Hamiltonian system of learning languages, and wrote an article to recommend it in the Edinburgh Review. He thus introduced the founder of it to Mr. Wellbeloved: —" The bearer of this is Mr. Hamilton, the author of the System of Languages. Pray see if his plans and books can be of any use to your College.   *We* reject everything new in our schools.   *You* are open to conviction."

After the publication mentioned in p. 116, Mr. Wellbeloved had printed in 1815 a sermon preached at an annual meeting of ministers held in Leeds, entitled, " The Religious and Moral Improvement of Mankind, the Constant End of the Divine Government."   The author acknowledges in a note that in the views taken of the nature and end of the divine dispensations, he had been much indebted to Bishop Law's Considerations on the Theory of Religion ; but he has added from his own stores some remarks on the relation of the Jews to the heathen world, in its bearing on the history of the preaching of the Gospel.   In 1818, he had published one of the most valuable of his printed sermons, entitled " The Doctrine of Instantaneous Conversion from Sin to Holiness, a Doctrine unsupported by Scripture."   The preacher convincingly shows, how unauthorized and how mischievous is the prevalent practice of applying indiscriminately scriptural language, which had an exclusive reference to the Jewish and Gentile world, as it existed in the days of our Saviour ; how it encourages fanaticism, and weakens the motives to avoid the formation of vicious habits.   One passage deserves especially to be quoted :—

" How unhappily is this gross and fatal delusion " (the efficacy of death-bed repentance) " kept up not only by the harangues of popular preachers and by the mistaken humanity of those who preside in our courts of justice, but by the narratives now so studiously presented to the public eye of the conversion and the religious fortitude and joy which distinguish the last moments of those, whose lives had been passed in one continued violation of the laws of God and man,—narratives which may well excite the most painful emotions in the mind of every one interested in the cause of human happiness. For their direct tendency is to encourage false and dangerous notions of the nature and sanctions of the divine moral government; to render men careless and unconcerned about the conduct they pursue and the character they form during life; and to undermine the important doctrine of reason and of revelation that 'whatsoever a man soweth that shall he also reap.' "*

He had taken an early interest in the Unitarian movement in India. His former pupil Captain Gowan (who afterwards assumed the name of Mauleverer), during his residence in Calcutta, had become well acquainted with Rammohun Roy, and in his correspondence with Mr. Wellbeloved had given him such an account of his character and talents, as to encourage sanguine hopes of the reform which he would effect in the Brahminical

* In consequence of the frequent practice of the Judges, to exhort criminals on whom they passed sentence of death to imitate the example of the "penitent thief," Mr. Wellbeloved, during a York assize, preached a sermon on the words of our Lord, Luke xxiii. 43. The under-sheriff, who was a member of his congregation, mentioned it to the Judge. When he came again on the Northern circuit, he abstained from alluding to this passage of Scripture, and, the same gentleman being in office, inquired of him for his friend Mr. Wellbeloved.

religion. When a Unitarian congregation was established in Calcutta, and a subscription opened for the purpose of building a chapel there, he entered warmly into the plan, and made an animated and successful appeal to his congregation in support of it, in a sermon from Acts xi. 9. Its publication had a great effect in stimulating the zeal of other congregations in behalf of a scheme which promised well, and which may yet be realized in the altered circumstances of India. A sermon on " Unitarians not guilty of denying the Lord that bought them," preached at Hull in 1823, and one on "The Mystery of Godliness," preached at Halifax in 1825, complete the list of his sermons on doctrinal subjects.

The next occasion on which Mr. Wellbeloved appeared as an author was in the character of biographer of his friend, the Rev. Thomas Watson, minister of the Presbyterian congregation of Whitby. The memoir was prefixed to a volume of sermons which he had not completely conducted through the press at the time of his death. There were many points of similarity in character and pursuits between Mr. Watson and his biographer, and since the death of Mr. Wood there had been no one with whom he had associated more agreeably or corresponded more regularly. They had both a taste for natural history, and when Mr. Wellbeloved visited Redcar, Scarborough, or Filey, they

usually contrived a meeting at some point rich in
specimens interesting to the naturalist.   Mr. Watson had not paid particular attention to biblical
studies, but he had read and reflected much on
Natural Theology, on Ethics, and on the Evidences
of Christianity—all subjects on which Mr. Wellbeloved delighted to converse with a man of congenial mind.   In religious opinion Mr. Watson was
an Arian, but he held this belief speculatively and
not dogmatically, and to Calvinism, under every
form and modification, he was as adverse as his
Unitarian friend.   His politics also were somewhat
more courtly; for he had been the intimate friend of
the first Lord Mulgrave, the celebrated Arctic navi-
gator, and was a frequent guest at Mulgrave Castle;
but this also was a difference which never interrupted the harmony produced by agreement on more
important subjects.   Mr. Watson was the author of
several works on the Evidences of Natural and Revealed Religion, and the Principles of Christianity,
which were favourably received, and rendered good
service in their day, by vindicating religion from
the attacks of infidelity, and substituting sober
and rational views of it for the fanaticism which
prevailed around him.   The posthumous volume,
of which Mr. Wellbeloved was the editor, contains
sermons preached at different periods of his long
ministry, which, in the prospect of speedily leaving
his flock, he was desirous should remain with them,

"that they might be able after his decease to have always in remembrance the important truths which it had been the great end of his public instructions to establish in their minds." "They for whose benefit it was immediately intended," observes the biographer, "cannot fail to receive and prize it as a sacred legacy from their aged and much-venerated pastor ; they will be reminded by it of the happiness they have so long enjoyed in listening to such instructions and incited to maintain with steadiness, and to adorn by a holy and consistent conduct, the truly Christian principles which have been inculcated upon them." In reading this just description of the feelings with which an attached congregation might be expected to receive a memorial of their minister's teaching, it is impossible not to regret that, by enjoining the destruction of his own sermons, he has precluded the possibility that his flock should enjoy a similar benefit. They would have received such a legacy with respect and affection, and throughout a much wider circle it would have been welcomed for its intrinsic value, and its associations with the memory of a tutor or a friend.

In the summer of 1826, Mr. Wellbeloved spent some time under the hospitable roof of Mr. Wood, at Platt, near Manchester, and was prevailed upon by him to sit to Lonsdale, for the portrait which has now become so extensively known by the

M

excellent engraving of Cousins. It was fortunate that the reluctance which he had always shown to have his likeness taken was overcome, by the desire to comply with the earnest wishes of a valued friend. It is a faithful representation of what he was in his 58th year; but his children cannot help regretting that they have nothing which recalls his venerable and engaging appearance in later life, and accords more exactly with the memories which they most delight to cherish. With the same friend, accompanied by his wife and son, Mr. Wellbeloved made a long tour in Scotland in 1828, some incidents of which are recorded in the memoir of him in the Christian Reformer. He twice again visited Scotland to attend the meetings of the British Association at Edinburgh and Glasgow.

In the midst of his various occupations Mr. Wellbeloved had never neglected his antiquarian studies, and he had endeavoured, but without success, in 1813, to form a small antiquarian society in York. The establishment of the Yorkshire Philosophical Society in 1822, afforded an opportunity of combining archæology, which was too weak to stand alone, with other branches of science. An incidental circumstance gave it a more important place in the objects of the Society's pursuit than it could otherwise have obtained. In 1827 the Crown granted a portion of the ancient site of

St. Mary's Abbey for the erection of a museum, and in excavating for the foundation, large portions of various monastic buildings came to light, which had lain buried since the time when the ground was converted into the terraced garden of a palace. The Society of Antiquaries were desirous of preserving a memorial of what had thus been disclosed, and Mr. Wellbeloved, on their application through the Director, Mr. Markland, undertook to illustrate the engravings which they published, as a portion of their work entitled Vetusta Monumenta. His labour comprises a history of this celebrated Benedictine foundation, with a description of the building, and the fragments of sculpture which had been excavated. Under his direction as Curator, the department of antiquities in the Society's Museum became one of the most important and interesting. A monthly meeting seldom passed in which he had not to present and explain some object which had been added to its antiquarian collections, and he frequently read papers illustrating at greater length the Roman or mediæval antiquities of York. At a later period, when these antiquities had accumulated to such an extent, as to be placed in a separate building in the Museum grounds, he arranged and described them in a Catalogue, which unites in a remarkable degree the two qualities of comprehensiveness and brevity, and may be recommended as a model for all similar works.　It was owing very much to his influence and example that the inhabitants of York, who had been previously very indifferent to the antiquities of their city, learned to place a pride on their preservation : one change he was mainly instrumental in effecting, the value of which every visitor to the city can estimate.　There is only one other place in England—Chester—where the ancient walls remain so entire as at York.　The circuit is not so complete as that of Chester, nor are the views so picturesque—less so now than ever, since the gardens of the Friars Preachers have been covered by the Railway station, and those of the Priory of Trinity by a modern chapel, and rows of brick dwellings.　Till a late period the Corporation, who were the natural guardians of these defences of the city, seemed indifferent to their preservation, or even desirous of their falling into complete decay, that they might appropriate the stone of the ruins and make a profit of the ramparts.　Mr. Wellbeloved had seen with regret that many a pleasant field walk, with which he had been familiar in early life, had been lost to the public, from the eagerness of the possessors of land in the neighbourhood of the city to exclude pedestrians, and he had joined with several other gentlemen, in an association for resisting such encroachments.　It was a happy suggestion that the walk around the walls should be taken under the protection of this association; and coming at a time when the inhabitants of York were beginning to set a value on the antiquities of their city, it was warmly taken up. By subscriptions in the city and county, and the proceeds of a ball, the sum of £3000 was raised, the breaches of the walls repaired, and a pleasant and healthy promenade secured to the citizens. He was looked upon henceforward as a sort of public guardian of the antiquities of York. When discoveries were made, his judgment was appealed to respecting their age and significance, and if the hand of the improver was lifted against any of its venerable monuments, his voice was sure to be raised in their defence.

The York Mechanics' Institute, or as it is now more appropriately called, the Institute of Popular Science and Literature, originated a little later than the Yorkshire Philosophical Society. Mr. Wellbeloved was one of its founders, and devoted a large amount of time and thought to its affairs, amidst the difficulties and discouragements with which it had to contend during the early years of its existence. In his capacity of Vice-President he delivered several addresses to the members, one of which, entitled, "The large extent of the Subjects of Knowledge a motive for Diffidence and Humility (1828)," was published. The beginnings of the Institute were humble, and its resources limited, and in common with all institutions for popular-

izing knowledge, it was frowned upon by the
higher classes of society in Church and State. The
present generation, which sees them patronized and
extolled by these same classes, can hardly estimate
the value of the service rendered to working men
by him and his coadjutors, whose zeal was not
checked by obloquy, nor chilled by the long delay of
success to their efforts. He had an opportunity of
explaining the motives of his exertions in this
cause, when his health was drunk at a dinner of the
supporters of the Yorkshire Philosophical Society
in 1830. In acknowledging the compliment, he
said :—

" When the York Mechanics' Institute was set on foot,
I took an active part in promoting it. I am proud that I
did so. I was told, in the outset, that I should do a great
deal of harm ; that society would be disorganized ; that we
should have no subordination, no inferiors ; that appren-
tices would be no longer bound by their indentures, but
would rise into journeymen ; that journeymen would leave
their masters, and set up as masters for themselves ; that
we should have no servants; and in short, that we should
have nothing but confusion. I have seen nothing of this—
I have heard nothing of it—of nothing approaching to it.
But I will tell you what I *have* seen. I have seen a
number of young people assemble night after night, for the
purpose of completing their necessarily deficient education.
I have seen others meet to improve themselves in architec-
tural drawing ; others attend lectures, and express the
greatest anxiety to procure information. I have seen them
devote hours, too frequently spent in debauchery and dissi-

pation, to the investigation of subjects interesting to all intelligent beings; and seeing this, I rejoice that I have been enabled to do anything to forward their views. I have seen, too, a number of young persons come, night after night, to the library,—which I regret to say, is not so well furnished as it ought to be,—for books which they carry home with them, to read by their fire-sides, instead of being induced to seek for recreation in the haunts of idleness, and amongst idle companions. Since the commencement of this beneficent institution, I have seen no other effects arising from it; and as long as this is the case, it shall have my services, and all the time I can bestow upon it. I think we are all bound to support such institutions. We have Infant Schools, Sunday Schools, National Schools, and Lancasterian Schools. What are they for, but to enable the population to read? When they are taught to read, will they not read? And *what* will they read? Are they to be left without guides to direct them what course to pursue? Mechanics' Institutes come in aid of these schools, to give the people proper books; and to keep them out of improper courses, which they would otherwise fall into. By instructing them, and cultivating their minds, we shall preserve them from the arts of Carlile and others, who go about the country, to induce the ignorant and uninformed to embrace their erroneous and pernicious doctrines. If, Sir (addressing the Chairman, the Rev. W. V. Vernon), all in a similar rank to yourself, would act as you do, and those who support you,—if they would employ their advantages in the same manner, there would be no danger of their ever being overtaken by their humbler brethren: they will always keep their station; and however long the spur may be in the toe of the mechanic, it will never reach the heel of the aristocracy."

This speech was appropriately followed by the

toast, proposed by Sir George Cayley, the President
of the Institute :—

The March of Intellect, with its true leaders in front.

Another of the public institutions of York in
which Mr. Wellbeloved was much interested and
took an active part in its management, was the
School for the Blind, which the County of York
established, as the most appropriate monument to
its eloquent and philanthropic representative, Mr.
Wilberforce. The Rev. William Taylor, F.R.S.,
its first superintendent, was his intimate friend.
None of his benevolent labours, I think, yielded
him such unmixed pleasure as he derived from his
office of visitor to this institution. The blind, as
they cannot be physiognomists, are quick to observe
the indications of character in the voice and manner of those with whom they have to do. He was
attracted by strong sympathy for the privation
under which they laboured; and watched with
interest the ingenious methods by which they supplied to themselves the lost faculty of vision.
Those of the pupils who remained long in the institution became strongly attached to him : they
watched for his step, expecting from him a kind
inquiry, or a playful remark; and when, owing
to his infirmities, he had ceased visiting the establishment, they expressed their regret that they
no longer heard his pleasant voice and his words
of friendly greeting.

Mr. Wellbeloved's admiration of the Minster, and his knowledge of its history, led him to employ his pen, though anonymously, in the controversy occasioned by the proposal to change the position of the organ-screen, after the fire of 1829. On Feb. 2nd of that year, which he has marked in his diary with two black crosses and "a most disastrous day," the choir had been burnt down, and the whole interior of that portion of the church laid in ruins. I was with him when he first visited the scene of desolation. It was a lowering, ungenial day, dark clouds traversing the sky, which was now its only covering. The beautiful carved work of the stalls and throne had been reduced to ashes; the pillars had been calcined, in some places almost to a thread; the floor was strewed with the half-burnt beams and bosses of the roof, which in their fall had dug deeply into the pavement. Mr. Wellbeloved had preserved tolerable composure amidst this wreck of the object of his admiration, but meeting Mr. Archdeacon Markham, the son of Dean Markham, to whom the fabric was indebted for its careful and accurate restoration, both were moved to tears. At the public meeting which was held in the Guildhall on the 11th of February, in seconding the motion for an address of condolence to the Dean and Chapter, and for a subscription in aid of the repair, he said :—

"It may, perhaps, excite some surprise that I, who am a Dissenter, should take any part in the proceedings of this day; but I willingly consented to do so, in order that it might be seen that dissent from the Established Church has no alliance with a blind fanatical zeal; that it does, not destroy the charities of our nature, and that religious party feelings do not mix themselves up with an event which has excited grief in the minds, not of the inhabitants of this city or this county only, but of the whole nation. In infancy I was baptized into the communion of the Established Church; in my boyhood I was instructed by her ministers. I thought it my duty to withdraw from her pale; but if dissent were necessarily connected with bigotry, if it enjoined me not to deplore a great calamity, because it had befallen the Church, nor to sympathize with those whom this calamity most nearly concerns, because they are clergymen of the Established Church, I should not long be found in the ranks of dissent. But it is not so. We Dissenters are, it is true, with few exceptions, averse to religious establishments; but we wish to live in peace, and, if we may be allowed, in friendship, with the members of the Church, and on all occasions to manifest towards them the sentiments and conduct which the most friendly dispositions can prompt.

"The day on which that sad calamity happened which has occasioned the present meeting, closed the thirty-seventh year of my residence in this city; and during the whole of this time I have experienced a daily and continually-increasing delight in beholding the beautiful and magnificent cathedral. From the frequent contemplation and study of that edifice, during the earlier part of my abode here, I was led to form a taste for English ecclesiastical architecture, which has largely contributed to the pleasure of my life. I cannot, therefore, but feel that in the destruction of so large and interesting a portion of that splendid fabric I have suffered a personal loss. What, then, must be the feelings of those to whose care this fine structure was committed, and who have shown themselves worthy of the trust by their anxiety to sustain it; who have displayed such sound judgment and correct taste in restoring the beauties which the hand of time had nearly destroyed, and preserving for the admiration of posterity what had been the ornament of York and the glory of the nation?"

The condition on which the subscription was raised, as announced on the part of the Dean and Chapter, was "absolute and perfect restoration," and they pledged themselves "not to depart from a model more excellent and beautiful than any which they could substitute in its place." Subsequently, however, the idea arose, that by the removal of the screen further to the east, leaving the eastern pillars of the great tower, against which the ends of the screen abut, clear in their original contour, the effect of the whole building would be greatly improved, and a resolution was passed at a meeting of subscribers held in London, recommending the plan to a meeting to be held at York. To this Mr. Wellbeloved and many other of the subscribers strongly objected, as a violation of the pledge given "to restore absolutely and perfectly, and not to depart from the model," as objectionable in point of taste, and as involving the hazard of destruction to the screen in the process of removal. Perhaps those who have seen the sublime effect produced in continental churches by the absence of any solid separation between the nave and the choir, giving an unbroken perspective from west to east, may have regretted that in our English cathedrals this perspective is so generally shortened, by the interposition of an organ-screen. They may have regretted that even so elaborate a piece of work as the screen of York Minster should have been placed where it not only produces this effect, but partially hides the beautiful bases of the great pillars of the central tower. But it had stood for more than three centuries where it was placed, and where alone the separation of nave and choir had ever been made, either in York Minster or the other cathedrals of England.*

The proposal to remove the screen excited great interest and strong opposition, not only in Yorkshire, but generally among antiquaries and lovers of ancient architecture. Mr. Wellbeloved began the discussion by a letter addressed to the subscribers, earnestly deprecating the change; Mr. Vernon (Harcourt), who had just printed a letter to Lord Milton in support of it, appended to his letter, when published, some strictures on Mr. Wellbeloved's. He replied in a letter to Mr. Vernon, who rejoined in a second letter to

* Mr. Wellbeloved notices an exception in the case of Ely, but it is an exception which confirms the rule.

Lord Milton, and Mr. Wellbeloved closed the controversy by a second letter to the subscribers. The meeting at York, where the influence of those who favoured the removal was naturally strong, decided for it; but the general feeling was so much against it, that in February, 1831, Dean Cockburn announced that, *for the present*, the screen was not to be removed; and we may predict that it never will, till the fabric itself shall crumble into ruins. Mr. Wellbeloved was encouraged in his opposition by eminent antiquaries in various parts of England, and on the question of the removal I believe the general opinion is that he was right. Mr. Vernon's access to the Minster records gave him an advantage in discussing a subordinate question—the time when the choir was finished, Mr. Wellbeloved fixing it in 1460, Mr. Vernon in 1373. According to the learned editor of the "Fabric Rolls of the Minster," the choir was begun in 1361, but not completed for thirty years. Both the disputants, therefore, appear to have overstated their case. Mr. Wellbeloved was desirous of bringing the time of the completion of the choir as near as possible to the erection of the screen, that it might appear as the designed consummation of the work; while Mr. Vernon wished the interval to be as wide as possible, to support his view, that the screen had intruded itself, at a much later period, into a place which the designers of the choir had not intended for it. As the screen, according to Mr. Raine, was erected between 1475 and 1505,* Mr. Vernon's estimate is nearer the truth. It is difficult, however, to see how the lateness of its introduction should be a reason, not for its banishment, but for its removal a few feet further back, which was the . measure for which he argued.

It is pleasant to observe, that this contest, notwithstanding the warmth of feeling shown by partizans, was carried on with entire courtesy and good temper between the two disputants. When Mr. Wellbeloved published his first letter, he sent a copy to Mr. Vernon, with the following note :—

"DEAR SIR,—You will, I trust, judge rightly of the motive by which I am induced to request your acceptance of a copy of a pamphlet of which, contrary to my wishes, you have been informed, I understand, that I am the author ; and I hope you will give me credit for perfect sincerity when I assure you, that I have felt great reluctance in publicly opposing a measure, which it is said you are anxious to accomplish. I would much rather use my humble endeavours to promote than to thwart any plan that you may approve. But in this case my judgment and my feelings

* Fabric Rolls of York Minster, edited for the Surtees Society by the Rev. James Raine, Pref. p. xiv. p. 79. Mr. Raine, I think, has also shown, that the place in which Archbishop Thoresby was interred, and to which he had removed the bodies of several of his predecessors, was the presbytery, or Lady Chapel, at the east end of the Minster, and not, as Mr. Wellbeloved had supposed, the chapel of the Blessed Mary and the Holy Angels, built by Archbishop Roger near the N. W. door of the Minster, and now destroyed. Pref. p. xvi.

have concurred in compelling me to adopt very different views, and exert myself in recommending them to others. When I first entered the choir of York, now nearly forty years ago, I thought it the most beautiful and the most perfect building of the kind that I had ever seen; and a very careful examination of almost every cathedral in England since that time has served only to confirm my earliest conviction. When it was destroyed by the late calamity, there was not one person, I will venture to say, more deeply affected than myself; when the promise was given that it should be exactly *restored*, there was no one who rejoiced more sincerely; and when contributions were required for this purpose, none cast in of their abundance more cheerfully than I did of my penury. Under the influence of past impressions, of disappointment as to the present, and of fears respecting the future, I could not remain silent. If, in censuring what I disapprove, and opposing what I am fully convinced will be injurious to an object of my most ardent admiration, I have gone beyond the line of fair argument, or violated the rules of decorum, which the keenest controversialist is bound to observe, I shall be truly concerned, and acknowledge that I justly deserve the consequence that must follow, the disapprobation of those to whose esteem I can never be indifferent."

Mr. Vernon replied : —

" DEAR SIR,—I should not have required to be informed who was the author of the letter which you have been so good as to send me. ' Ex ungue leonem.' I now send you, in return, a letter of my own, and a postscript in reply to yours, written, I hope, in a no less amicable spirit of controversy. You will find that I have made free with your facts and inferences, but I hope I have never, even in

retorting upon the anonymous assailant, lost sight of the
respect very sincerely felt for yourself by

" Yours very truly,
" Wm. V. Vernon.

" The Rev. Charles Wellbeloved."

The following letter was addressed to Mr. Wellbeloved by the Archbishop, to whom he had sent a
copy of his "Second Letter : "—

" Revd. Sir,*—I beg to offer you my best thanks for your
obliging attention in sending me a copy of your ' Second
Letter to the Subscribers.'

If the perusal of it has not made me a convert to your
opinion on the question at issue, be assured that *I give you
full credit* for the ability and good temper with which you
have argued it.

" I am, Revd. Sir,
" With regard,
" Yours faithfully,
" E. Ebor."

The fire in the Minster, by laying open portions of

---

* Mr. Wellbeloved's correspondents were not all so courteous in
their mode of address. One of them, an aristocratic antiquary,
having directed his letter to Mr. Charles Wellbeloved, says in explanation, " as a strong conservative and a man firmly attached to
our institutions of Church and State, I do not allow the title of
' Reverend ' to a Protestant Dissenting Minister, any more than
' Lord ' to a Popish bishop." Mr. Wellbeloved in reply said, that
the address of a letter had answered its purpose when it had enabled
the postman to find the person for whom it was intended ; that he
never *took* the title of Reverend, but that it was *given* him in notes,
which he had the honour to receive from the Archbishop of the Pro-
vince and his son.

more than one ancient structure which had preceded
all that was above ground, had added largely to the
materials for a more correct history of the fabric.
Mr. Brown, an ingenious artist of York, who had
long made the Minster his study, and by his minute
knowledge of its architecture had materially assisted
Mr. Wellbeloved in the screen controversy, projected a work in which the various stages of its
architecture should be illustrated by drawings, and
its history elucidated by original documents. Being
more practised in the use of the pencil than the
pen, he relied very much on Mr. Wellbeloved for
assistance in the literary portion of his labours.
The MS. was submitted to his revision, and some
parts were written by him. His graceful and flow-
ing style cannot fail to be recognized, for example,
in the introduction to the chapter on the symbolical
character of ornamental foliage.

" There is scarcely any feature of what is usually called
Gothic Architecture more strikingly characteristic, than the
sculptured foliage with which the more magnificent buildings
of this style are so richly adorned. In the Saxon architecture, if indeed we have any remains of that style to guide
us, it appears to have been very sparingly used. In the
Norman it occurs, yet not very commonly, among zigzag
mouldings and grotesque devices of animals. But when we
come down to the period of that which is denominated the
Early English, and especially as we advance to that which is
called the Decorated, we find it pervading almost every part
of the sacred edifice. It decorates the capital of the column
and the pier; it insinuates itself into the hollow moulding,

N

and issues thence to adorn the head of the neighbouring
shaft; it springs from the wall in the graceful forms of
brackets and corbels; it creeps along the canopy of windows
and doors; it rises in the crockets of pinnacles, which it
crowns with the leafy finial; it gives beauty and variety to
the numerous intersections of the ribs in the groined roof;
it drops in curiously-wrought pendants from canopied stalls,
or the richly-carved ceiling of the Tudor age."*

The year. 1830 witnessed the commencement of
the suit instituted by the Independents against the
Trustees of Lady Hewley's estates and hospital,
which, in its several stages, occupied the Court of
Chancery and the House of Lords for twelve years.
Its object was to obtain a decree, that those ministers who denied the doctrines presumed to be held
by Lady Hewley and the Protestant Dissenters of
her day, were not fit recipients of exhibitions from
her bequest; and the removal of the trustees, as
having violated their duty in granting them.   Mr.
Wellbeloved was specially aimed at in these proceedings on several grounds.   He was not a "godly
preacher of Christ's Holy Gospel," because he was
a Unitarian; he was theological tutor in a Unitarian College, and Lady Hewley could never have
designed that her exhibitions to students should
be the means of training young men in doctrines

* Mr. Wellbeloved was applied to, to furnish an account of York
for Lewis's Topographical Dictionary.   The description of the
Minster in that work is certainly his; I doubt as to the rest of the
article.

which she held in abhorrence ; he was in the receipt of £237 annually from the College funds, as salary and fees, and, therefore, not being in the terms of Lady Hewley's deed, a "poor preacher,"* the grant of £80 a year to him as minister of the St. Saviour-gate chapel was unjustifiable.

Preparations for this suit had long been covertly made. In 1816 a person resident in York had obtained from Mr. Wellbeloved a copy of Dr. Colton's funeral sermon for Lady Hewley, under the plea of preparing a memoir of her for the Evangelical Magazine. On his letter Mr. Wellbeloved has written "*stratagem,*" finding afterwards that it had been drawn from him, in order to be used as an evidence of Lady Hewley's theological opinions.† The Commissioners appointed to inquire into the administration of public charities visited York and summoned him before them, in 1824 ; but no spe-

---

* " We see, in these remarks on Mr. Wellbeloved's income, what men of attainment have to expect, when men like the writer of this pamphlet have the regulation of the incomes for the higher services in society. Mr. Wellbeloved's life has been one of great labour; and if he had received twice as much as he has received, he could not, on any fair comparison of service and reward, be thought overpaid." Historical Defence of Lady Hewley's Trustees, by the Rev. Jos. Hunter, F.S.A., p. 75. The pamphlet referred to was from the pen of Mr. George Hadfield.

† It was quite in accordance with this mode of obtaining evidence, that, as was stated by Mr. Bickerton Williams, the orthodox Commissioner, the Relators were prepared to prove that Mr. Wellbeloved denied the Trinity, by the evidence of a person who had listened at the chapel door during his sermon.

cific inquiries were then made into the Hewley charity. In 1826 they renewed their visit, and he underwent a long examination by them, the results of which are detailed in their Report presented to Parliament in January, 1827. A fierce controversy had been going on in Lancashire, originating in a speech made at a dinner in Manchester, on occasion of a testimonial presented to the Rev. John Grundy. In a letter addressed to the *Manchester Gazette* by Mr. Hadfield, the Unitarians had been charged with appropriating to themselves chapels and endowments which belonged to the orthodox, and replies had appeared from Mr. Tayler and Mr. Wood. The Charity Commissioners, one of whom was the son of the steward of Lady Hewley's estates, evidently entered on their work well instructed by the party hostile to the Trustees; for in the notes appended to their Report they allude to the complaints and claims of Trinitarian Dissenters. They say—

"On the examination of the Rev. Charles Wellbeloved, Minister of the chapel in St. Saviourgate, we find that the congregation of that chapel are denominated English Presbyterians ; that Unitarian tenets or principles are taught and inculcated in the chapel, and that the same were maintained by the last minister, the Rev. N. Cappe. Mr. Wellbeloved also states, that he does not know whether the same religious tenets were held by Mr. Hotham, who was minister before Mr. Cappe until 1756, but that Mr. Hotham's predecessor, the Rev. Dr. Colton, during whose ministry Lady Hewley attended the chapel, was certainly not a Unitarian, and Mr. Wellbeloved concludes, from Lady Hewley's attending at the chapel during Dr. Colton's time, and from the general state of religious opinion, that she did not entertain what are commonly called Unitarian opinions."

In a note they add—

" The Rev. Charles Wellbeloved, who is ·the theological tutor of Manchester College, states that the design of that Institution is to instruct young men for the ministry among Protestant Dissenters; that the College is principally resorted to by persons intended for the ministry among Presbyterian Dissenters, and the subscriptions to the Institution are contributed for the most part by Presbyterians, but the College is open for students of any denomination ; that they are carefully instructed by him in biblical criticism; but no particular doctrines or tenets of faith are inculcated, and the students are allowed and encouraged to study the scriptures and to judge for themselves on every point of doctrine ; that most of the students who come to and leave the College entertain Unitarian sentiments, but, he adds, do not, on leaving the College, entertain those sentiments in consequence of any influence which he, as their tutor, exercises."

Had Mr. Wellbeloved possessed less of the "charity which thinketh no evil," and more of "the wisdom of the serpent," the want of which he lamented, he would have declined to answer interrogatories respecting his own religious opinions—a point clearly not within the competence of the Commissioners to investigate. In their Report they acknowledge, that all the proceedings of the trust are carried on with propriety, "unless it

should be considered a departure from Lady
Hewley's intentions, that part of the revenues
should be applied in favour of dissenting ministers
who entertain and preach Socinian or Unitarian
sentiments, or in the allowance of stipends to
widows of such ministers, and exhibitions to students brought up in such sentiments." And they
refer to the Wolverhampton case, as rendering
it at least very questionable, whether preachers or
students of Unitarian belief can properly receive
such exhibitions, recommending that the question
which has arisen should be submitted to a Court of
Equity. This hint was not lost, and the Attorney-
General, Sir James Scarlett, was applied to by the
Independents, to file an information against the
Trustees. He declined to do so, alleging that he
saw no reason to disturb an administration which
had gone on satisfactorily for seventy years.* A
change in the law, however, took place, making it
imperative on him to commence proceedings on the
instance of parties, if his costs were guaranteed;
and this being done the suit "The Attorney-Ge-
neral v. Shore and others, on the Relation of
Thomas Wilson and others" began. On the 28th
of June, 1830, a strip of parchment, looking as if
it might have been the lost direction of a hamper,
was delivered at Mr. Wellbeloved's door, which on
examination was found to bear the names of Cour-

* Speech of Atty.-Gen.   See Christian Reformer, 1839, p. 381.

tenay and Vizard, calling on him to appear in
Chancery on the 30th of the same month. The
declaration of the Relators, besides praying for the
discontinuance of the exhibitions to Unitarians,
and especially to Mr. Wellbeloved, and for the
removal of the Trustees,* called on the Court to
pronounce only those Dissenters to come within
the scope of the charity, who were protected by
the Toleration Act; *i.e.* those who did not deny
the Trinity.

It was not till December 1833, that the cause
came on for hearing before Sir Lancelot Shadwell,
the Vice-Chancellor. In the preliminary proceedings the defendants objected to answering interrogatories respecting their religious opinions. In
this I conceive they were perfectly justified.
They found no doctrinal test in the deed whence
their trust was derived; no question respecting
their opinions had ever been asked of them or
their predecessors; they had asked none of those
to whom they administered the bounty of their
Foundress. They had, therefore, good reason for

---

* There were two sets of Trustees—the Grand Trustees, in whom
the property was vested, and the Sub-trustees, who had the management of the Hospital for aged women in Tanner Row. Both were
ultimately included in the suit. Mr. Wellbeloved and myself were
Sub-trustees. It was directed by the deed relating to the Hospital
that every almsbody should be able to repeat the Commandments,
the Lord's Prayer, the Creed, and Mr. Bowles's Catechism.

declining, unless compelled by the highest legal
authority, to say whether they were Unitarians or
not. Lord Chancellor Brougham on appeal decided that they must answer as to their religious
opinions, and a string of interrogatories was
framed by the Relators, with a view to extract a
confession of faith from them. Mr. Wellbeloved
was advised to frame his answers entirely in the
words of Scripture, and he did so, the other Sub-
trustees concurring. This was perhaps to be regretted. It was not likely that the Court would
be satisfied with answers, which gave no information on the point on which it required to be
informed ; it wore the appearance of *fencing*, which
judges always interpret to the disadvantage of those
who resort to it, and it gave a handle to the opposite party, to impute to the defendants a desire to
conceal the truth, though Lord Lyndhurst in his
judgment exonerated Mr. Wellbeloved from the
blame which Mr. Knight had heaped on him for
these answers. A commission having been sent
down to York to obtain evidence, the matter was
argued for several days in December, 1833, before
the Vice-Chancellor, whose mind had evidently been
made up from the beginning against the Unitarians.
He pronounced as his decree, " that no persons who
deny the divinity of our Saviour's person, and who
deny the doctrine of original sin, as it is generally

understood,* are entitled to participate in Lady
Hewley's Charity ; and that the trustees must be
removed." The judgment was principally occupied by a criticism of the learned judge's on the
Improved Version, for which he attempted to make
Mr. Wellbeloved responsible, on the sole ground
that he was a subscriber to the Unitarian Association, by whom it was circulated, though he had
never taken any active part in the management of
the Association, had had no share in the preparation of that Version, and, if the matter had been
inquired into, might have been known to disapprove many things which it contained. The Relators themselves had withdrawn this work from
before the Court, but the Vice-Chancellor did not
allow this circumstance to deprive him of the opportunity of displaying his prejudice against the Unitarians, and his mastery of Greek criticism.†

* So his judgment is worded, in the pamphlet entitled "The Unitarians defeated, printed by permission of the Vice-Chancellor." In
the formal decree it stands "Ministers or Preachers of what is commonly called Unitarian belief and doctrine."

† One or two of his observations may serve to show how thoroughly
*un*judicial was the temper in which he exercised his function of judge.
Animadverting on the Improved Version, for printing the first chapters of Matthew and Luke in Italics, he says, "In the progress of
improvement it may be discovered that no parts of Scripture are
genuine and authentic, except the first verse of Genesis and the last
of Revelation ; and, according to the argument for the defendants,
the preachers upon these two verses only might still be considered as
' godly preachers for the time being of Christ's Holy Gospel,' within
the intent and meaning of Lady Hewley's Trust Deeds." Com-
menting on an expression in Bowles's Catechism, " the infinite love

An appeal from this judgment was made to the Lord Chancellor Brougham, and in the course of the year 1834 the whole case was reheard before him, Baron Parke and Mr. Justice Littledale sitting to assist him.

The Hewley case was curiously affected by the political vicissitudes of the times. It was begun in the Chancellorship of Lord Lyndhurst, who was soon succeeded by Lord Brougham. He had heard the pleadings, in 1834, with the exception of Sir Edward Sugden's reply, when the administration of which he was a member was displaced, and as the Relators declined to take his judgment when out of office, the whole case was heard again before Lord Lyndhurst, assisted by Baron Alderson and Mr. Justice Patteson in April, 1835. Again a change of ministry occurred, and Lord Lyndhurst resigned the seals; but it was agreed by the defendants to take his judgment, which was accordingly delivered in February, 1836. It stands in remarkable contrast with that of the Vice-Chancellor, and with the opinion of Mr. Baron Alderson, whose tone was that not of a judge but of an eager partizan. Lord Lyndhurst is so far from finding Bowles's Catechism " racy with Trini-

---

of Christ," he says "none but a divine being could have infinite love." " On such reasoning," says Mr. Stock, in his able Observations, "a rival metaphysician might affirm the divinity of his Honour's self, for does he not hope for the enjoyment of infinite happiness hereafter?"

tarianism," as Dr. Bennett had called it, or " a
stream from the same fountain as the Assembly's
Catechism," as Dr. Pye Smith had sworn, that in
alluding to its teaching the doctrine of the Trinity
he is careful to guard himself by such expressions
as "passing over the question relating to the
Trinity ;" " *if* we may rely on the testimony of
those witnesses who have been examined, that this
is a Trinitarian Catechism "—pretty plainly showing that he did not rely upon it.   The only doctrine laid down in the Catechism, which he found
to be denied by the Unitarians, was that of original
sin.   According to the Catechism, the respondent
declares, "that he was born in a sinful and miserable condition ;" the defendants stated it as their
belief, that without actual sin committed, he was
not liable to the wrath and curse of God.   The
evidence of their Unitarianism he found in a
less questionable source, sermons preached by Mr.
Wellbeloved and myself, in which our dissent from
the doctrines of orthodoxy was plainly and broadly
stated ; and these sermons having been preached
before assemblages of Unitarians, and published at
their request, it was no unfair inference, that they
represented the convictions of the body at large.
As it had hardly been denied that the Presbyterians
of Lady Hewley's day were generally Trinitarians,
and the evidence of her personal sentiments, as far
as any evidence could be produced, was in favour

of her orthodoxy, the critical question of the cause
was, were the defendants justified in presuming
that she was imbued with the liberal principles of
some of the Presbyterians of her age, and had pur-
posely abstained from defining the faith of the recipients of her bounty, leaving a large discretion to
her successive Trustees? This had been inferred
from the liberal character of those in whom the
trust was originally vested, but the Chancellor
thought this inference not supported by evidence,
and rather concluded that she could not have
meant her bequest to be applied for the benefit of
those who denied the doctrines which she held. He,
therefore, confirmed the Vice-Chancellor's decree,
and condemned the Trustees to pay their own
costs.

This decision had prospective results more important than the withdrawal of the exhibitions to
Unitarian Ministers and their widows, and to the
students of Manchester College. It had been
avowed by Mr. Knight, that this suit was only
preliminary to an attack upon all the Presbyterian
chapels and endowments throughout the kingdom,
which were in the hands of the Unitarians—an
avowal which evidently made a great impression on
the Chancellor's mind, as he desired the Counsel to
repeat it. It became, therefore, a question no
longer between the Trustees and the Relators, but
between the whole body of Unitarians and the In-

dependents. It was felt to be a duty, in a matter
threatening such momentous consequences, not to
accept as final the decision of any inferior court,
but to carry it by appeal to the House of Lords.
And as the Trustees could not be expected to fight,
at their personal cost, the battle of the whole denomination, a subscription was entered into for
defraying the expense of the appeal. I do not
believe that any strong expectation was entertained
of a reversal of the decree by the House of Lords,
but it was considered, that until the highest authority had declared the law, it would be premature
to seek relief from the Legislature. The Appeal
was heard in 1839, but judgment was not given
till August, 1842, when another turn of the political wheel had placed Lord Lyndhurst again in
the Chancellorship. As a preliminary to the judgment, a number of questions, comprising all the
principal points of the case, were, in May, 1839,
submitted by Lord Chancellor Cottenham to the
Judges, seven of whom delivered their opinions.
On the part of the Appellants, a full statement of
their case was furnished to the House, the materials
for which, as far as the historical question was concerned, had been supplied chiefly by the Rev.
Joseph Hunter, F.S.A., who had already vindicated the character and proceedings of the Trustees, in his pamphlet entitled An Historical Defence
of the Trustees of Lady Hewley's Foundation. Of
the seven Judges who delivered their opinions, Mr.

Justice Maule alone was in favour of the Appellants on all the six questions.* Mr. Justice Erskine, Mr. Justice Coleridge, and Mr. Baron Gurney, all of whom treated the question under the influence of their own religious belief, gave it as their opinion that the words of the deed excluded Unitarians. Mr. Justice Williams said "understanding as I do the language of the foundation deed and the belief and doctrine which I collect to be attributed to the Unitarians (though upon this, as not being in any degree a legal question, I speak with great uncertainty) I think they are excluded from being objects of the charities of that deed." Baron Parke and Lord Chief Justice Tindal,† two of the most sound and learned judges on the bench, gave it as their opinion, that all the evidence which had been brought forward from the wills of Sir John and Lady Hewley, from the funeral sermon of Dr. Colton, in the depositions of Dr. Pye Smith and Dr. Bennett, was irrelevant and inadmissible. They

* " With regard to the amount of error of the Unitarian doctrines, excluding those who profess and preach them, I cannot think that temporal courts can conveniently entertain the question of more or less of theological error. I think that those who framed the deeds endeavoured, and on a true construction successfully endeavoured, to exclude such an inquiry, my opinion being, that according to the use of the words under consideration in the deeds in question, they are not exclusive of any class of Christian Protestant Nonconformists, and that Unitarians are commonly, and always have been, considered as forming a part of the Christian community."

† Sir W. Follett, in his speech on the Chapels Bill, says of this opinion of L. C. J. Tindal, "that it is entitled to the greatest respect and reverence."

were both of opinion, that the deed of 1707, which directed the use of Mr. Bowles's catechism in the Almshouse, could not be applied in explanation or restriction of the deed of 1704, which established the exhibitions to preachers and students. But they agreed with their brethren that the denial of the doctrine of the Trinity having been illegal, at the time when these deeds were framed, its impugners could not have been within the scope of Lady Hewley's charitable intentions; and that the subsequent removal of the penalties against antitrinitarians did not authorize an application of her bounty to them. As might be expected, therefore, the House of Lords affirmed the decree of the Court below, Lord Cottenham, who moved the judgment, expressing his opinion, in which Lord Brougham agreed, that much doubtful and exceptionable evidence had been received in the course of the cause.

Looking back over the interval from the Vice-Chancellor's decree, to the final decision of the House of Lords, it is instructive to observe, how one after another the branches of evidence by which it had been supported had been lopped off, by sounder lawyers. The Improved Version, which occupies the front rank in the Vice-Chancellor's invective, was withdrawn by the Relators themselves, and can only have been introduced, in order to rouse his religious prejudices. The ingenious

efforts of Dr. Bennett and Dr. Smith, to prove that
the Independents of their day were identical with
the Presbyterians of Lady Hewley's, went for
nothing, any more than the labour with which they
had strained one drop of orthodoxy from Mr.
Bowles's Catechism. The decision came finally to
rest on the naked ground of the penal statutes
against Unitarians, which the bigotry of a former
age had enacted, and the liberality of the present had
repealed—a fact which the Relators have studiously
kept out of view.

Without presuming to call in question the decision of the House of Lords, I may observe, that,
the principle on which it proceeded was found to be
fraught with consequences so hard and unjust, that
the Dissenters' Chapels Bill was passed in order to
prevent them. By that Act, introduced by Lord
Lyndhurst himself, it was enacted, that applications
of charitable funds which had been unlawful before
the passing of the Act by which impugners of the
Trinity were relieved from penalty, should be considered to have been lawful from the beginning.
It further established the principle, that where no
religious doctrines appear on the face of a deed
creating such a charitable foundation, the usage
of a quarter of a century should legalize its application. Coupling this with Lord Lyndhurst's
own admission, in his speech on introducing the
Chapels Bill, that in the deed by which Lady

Hewley's charity was founded there was no express declaration of the doctrines which she intended to be inculcated, I think I am warranted in asserting, that the Unitarians were sufferers by an unjust law, which had been allowed to remain unaltered, only because it had not been perceived to what purposes it might be applied by bigotry and self-ishness.

As an epilogue to this history I insert a correspondence arising out of it. After much wrangling in the Court of Chancery between the Independents, who having fought the battle wished to seize on the whole of the spoil, the Scotch Presbyterians, who had always had a handsome share of Lady Hewley's bounty, of which they foresaw the loss, and the Baptists, who claimed as orthodox Nonconformists, the Court divided the seven Trusteeships among the respective claimants. The following letter was addressed to Mr. Wellbeloved by one of the new Trustees:—

"Manchester, 24th Feb., 1854.

"REV. SIR,—Some time ago I had the pleasure of seeing the portraits of Sir John and Lady Hewley in the Vestry of the Chapel of which you are Minister at York, and I hope you will excuse the liberty I take in asking you if you would feel disposed to part with them, and for what consideration. I had nothing to do with the movement which transferred the Hewley charity to a new set of Trustees, but was appointed one of the Presbyterian Trustees, under the new management, by the Court of Chancery. Feeling,

O

consequently, an interest in the mementos of the prefixed
(*sic*) individuals; and as they may not have the same
interest in your estimation that at one time they had, perhaps you may feel disposed to part with the portraits.   I
am well known to your friends here, and have the honour to
remain,

" Rev. Sir,

" Yours respectfully,

" ROBERT BARBOUR.

"Rev. Charles Wellbeloved."

The following was Mr. Wellbeloved's reply :—

" SIR,—The portrait of Lady Hewley is not mine; it
belongs to the members of my congregation.   It is now in
its proper place, the vestry of the chapel which Lady
Hewley zealously assisted in founding, and in which, during
many years of her life, she was a constant worshipper; and
from that place I trust it will never be removed.

"It is true that I have been deprived of that share of her
bounty which, as minister of that chapel, I for many years
received, and which would not have been withdrawn had
her views and intentions been rightly interpreted.   But this
circumstance, however it may affect the character of some
persons, reflects no dishonour on the memory of that benevolent lady, nor weakens in the least degree the obligations
of esteem and gratitude towards her by which I have ever
held myself bound.   And I cannot but express my surprise
and regret that it should for a moment be imagined, that
because I am no longer benefited by her bounty, the
memorial of her, so much coveted by some who have little
sympathy with her real character, 'has not the same
interest in my estimation that it once had.'   The fact is,
that this memorial came not into my possession till I had
ceased to be a recipient of her charity.   But I gratefully

received it from an ancient friend, and highly valued it; and as long as I live I shall continue so to value it, as a memorial of one of the excellent of the earth, who deserve to be held in everlasting remembrance.

> "I have the honour to be,
>> "Your obedient servant,
>>> "CHARLES WELLBELOVED.

"R. Barbour, Esq."

Had these portraits been obtained they were destined for the library of the Lancashire Independent College, and, placed there, would, no doubt, have been considered as evidence, that the Independents were the legitimate representatives and successors of the Presbyterians of Lady Hewley's day.

Desirous of carrying on without interruption the history of this cause, in which Mr. Wellbeloved was, on public and personal grounds, so deeply interested, I have passed over the events of many years of his life. The marriage of his third daughter to the Rev. J. R. Wreford, D.D., in 1827, and of his youngest to Sir James Carter (now Chief Justice of New Brunswick), in 1831, left him with his second daughter only as a companion. A change had taken place in the management of the College in 1827, by the retirement of Mr. Turner,* and the appointment of the Rev. William Hincks, the son of Mr. Wellbeloved's old

* Of this able and excellent man, my colleague during seventeen years, see a Memoir in the Christian Reformer, vol. x. p. 159.

o 2

college friend, and a pupil of his own, as his successor. The establishment of the University of
London, as it was then called, now University
College, had at first an unfavourable effect on. the
resort of lay-students to the College at York.
Hitherto it had possessed the recommendation to
Dissenters of being the only place in South Britain
where a complete academical education could be
obtained, without the necessity of subscription to
articles of faith, or conformity to the worship of
the Church of England. The new University disclaimed all tests, and all interference with the
religious opinions or duties of its pupils. It was
natural to suppose that education would be more
effectively carried on in a Metropolitan University,
by a body of professors, severally representing
every branch of human knowledge, than in a provincial institution, where the whole course of
secular instruction was committed to two individuals. The difficulties which arose in the early
years of the University counteracted for a time
this tendency, but when its plans were better
arranged, and the confidence of the public re-
vived, Manchester College again felt the effect in
a diminution of the number of its lay students.
Doubts began to be entertained among the supporters of the College, whether the education of
the divinity students might not be more advan-
tageously carried on by a removal to London,

where the secular portion of their instruction might be obtained from the Professors in the University, the College being converted into a theological seminary. Others again favoured its removal to Manchester. It was thought that if re-established there, in the midst of the numerous, wealthy, and intelligent communities of Lancashire, the numbers of its lay students could not fail to be largely increased, and the benefits of its course of study thus greatly extended. Some, who thought that the training of the divinity students had hitherto been too much literary and scientific, and had not sufficiently prepared them for the active and popular duties of their profession, regarded Manchester, with its influential body of Dissenters, its flourishing congregations, and its numerous educational and philanthropic institutions, as a fitter school for the acquirement of the habits and turn of mind which a minister should possess than York. From the combined influence of these various causes a general feeling had arisen, that a removal from York, either to Manchester or London, was desirable—to which of them, was a question pretty equally dividing the supporters of the College. The state of my eyesight and my health had prevented my fulfilling my academical duties in the greater part of the session of 1837–8, and had led to the resignation of my office, and my going to winter in Italy in the autumn of

1838. Mr. Hincks had intimated his intention to resign at the end of the session 1838–9. These circumstances induced the Committee of the College to consider very seriously the question of a change of locality, and they addressed letters to various ministers and laymen, asking their opinion, first, on the general question of a removal from York; and, secondly, on that of the place to be fixed upon, if such removal were determined. Of the eighteen persons thus consulted, all except two, and one who was of doubtful opinion, agreed that a removal from York was desirable. They, however, as well as the Committee, were divided on the second question; some inclining to London, some to Manchester, or a provincial centre in the North of England. The difficulty of deciding among such conflicting opinions induced the Committee to request Mr. Wellbeloved to continue his services for another session, during which some temporary arrangement was to be made. In communicating to him the state of opinion which they had ascertained, and the difficulty of an immediate decision, the Committee thus express themselves, by their chairman, Mr. Harrop:—

"In conclusion, my dear sir, I have only to express to you, on behalf of every member of the Committee, their deep sense of your invaluable services to their Institution, their earnest wish to make every possible arrangement for your future comfort and happiness, and their fervent prayer, that if the consultations in which they are now engaged should lead unavoidably to the dissolution of a connection which has to them been productive of such entire satisfaction, you may carry with you into your retirement the best reward of a life unweariedly devoted to the highest interests of humanity—the inward approval of your own mind, and the affectionate respect of all who have benefited by your instructions and example."

It was not till the close of the year 1839 that the question was decided. On the 20th of December, a special general meeting of the Trustees of the College was held, at Manchester, at which, after a long discussion, the decision was in favour of Manchester as its future site. The majority was small, and an accidental circumstance made it larger than it would otherwise have been. The opinion of a legal member of the Committee, that there were obstacles to the removal to London (an opinion which subsequently proved unfounded) contributed to the decision in favour of Manchester. Mr. Wellbeloved's connection of thirty-seven years with the College consequently ceased, at the Examination in the last week of June, 1840. As he had entered his seventy-second year, his retirement from an anxious and laborious office could not be called premature, and, had he held it longer, illness or failing power might have compelled him to resign it under more painful circumstances. I believe, however, that at the time of his actual retirement, his ability to discharge its duties was in no important respect impaired.

Nothing could be more gratifying than the proceedings of the last day of the Session of 1840. It had been resolved by his old pupils and friends to present him with some substantial and permanent mark of their gratitude and esteem, and a sum of £300 was subscribed, of which one hundred was expended in the purchase of a silver salver, and the remainder presented in a purse.* It may interest those who presented him with this splendid testimonial to know that it has been left ultimately as an heirloom to his grandson, J. C. Addyes Scott; and that the accompanying purse enabled him to purchase many costly volumes of antiquities, without which he could not have carried on the studies which

---

* The salver bore the following inscription :—

VIRO·REVERENDO·CAROLO·WELLBELOVED

COLL. MANCVN. APVD. EBORACENSES. PRÆFECTO. IBIDEM. THEOLOGIÆ. PROFESSORI

PER. XXXVII. ANNOS. LITERARVM. SACRARVM. DISCIPLINAS

MVLTIPLICI. DOCTRINA. SINE. PARTIVM. STVDIO. TRADENTI

IN. DISCIPVLORVM. CONFORMANDIS. REGENDISQVE. MORIBVS. GRAVITATEM. COMITATE. TEMPERANTI

IN. OMNI. VITÆ. RATIONE. SANCTO. SIMPLICI. BENEVOLO. STRENVO

PRÆCEPTORIS. MVNVS

EXIMIA. FIDE. RELIGIONE. DILIGENTIA. ADMINISTRATVM

IAMIAM. DEPOSITVRO

EX. ÆRE. CONIATO. DONVM. DEDERVNT

PII. GRATI. VENERABVNDI

COLL·MANCVN·ALVMNI

VII. KAL. IVL. ANNO. MDCCCXXXX

afforded him so much amusement in the later years of his life, and enabled him to produce those works, which established his reputation as an archæologist.

Sixty-eight gentlemen, most of them old pupils of Mr. Wellbcloved, assembled on this occasion, and after a dinner, at which the late Robert Philips, of Heybridge, presided, the testimonial was presented by Mark Philips, Esq., M.P., on the part of the lay students, and the late Rev. J. G. Robberds, of the divinity students. The speech which Mr. Wellbeloved delivered in answer has been printed more than once, yet it is proper to preserve it in this memoir of his life, as the expression of the feelings with which he had discharged, and with which he laid down, his office.

He addressed the meeting in the following terms :—

" Mr. Philips, Mr. Robberds, and gentlemen ; my highly-valued and most-respected pupils that have been ; it is not, I assure you, a mere formal, empty profession that I make when I declare that I cannot express to you the sentiments of my heart on this most interesting occasion. ' *Out of the abundance of the heart*' we are told, on the highest authority, ' *the mouth speaketh.*' But the abundance of the heart may be so great that the mouth may be altogether incapable of relieving it, and of giving utterance to its emotions. So I now find it to be with myself. And how should it be otherwise ? I should be unworthy of the extraordinary tribute of respect which I am now receiving, if I were not overpowered by it. You will give me credit, I am sure, for all those emotions, which a heart in its right place, and a heart properly disciplined, must in such cir-

cumstances feel, but which I cannot fully describe. I must
refer you therefore to your own breasts, in order that you
may judge rightly of the state of mine. . Great, very great,
as is the kindness which has prompted you to offer this
testimony of your esteem to me, my gratitude on receiving
it, I trust you will believe, cannot be less. The hearts of
those who have given, and the heart of him that receives, I
am confident, must truly respond to each other. Accept,
then, my offering of thanks, my dear friends,—that offering
which I can present you in words; imagine all that is
possible of kind and grateful feeling, which no words can
express. Had I been permitted to retire from the situation
I have so long held, in the same silent, unmarked, and un-
ostentatious manner, in which I entered upon it, I should
have been perfectly satisfied; assured, as I could not fail to
have been, by what I had experienced during the whole of
that long period, from, I will not say every individual, but
from the great majority of all those who have been under my
care: from the experience that I had of them while they
were in the College; I was sure that I should carry with me
into retirement, all the affectionate regards of those with
whom I had been so happily and so long connected, that I
deserve to possess. My habits and feelings would have led
me to prefer this, if the choice had been left to me; but
your kindness would not suffer that; and since I know that
it is the most gratifying to you, if on no other account, on
this alone, it must be most gratifying to me. I need not
assure you that I shall ever most highly prize this costly
token of your kind regard so long as life or the power of
perception shall last,—not for its own sake, not on account
of its intrinsic value, great as it is, or of the beauty of its
workmanship, but for the sake of the testimony it bears, in
that beautiful inscription, of your approbation and esteem.
‘ *Laudari a laudato viro* ’ was of old, and must ever be,
considered a high and enviable distinction. You have conferred this distinction upon me, and this splendid gift will

ever remind me of the honourable privilege of being respected and esteemed by those who are themselves, in their
several stations, esteemed and respected by the wise and
good around them,—whose character for intellectual and
moral worth is such as to reflect true honour on all who are
the objects of their praise and friendship. This token of
your esteem will be highly valued by me as a pleasing
memorial also of my long-continued connection with an
Institution, from the most zealous friends and supporters of
which I have received such numerous marks of kindness
and friendship, which has also been the means of uniting
me in ties of the purest friendship with many of the most
excellent of the earth, and of continuing and of strengthening the ties of valuable and early friendship. Nor shall I
ever look on this memorial of your kind regard, I trust,
without feeling my gratitude excited and increased towards
that great and good Being, whose providence has enabled
me to exercise so long, and with so little interruption, that
portion of talents which it has pleased him to grant to me,
in promoting the interests of scriptural truth and virtue ; in
endeavouring, I hope not unsuccessfully, to communicate
religious information to those who were willing to receive it,
and in aiding many to become the guides and instructors of
others in the attainment of true honour and substantial
happiness in this world, and of life eternal in the world to
come. And at the same time the conviction, which I now
so strongly feel, and which I shall, I am persuaded, ever
retain, that this testimony of your regard and esteem far
exceeds my deserts, ('No, No,' from all parts of the room)
—will keep alive in me that humility of spirit which is
becoming in everyone, however extensive his knowledge and
brilliant his talents, and especially becoming in him who now
thus imperfectly addresses you, and who claims for himself no
other merit than that of having laboured to the utmost of
his ability to serve the best interests of those who have been

confided to his care with fidelity and diligence, as ever in
his great Taskmaster's sight. And now, my kind and
valued friends, I entreat you once more to accept the best
thanks I can offer,—thanks very inadequately, very imperfectly expressed,—for this splendid testimony of your esteem
and approbation, and for having added so much to its value
by your assembling here on this occasion in such numbers,
at, I fear, no little trouble and inconvenience to yourselves.
And may God Almighty grant you all, his choicest blessings
in this life, and unite us all again, in the bonds of uninter-
rupted and everlasting friendship, in a better world, when
this life shall have passed away."

As a sequel to this account, I record with pleasure, that in the year 1843 the sum of a thousand
pounds was presented to Mr. Wellbeloved by old
friends and supporters of the College, who, in the
language of· Mr. Wood in announcing the dona-
tion, "were desirous that he should receive some
substantial proof of public gratitude for those
laborious, faithful, and successful services which
he had rendered to the College as its theological
tutor." It was dictated by a kind and thoughtful
regard to the circumstances in which Mr. Wellbeloved was placed by the removal of the College.
His income from it ceased entirely. Mr. Harrop's
letter had hinted at an annuity from its funds, but
Mr. Wellbeloved knew that whatever was devoted
to his use from this source must be withdrawn
from the objects for the promotion of which it had
been established, and his friends were aware that

he had a strong repugnance to being the cause of
such a diminution of its resources. Ever since the
commencement of the Hewley suit, the grant of
80*l.* a year—one-third of his whole income from
his profession as a minister—had ceased; he had
suffered very severely by the profligate management of the Bank of the United States, after it
became a local, instead of a national, institution.
Such losses when they occurred could not fail to
affect him, but the painful feeling soon passed
away, and his relief was to turn his thoughts to
the various labours, in which he was engaged for
the good of others. His own liberal temper and
the demands of his family had been alike unfavourable to any accumulation of property. His
neglect, indeed, of his pecuniary affairs might be
reckoned as a fault, if it had not been so closely
connected with the virtues of his character. "I
can keep other people's accounts," he once said, in
reference to this subject, "but I cannot keep my
own."

On laying down his offices of Principal and
Theological Professor in the College, Mr. Wellbeloved was appointed joint visitor with the Rev.
William Turner, and in that capacity delivered an
address to the students at the close of the first
session, which is printed in the Christian Reformer
for 1841. He had prepared another for delivery in
1843, when the state of his health prevented his

visiting Manchester. Although he never ceased to regard the College with affectionate interest, he took no active part in the discussions which subsequently arose respecting its management and its locality. Nor did he join in the controversies which from time to time divided his own denomination. "We missed him," says Mr. Hincks in his funeral sermon, "in the conflict of schools, and the debate on sectional differences." His own opinions were firmly fixed; and though by no means unobservant of what was passing, or indifferent to the growth of what he believed to be erroneous and even pernicious doctrines, he had entire confidence in the power and ultimate ascendancy of truth.

Questions of politics, into which we have seen that Mr. Wellbeloved had entered warmly in early life, had for many years occupied a very subordinate place in his thoughts. The republican ardour of his youth had long subsided into a sincere attachment to constitutional monarchy, not precluding a lively sense of the imperfection and injustice of many parts of our laws. He had joined in every movement for social, religious, and political reform, but had studiously kept aloof from local politics, and, although strongly attached to Whig principles, had declined the office of Vice-President of the York Whig Club, which had been offered him in 1821. There was one remarkable exception.

After the passing of the Reform Bill, it was hoped that the electors would renounce the corrupt practices of preceding times, choose members for their merits, and expect nothing from them but faithful and disinterested service.   Mr. Dundas (now Lord Zetland), the Whig Member for the city of York, had lost his election in 1832, notwithstanding his high personal character and the long connection of his family with the city, by his scrupulous abstinence from all the ordinary means of corruption and influence.   In recognition of his honourable conduct, many of his fellow-citizens of all parties entered into a subscription to present him with a silver candelabrum, and Mr. Wellbeloved was requested to be their spokesman.   In addressing Mr. Dundas, he said, speaking in their name :—

"They were convinced that the changes of the constituency introduced by the Reform Bill were comparatively of little value, unless they were accompanied by a total change of the corrupt system which had so long prevailed, unless bribery in all its forms were wholly rooted out. They therefore observed with admiration how carefully you abstained from every practice, however it might be sanctioned by long and general usage, that was in the slightest degree adverse to perfect purity of election; how religiously you adhered to the resolution which from the first you avowed, that you would not interfere in any instance or in any degree with the unbiassed suffrages of the electors; how scrupulously you sought to throw no temptation in the way of the neediest voter to make a profit by his vote; how studiously you rejected all those means of undue influence,

of corruption and bribery which have been commonly, not
to say universally, employed in contested elections, but
which are ever attended with consequences most pernicious
to private and public .morality.   Many have talked loudly
of purity of elections; many have professed an anxious
desire that it could be preserved inviolate.   You, Sir, were
not satisfied with professions; the most scrutinizing eye
was not able to detect the slightest discordancy between the
principles you adopted and the conduct you pursued."

He justified himself for undertaking this duty
by observing, that he had most carefully through
life abstained from any active concern in either
promoting or opposing the interest of any political
candidate; but that the object of the present
meeting was to express disapprobation of practices
which are invariably connected with the most
deplorable evils, and to pay a tribute of respect to
one who had done all in his power to put an end
to them.   The year 1859 has afforded lamentable
proof how small has been the influence of Mr.
Dundas's honourable example.

CHAPTER V.

LIFE SUBSEQUENTLY TO THE REMOVAL OF THE COLLEGE TO MANCHESTER.

1840—1858.

IN the years which immediately followed the removal of the College to Manchester Mr. Wellbeloved was much occupied in the composition of his "Eburacum; or, York under the Romans," which was published by subscription in 1842. In a city like York, which conceals beneath its surface the records of so many vanished centuries, and such various stages of civilization, the discovery of antiquarian relics is, of course, not uncommon; but just before he undertook the composition of his work several circumstances had much increased their number. A new entrance had been formed into the city from the north, which had brought to light a large portion of the walls of the Roman station. The visitation of the cholera had roused the citizens to provide a better drainage, and the excavations made for this purpose had furnished the means of tracing the outline of Eburacum. The introduction of the railway within the walls of the city, much as it was deplored by the lovers

P

of antiquity, served the cause of archæology by
laying open the Roman baths which occupied the
site of the railway station.   Mr. Wellbeloved's
volume had been produced by a gradual expansion.
Its germ was in some papers read before a select
number of the members of the Yorkshire Philosophical Society; these were enlarged into a course
of seven lectures on the antiquarian contents of
the museum, delivered in 1840; and finally assumed the form of an 8vo volume, with numerous
illustrations.   The author had intended originally
to confine himself strictly to the history and antiquities of Eburacum, but he found, that to make
these intelligible, it was necessary to connect them
with the conquest and occupation of Britain by
the Romans, and to compare the remains of their
works here with the other traces of their settle-
ments.   Instead of a monograph of the antiquities of York, it thus became a general history of
Roman dominion in Britain; and the learning and
research with which it is executed have procured
it a place among our standard works of archæological literature.*

* Dr. Whitaker, in his edition of Thoresby's Ducatus Leodiensis,
p. 105, speaking of Sir Thomas Fairfax, expresses his surprise that
the " drowsy humour of the Presbyterian," a phrase which he bor-
rows from Lord Clarendon, "should have been united with the zeal
of an ardent antiquary."   To the names of Thoresby and Horsley,
which might have induced Dr. Whitaker to refrain from this sarcasm
on Presbyterianism, may now be added those of Wellbeloved and

From this time, till even the last weeks of his life, antiquarian studies occupied a chief place in Mr. Wellbeloved's employments. They were an unfailing source of interest. New discoveries were made from time to time in York and its vicinity, and it was to him that archæologists looked for an account and an explanation of them. Seated in his study, with his books around him, even when confined to the house by indisposition, he could classify and describe the smaller objects of antiquity which were brought to him from the museum, and many an hour, which would otherwise have passed wearily, was thus beguiled. He combined several qualities which are conducive to success in archæological pursuits — an almost microscopical power of sight, which even extreme old age did not impair; sagacity in drawing inferences from faint and doubtful appearances, and patience in proving and confirming them into certainty. To these special qualifications of the archæologist he joined a cultivated taste and extensive knowledge of history, which are necessary to relieve the dryness of mere archæology, to prevent it from degenerating into pedantry, and to connect it with the higher departments of knowledge. In the year following the publication of Eburacum he con-

Hunter. With Mr. Hunter, Mr. Wellbeloved continued in friendly correspondence to a late period of his life, and never applied to him in vain for information respecting Yorkshire antiquities.

tributed to the Penny Cyclopædia the article on York.

He exerted himself in the establishment of the School of Art in York in 1842, and several times addressed the pupils on delivering the prizes. The address of 1844 produced a letter of thanks from Etty, the painter. He had been instrumental in obtaining for his native and beloved city the distinction of being the seat of one of these institutions, which had been coveted by some of the manufacturing towns of Yorkshire. Mr. Wellbeloved's practice of the art of design did not advance beyond the making of a pencil sketch; but if he had had leisure to cultivate it, his quick eye and ready hand would have enabled him to excel. Without practical skill in design, however, his taste, knowledge, and experience of instruction enabled him to give valuable advice to the pupils, especially in directing them to the beautiful models which the Minster affords. The sentiments expressed in the following passage were not so trite in 1844 as they have since become.

"The best remuneration of the designer will be derived from the application of his art to those articles which minister to the luxury of the wealthy. I hope, however, you will not disdain to bestow your labours on articles of a less splendid description, but that, as far as may depend upon yourselves, you will promote, by your skill and taste, the cultivation of pure taste among those who hold inferior rank in society. Why should not the dress of the cottager, and the furniture of his cottage display good taste, as well as the dress of the rich, and the furniture of the palace? Why, to take for example a common article of table furniture, why should not well-drawn landscapes, or some beautiful plant, or simple groups of figures, take the place of those absurd, incongruous jumbles of Chinese bridges and pagodas, and Chinese men and women which, in utter disregard of proportion and perspective, are commonly presented on the pottery in daily use? I can only hint at this; but I feel that it is a subject of moral importance. There is, I am persuaded, some connection between a good taste in personal and domestic decoration and good taste in respect to the conduct of life; between the perception of natural or artificial and that of moral beauty. Let a man have a decent pride in the neatness of his abode, and in the simple elegance of its furniture, in the trim and gay appearance of his little garden, and he will have a just pride in that decent conduct, without which these comforts of life cannot be obtained and enjoyed. I reckon among the benefactors of society those who employ their taste and skill in opening the eyes of the multitude to the beauties of nature and of art, and who furnish them with elegancies, the manifest tendency of which is to soften and refine their sentiments and manners. Be prepared, then, to employ your talents so as to improve the perception of beauty among those who compose the mass of the community, remembering the words of the philosophic poet—

> "Thus then at first was Beauty sent from Heaven,
> The lovely ministress of Truth and Good
> In this dark world. For Truth and Good are one;
> And Beauty dwells in them and they in her."
>
> AKENSIDE.

In the year preceding the delivery of this

address, he lost one of his most valued friends, Mr. Thrush. Their common warfare in defence of what they believed to be gospel truth had united them more closely in mutual esteem, and a year seldom passed in which Mr. and Mrs. Thrush did not spend some weeks in York. Mr. Wellbeloved, who was not accustomed to push a principle to an extreme, did not agree with his friend in considering war, under all circumstances, as forbidden to a Christian; but he honoured him for the boldness with which he promulgated so unpopular an opinion, and the disinterestedness with which he sacrificed the emoluments of a profession which he regarded as unlawful. He also highly appreciated the character of his wife, who had cheerfully shared the trials of her husband, and, at her request, undertook to write a memoir of him, which was published in 1845. The incidents of Mr. Thrush's active life were not numerous or important; but, by a faithful delineation of his character, and the introduction of his letters, which are true pictures of his upright mind, the biographer has succeeded in exciting an interest in his simple history. Mrs. Thrush survived her husband several years, and the friendship between her and Mr. Wellbeloved continued to the end of her life. In the year 1845 he passed several weeks, with his family, in her house in Harrowgate. His health had remained tolerably good for the few first years after

the removal of the College.   An accident which
occurred in the autumn of 1841, the partial rup-
ture of a tendon, had confined him to the house
for six weeks, but it had not impaired his power of
walking, or affected his general health.   In 1844,
however, he had an illness of so severe a kind, that
for four months he was unable to preach.   On the
15th of September he again appeared in the pulpit,
and preached from Ps. lvi. 3, "What time I am
afraid I will trust in thee."   This illness he regarded as a warning, that he must not reckon upon
being able in future to discharge the whole of his
ministerial duties, and he was desirous to engage
an assistant.   His son, Mr. Robert Scott, ever attentive to the comfort of his father, undertook to
supply the means of doing so.   The letter addressed to him by the congregation, in answer to
his announcement of his wish to appoint an assistant, contains sentiments so honourable to both
parties, that I will here insert an extract from it.

"Whilst we beg, in reply to your communication, to
assure you of our affectionate interest in your health, and
our deep regret that its present uncertain state will not
admit of the regular performance of your ministerial duties,
we beg to offer you the sincere tribute of cordial approbation, respect, and affection, with which we unanimously
regard this additional manifestation of your anxiety to promote our spiritual welfare.   We rejoice, too, in the assurance which it affords us, that a connection which commenced in satisfaction and hope with our predecessors and

fathers, and which has continued in mutual affection, respect, and harmony with two generations of worshippers,
will be dissolved only by death.   And we venture to hope
that this appointment will prove largely conducive to your
own comfort and health, and thereby extend, through the
blessing of God, the duration of that connection, which is
endeared to us by so many of the happiest and holiest associations of our lives."

After the close of the session of College in 1845,
Mr. John Wright, who had just finished his course
of theological study at Manchester, entered upon
his office as assistant minister.   He was introduced
by Mr. Wellbeloved to his flock, in this relation,
on a very interesting occasion—the presentation of
a silver tea-service to him on the part of the congregation.   The time chosen for it was the week
of the first quinquennial meeting of the students
of the College, of whom a considerable number
were present to join in this tribute of respect.   In
acknowledging the kindness of his friends, Mr.
Wellbeloved took occasion to review the course of
his ministry, and to express the principles by
which he had been guided in the exercise of its
duties.

"It is with deep and unfeigned humility that I review
the extended period of my ministry.   I need no one to
remind me of my own faults and imperfections.   Yet I
trust I can truly declare, that in conducting the public services it has ever been my most anxious desire to secure the
greatest possible benefit to my hearers.   I may have erred

in my judgment, I may not have chosen the best means of attaining the end which I had in view ; but I can conscientiously say, that your religious instruction, your moral and spiritual improvement, not your entertainment, has ever guided me in the selection of the subjects to which, in the course of my preaching, I have directed your attention. I have studiously avoided preaching, in any sense or in any degree, myself. My desire has been to preach Christ Jesus, my Lord. My anxious inquiry from week to week has been 'How shall I best open the Scriptures to those who hear me ? How shall I most powerfully excite and help them to sustain their devotional feelings ? How shall I most effectually persuade them to keep themselves in the love of God and of Christ ? How shall I kindle in them a warm desire after holiness and virtue, and most successfully urge them to be and to do all that the Lord their God requires of them ?' I have never sought to amuse you by curious speculations, or the sallies of a lively imagination, or by a studied display of eloquence; nor have I perplexed you, or endangered your Christian charity, by setting before you subjects of a controversial character." In concluding his address he said, " My term of service in the ministry of the Gospel has been protracted beyond the ordinary limit.* In the common course of nature it cannot be extended much farther. I have lately, as you know, received a serious warning of its approaching close. While a gracious Providence shall uphold me in life, and continue to me the use of my mental and bodily powers, it will still be my greatest happiness to employ them in your service, in the work to which I have been so long devoted. And when it shall have pleased the Allwise Disposer of events to remove us all from this scene of mortality, may we meet again

---

* He was in the seventy-sixth year of his age, and the fifty-fourth of his ministry in York.

in the mansions of everlasting blessedness, to aid each other in our never-ending progress towards the perfection of knowledge, virtue, and happiness."

This solemn and pathetic appeal drew tears from many of those to whom it was addressed. His people had the happiness of hearing him frequently again from the pulpit, but this was the last time that he met them collectively on any social occasion.

A painful visitation was awaiting him. He had already been severely tried, as we have seen by domestic losses. In 1842 his youngest daughter Emma, had died at Fredericton in New Brunswick, after a long and painful illness. She had been a sufferer, even in childhood, from ill-health, which she had endured with a gentle patience that greatly endeared her to her parents, and as she grew up, her graceful manners, the natural expression of a pure, guileless, and affectionate disposition, and the refinement of her tastes and accomplishments, made her the delight of every circle in which she was known. She had visited England with her husband, but had returned to New Brunswick in the autumn of 1841, in a state of health which gave little hope of recovery, and our forebodings were realized, after many months of anxiety on her account, in July of the following year. Towards the end of 1845 his second daughter Anne, who had been his sole domestic companion since the marriage of the youngest, showed symptoms of declining health, which in the following spring assumed the unmistakable character of consumption. An illness almost in infancy had enfeebled her frame and made her health precarious, and this, joined to an uncommon sweetness of disposition, had given her a precedence in her father's affections, which never caused a moment's jealousy in the other members of the family, so confident were they in her rectitude and disinterestedness. As she had lived so many years alone with him, she knew more of his inner thoughts than any other of his children; he reposed great confidence in her judgment, which, notwithstanding her limited experience of the world, was remarkably sound; and her perpetual cheerfulness and good humour could dissipate the clouds which occasionally gathered around him. She had all her father's religious sensibility with a more hopeful disposition, and she bore with admirable patience and resignation the weakness and pain of the decline which preceded her death. Her chief anxiety was to conceal from him the real nature of her complaint, and to avoid adding to his distress, by allowing him to perceive what she was suffering. He on his part clung to the hope of recovery, when every one else felt it to be vain, and till a short time before the termination of her illness, had not, I believe, allowed himself to think that it was beyond the power of medical skill. The last week of her life was that of the meeting of the Archæological Institute at York, in July, 1846, and he took a part in its proceedings during the three first days. His exclamation on hearing of her death, which occurred during the night of July 25, "Thank God that I am an old man!" expressed at once the feeling that the remainder of his life must be darkened by a sense of his loss, and the consoling thought, that he should not long be separated from the object of his love. The distress of the few first days cannot be described; he soon, however, returned to his ordinary occupations, and found relief in his pulpit duties, which he resumed on Sunday, August 10. But the wound was too deep ever to be entirely healed, and from many touching incidental proofs I have learnt, how long and how tenderly he mourned for his lost child. In consequence of her death and his advanced age and increasing infirmity, we were desirous of occupying the house immediately adjoining his own; but so unwilling was he that others should make any sacrifice for him, that it was only by persuading him that our comfort would be greatly increased by the removal, that we prevailed on him, after a time, to accede to it. The change of our residence did not take place till Midsummer, 1849. I resigned the offices which I held in connection with Manchester College, and which imposed the necessity of a residence there during several weeks of the session, at the close of the following year.

His health had been seriously impaired in the beginning of 1848, an eruptive complaint, with which he had been attacked towards the end of the preceding year, having increased so much, as to confine him to the house from the beginning of January to the end of May. He did not enter his pulpit till the first Sunday in July. His reappearance there was hailed with great delight by his flock, and an address of congratulation was presented to him by the younger members, to which he made the following reply :—

"Monkgate, July 4th, 1848.

" MY DEAR YOUNG FRIENDS,

"I am greatly obliged to you for your kind congratulations on the improved state of my health, and on my having been able once more to address you from the pulpit. This affords me a pleasing and consoling proof that, although inevitable circumstances have prevented me from imparting religious knowledge and counsel to you individually and in private, my ordinary public ministrations have not been unacceptable or fruitless. In return for your kind sympathy in my sorrows and sufferings, let me assure you of the deep interest I feel in your future honour and welfare, both temporal and eternal. I am old, and leaving the world ; you are young, and the world with all its enjoyments, and all its trials, is opening before you. Neither Reason nor Religion forbids you to enjoy the world. God has made it, in part at least, to be a place of enjoyment for his rational creatures.

Its trials you cannot escape. But there can be no *true* enjoyment of the world, separate from the fear and love of its Maker : none, where the counsels of wisdom are neglected, and higher interests and purer enjoyments are not deemed superior objects of desire and pursuit. The delights of life are most fully experienced by those whose first concern it is to lead a devout and a religious life : and the trials of life are best sustained, and turned to the best account, by those whose daily study it is to do the will of Him who orders all the circumstances of being. Let it be your endeavour, my young friends, to attain to such a character. Let the performance of your duty be your chief aim, and your highest delight. In whatever station the Providence of your heavenly Father may hereafter place you, let it be your increasing endeavour to discharge the duties of that station. Improve all the religious and moral advantages it affords to the utmost of your ability. Consider well its peculiar temptations, and prepare to meet them and to overcome them. Connect, in your thoughts, as much and as constantly as you can, this present fleeting world with that abiding world that is to succeed it. Habitually revere and love and obey God. Study the life and character, and imbibe the spirit of your Lord and Master, Jesus Christ. Be ever, as he was, sincerely pious, actively benevolent, pure in heart, blameless, virtuous and holy in life. You cannot be too assiduous in obeying God, in serving others, in governing your own hearts and minds. However diligent you may have been in health, when sickness comes you will regret that you have done no more. At the close of the longest life, however wisely you may have improved the talents entrusted to you, you will lament that many things have been left undone, which you might have done. ' Be diligent then in business,' both as it respects the world on which you are entering, and preparation for a world to come ; at the same time ' be fervent in spirit, serving the Lord.'

That in all cases you may have wisdom to discern what is right, and in all circumstances, patience, fortitude, and zeal to pursue it, is the sincere and earnest prayer of,

  " My young Friends,

   " Your faithful friend and affectionate pastor,

     " CHARLES WELLBELOVED."

As the complaint with which he had been troubled seemed not likely to be removed by medicine alone, he was advised to try the effect of the water of the Dinsdale Spa, near Darlington, and he accordingly spent many weeks in the summer and autumn of 1848 at Middleton-one-Row, a small retired village, near Dinsdale, wholly free from the bustle and the crowd which make our watering-places resemble more places of amusement than of health-seeking. It stands on the northern side of the valley of the Tees, which winds among woods at the foot of a rocky bank, and commands a rich home view, and a more distant prospect of the Cleveland hills, with which, from his former visits to Marske, Redcar, and Seaton, Mr. Wellbeloved had become so familiar, that he knew every summit and every valley throughout the range. The purity of the air, and the use of the waters, had a very beneficial effect upon his health. For in-door occupation, he had brought with him a large collection of the Northumbrian stycas, recently discovered in York and its neighbourhood, which he deciphered and cata-

logued for the Yorkshire Philosophical Society.
Another of his employments was the revision
of his version of the Minor Prophets, which he
had before prepared as a portion of his Bible,
though with little hope at that time that it would
ever be published. The vicinity of Middleton to
Stockton-on-Tees, gave him frequent opportunities
of intercourse with his friend, the late Mr. Wright,
of Stockton, who joined to an amiable and benevolent temper, and a modest and candid mind, a
knowledge of theological literature not often found
in a layman. It was not till the beginning of
November, 1848, that he returned to York, much
improved in health ; and during the ensuing winter
and spring he was able, with rare exceptions, to
take the services of Sunday morning.

In the summer of 1849, he had the pleasure of
seeing in York the associate of his early years,
Arthur Aikin. He had announced his intended
journey in a letter, which I have much pleasure
in inserting, as a proof how little change time had
made in the friendship which had begun sixty
years before :—

"MY DEAR CHARLES,—Although for a long time we have
had no intercourse either personally or by letter, yet I am
sure that our mutual regard has undergone no diminution.
We have each of us experienced the necessary consequences
of protracted life, and our lost, our loved, our mourned are
constantly drawing our hearts there where our treasure lies.

Wretched, indeed, would be the state of old age, with its consciousness of failing powers of body and of mind, if the hope of again joining those who have gone before us did not become more distinct, as the distance between us diminishes.

"I have a great desire that we should once more meet, and therefore, if no other engagement of yours forbids, I will spend a week with you early in next month."

The visit took place, and produced the pleasure which both the friends anticipated from it. They explored together the scenes, now much changed indeed, of their early rambles around York, and visited the instructive remains of the ancient Isurium at Aldborough. Mr. Aikin was a man not only of encyclopædical knowledge, but of that comprehensive culture of mind which enables its possessor to appreciate and enjoy whatever is curious or beautiful, though lying beyond the sphere of his special studies.

The cure of his complaint not having been quite completed, Mr. Wellbeloved returned to Middleton in 1849, and again derived great benefit from his residence there. An alarming rheumatic affection of the head and limbs with which he was attacked in March, 1850, and which confined him for fourteen weeks to his chamber, prevented his leaving home in the two succeeding years; but in 1852 he visited Middleton for the third time. On the first Sunday of July in that year he was able to administer the Lord's Supper, his first participation

Q

in any ministerial duty since March, 1850. After his return from Middleton he was able to attend public worship, with few intermissions, for the remainder of the year. In January, 1853, he had the first attack of violent neuralgic pain in the ear and throat, by which he was confined to the house till summer, when he was again able to attend public worship, and to visit the Museum. On the first Sunday of August he administered the Lord's Supper. He paid a fourth visit to Middleton in the autumn, but without experiencing so much benefit from it as on former occasions. This was the last of his distant journeys. He had hoped to spend some time at Thorp-Arch in the autumn of 1854, but the recurrence of indisposition in the beginning of September prevented his leaving home. The spring of 1855 brought back the neuralgia with more violence than before, so as to excite apprehension that the intense paroxysms of pain, and the difficulty of swallowing food, must exhaust his strength. In the month of May violent sickness was added to the other causes of alarm. The excellence of his constitution happily enabled him, as the summer advanced, to throw off the complaint for the time, but he was never free from the apprehension of its return. It left him also much reduced in bodily strength, so that he depended chiefly on a Bath chair for the enjoyment of the open air.

The beginning of 1856 was saddened by the death of his son, Robert Scott, in the month of February. So rapid had been the progress of the disorder by which his valuable life was terminated, that the first tidings of illness were almost immediately followed by the announcement of imminent danger. Though he had been long removed from his home, and had entered into a variety of new relations in life, his dutiful affection and reverence for his father had suffered no diminution, and, in return, his father reposed the most entire confidence in him. The loss of his sympathy and aid, never wanting in seasons of affliction, whether produced by sickness or domestic trials, was painfully felt in the interval between this time and his father's death. At the time of the decease of his brother, in 1819, he was just finishing his preparatory education, and knowing how much his father's heart was set on bringing up a son to his own profession, he requested to be allowed to change his destination, which was the law, and devote himself to the ministry. In some respects he was well qualified for it; his mind was serious and reverent; he had a great desire of usefulness; and he would have been diligent in acquiring the knowledge which the profession of a minister demanded. But his father rightly judged that he was more fitted for active life, and he pursued his original purpose, going through the training of a solicitor's

office, and being ultimately called to the Bar. His
father had followed with great interest his subsequent course, which had placed him in an honourable and influential position, both among his own
religious denomination and in general society.*   I
have already mentioned the liberality with which
he had enabled him to relieve himself of a part of
his duties by engaging an assistant.   He showed
the same thoughtful consideration in the disposal
of his property, providing him with the means of
obtaining every comfort which his old age might
require.

The year 1856 was remarkable, as completing a
hundred years since the commencement of Mr.
Cappe's ministry.   Of this period his pastorate had
occupied forty-four years, and Mr. Wellbeloved's
fifty-six.   It is not common to find a pastoral
connection lasting even for the shorter of these
terms; that two in succession should fill up a
century must be a very rare occurrence.   It appeared to Mr. Wellbeloved's congregation to be
an event capable of suggesting important reflections, and at their request a special service was
devoted to its celebration, on the 25th of May,
in which, however, he was himself unable to take
part, even as a hearer.   Such had been the changes
produced by various causes in the composition of

* See a Memoir of him in the Christian Reformer, vol. xii.
pp. 102—220.

the congregation, that it contained, in 1856, only
one member who had been living at the commencement of Mr. Wellbeloved's ministry, and not a
single representative of those by whom Mr. Cappe
had been invited.*

At the beginning of the year 1857 Mr. Wellbeloved was sufficiently well for us to undertake
together the final revision of the text of his translation of the Pentateuch, to which we devoted
an hour and a half or two hours every forenoon,—
as long a time as he was able to bear continued application. The plan of republishing his translation
has been already mentioned as originating in 1849,
but from various causes its execution had been delayed till now. The revision occupied us constantly
during the months of January and February. The
principles on which it was undertaken have been
briefly explained in page 130, and in the Preface to
the first volume, lately published.† It was evident,
in the course of our joint labour, that his memory
served him less promptly in the production of his
stores of knowledge than formerly, and the difficulty of deciding in doubtful cases, which he
had always felt, was increased; but his judgment

---

* See Christian Reformer, vol. xii. p. 433.

† The Holy Scriptures of the Old Covenant, in a revised Translation, by the late Rev. Charles Wellbeloved, the Rev. George Vance
Smith, B.A., and the Rev. John Scott Porter. Vol. I., containing
the Five Books of Moses, with the Books of Joshua, Judges,
and Ruth, by the late Rev. Charles Wellbeloved.

was as clear and sound as it had ever been, and though protracted mental exertion was irksome to him, he would never slur over a difficulty. We had not accomplished more than the revision of Genesis when he had a new and more violent attack of neuralgia, about the middle of March, which rendered him frequently incapable of continuous application, and was at times so severe as to excite in himself serious apprehensions. There were intervals, however, in which we were able to proceed through the Pentateuch, and he inspected the proofs when the printing began in the month of May. The disorder abated as the summer came on, but it left behind it increased weakness, and I could not venture to ask his judgment of the revision which I undertook of the books of Joshua, Judges, and Ruth, with the help of the materials which he had prepared some years before. The remainder of the year passed away with frequent recurrence of illness, but happily without violent pain. He was able to occupy himself with reading and writing, and could enjoy conversation, especially with two antiquarian friends, whose visits never failed to interest and enliven him.*   He was also engaged in preparing for the press a third edition of his Catalogue of the Anti-

---

* Robert Davies, Esq., F.S.A., and the Rev. James Raine, the Editor of the Testamenta Eboracensia, and the Fabric Rolls of York Minster.

quities in the Museum, which was published in the spring of the following year. During the early months of 1858 he had several attacks of indisposition, one in April of an alarming character, and in May a return of neuralgia, but not so severe as in former years. Amidst the languor and pain of the last months of his life, the election of the Rev. George Vance Smith as his assistant and successor, was an event which he regarded with great interest. Mr. Smith had been his pupil in the last years of his connection with the College, and when the Professorship of Theology at Manchester became vacant, by the resignation of Mr. Wallace, he had joined in recommending him as his successor in that office. The unanimity with which the congregation in St. Saviourgate concurred in the appointment of Mr. Smith was very satisfactory to him, as it gave him the assurance that " Mr. Cappe's pulpit " (for so he spoke of it, and not as his own) would be filled by a man of education and biblical learning.

As there seemed no special cause of apprehension at the time, we left him in the beginning of August to go to Harrogate, being assured by his medical attendant, who watched over him with more than merely professional assiduity, that he saw no reason to fear any immediate change. I visited York again on the 14th, and returned to Harrogate ; but the intelligence which we received on the morning of the 25th induced us immediately to set off for York, and we found him alarmingly ill. It was evident from the first that unless the disorder from which he was suffering could be checked, his strength must sink under it, and none of the means adopted produced any effect. On the night of Saturday, the 28th, we were informed that all hope of recovery was at an end. The final change took place a little after five o'clock on Sunday morning. His last illness had been throughout rather harassing and exhausting than painful, and its close was happily free from any severe suffering.

There is a natural curiosity to learn how the approach of death is regarded by good men, and character is sometimes estimated even more from the sentiments uttered in the prospect of dissolution than from the actions of the past life. It is, indeed, pleasant and soothing to be able to recall the parting counsels, the farewell blessing of a parent, and an aggravation of sorrow when there is no such relic for the memory to treasure.* During the week of his illness Mr. Wellbeloved's strength was so much reduced that he spoke little, except to his medical attendants, or to the faithful servant who had passed sixty-three years in his family, and

---

* Οὐ γάρ μοι θνήσκων λεχέων ἐκ χεῖρας ὄρεξας·
Οὐδέ τί μοι εἶπες πυκινὸν ἔπος, οὔτε κεν αἰεὶ
Μεμνήμην νύκτας τε καὶ ἤματα.—Il. ω', 743.

who was ever at his side, attentive to the faintest expression of his wishes. It was of the utmost importance that he should be kept free from every source of agitation. His children needed no other assurance of his affection than the experience of their whole lives had furnished. He himself required no sudden or artificial preparation for his departure from the world. His days had been passed in virtuous activity; he had borne afflictions of no ordinary severity in resignation to his Heavenly Father's will; his faith in the promises of the Gospel was unshaken. He had spoken to us, when former attacks of illness had led him to apprehend the approach of death, in the language of humble submission and tranquil hope. And although it was not permitted us to know the thoughts which were passing in his mind in his last hours, we felt an entire conviction that they were in accordance with the principles which he had professed and acted upon during life.*

* He has beautifully described the feelings of children placed in the same circumstances as his own descendants, in the contemplation of a parent's death. " The afflicted family follow to the grave the venerable parent, by whose kind and pious care their early feet were led into the paths of integrity and virtue ; their tender minds were directed to the love of God and the desire of his approbation ; their youthful affections were set upon those great objects which are most worthy of the regard of rational and accountable creatures. Thus instructed, they have acquitted themselves in the world with honour and usefulness ; their growing excellences have cheered the declining years of their parent; their filial piety has supported his feeble steps, as he was descending into the valley of the shadow

Unusual marks of respect were paid to his memory by those who were not connected with him in religious belief, but who knew the worth of his character, and were grateful for his services to his fellow-citizens. The Council of the Yorkshire Philosophical Society, including the Rev. W. V. Harcourt, one of the Vice-Presidents, and the Committee of the York Institute, besides passing resolutions expressive of their sense of his services, resolved to attend his funeral, which took place in the ground behind the chapel on Friday, Sept. 3, his remains being laid in the same grave to which, twelve years before, he had consigned those of his beloved daughter. Several of them were present on the following Sunday, when his funeral sermon was preached by his former pupil, the Rev. Thomas Hincks, of Leeds, who gave a just and discriminating view of his character. His discourse was, at the same time, well calculated to remove any prejudice which might have existed in the minds of the hearers against Mr. Wellbeloved's religious principles. Subsequently, at the annual meeting

of death. To stand around such a grave is a painful task; but how sure an alleviation of the mourner's sorrow is the certainty which the Christian doctrine affords, that beyond the grave are the mansions of blessed spirits, regions of immortal joy, into which they also will, at no distant period, be conveyed, and there once more join their beloved parent, listen again to the accents so long dear to them, and aid the general song of praise to him who has realised all their glorious hopes."—Sermon on the Death of Robert Cappe, M.D., p. 23.

of the Philosophical Society, it was determined to place some permanent memorial of him in the Museum. A tablet, with an inscription commemorating his services as Curator, and his writings in the department of archæology, has accordingly been erected in the upper room of the building, in which the antiquities arranged and described by him are deposited. On the application of the Society, Mr. W. R. Wood kindly allowed a copy of the portrait referred to in page 161 to be made, which has been placed in the vestibule of the Museum. Another copy, subscribed for by members of the congregation, has been placed in the vestry of the chapel, which thus contains, along with the portraits of Sir John and Lady Hewley, those of the entire succession of ministers since the foundation in 1692—Dr. Colton, Mr. Hotham, Mr. Cappe, and Mr. Wellbeloved. The York Subscription Library and the York Institute have also placed on their walls a copy of the engraving. His pupils, in various parts of England, did not allow his death to pass without expressing in their public services their veneration for his character and their gratitude for his instructions. The Rev. William Gaskell, who had been prevented, by absence in Scotland, from filling the pulpit in St. Saviourgate on the Sunday after his decease, published, at the request of his hearers, the sermon which he preached in Cross Street Chapel, Manchester, in which ample justice

is done to the services which he had rendered to
the world, and his devotion to the cause of Christian
truth.

———————

The narrative of Mr. Wellbeloved's life will, it
is hoped, have afforded even those to whom he was
not personally known a distinct idea of his intellectual and moral character, and precluded the necessity of a formal summary. There may, however,
be some traits of both which it is the duty of
a biographer especially to bring into notice.

His acquisitions of knowledge were laboriously
made. He was accustomed to speak of his own
memory more disparagingly than accorded with
the extent and variety of the objects which it
embraced. But it was not a philological memory,
and his principal and professional studies lying in
this department, he felt the want of facility in acquiring a knowledge of language, which he endeavoured to supply by classification, by laying hold
of the rational and philosophical principles of ety-
mology and grammar,* and by the copious use of
extracts and memoranda. His attainments in philology were, nevertheless, very extensive. Besides

* One of the projects of his earlier life had been an English
Grammar, on the principles of Horne Tooke.

reading with facility Greek and Latin authors, he had a thorough knowledge of Hebrew, Chaldee, and Syriac, and was sufficiently versed in Arabic for the purpose of comparative criticism. French and Italian were familiar to him, and he understood German so far as to be able to avail himself of translations and commentaries in that language. The results of his careful investigations might be relied on for their accuracy, though he had not that promptitude in producing what he knew, which sometimes gains the possessor credit for more knowledge than belongs to him. The consciousness of a want of the quickness required for extemporaneous discussions, joined with general diffidence, made him always reluctant to engage in them, lest he should do injustice to his own convictions of truth. Extemporaneous speaking, indeed, though the occasion was foreseen, was always a painful effort to him.

His literary tastes partook of the simplicity and purity of his moral nature. His own style, somewhat diffuse in his pulpit compositions, was perfectly free from affectation and artifice. He never aimed at effect by antithesis or rhetorical ornament. He dealt sparingly in figures, and used them, when at all, not for colouring but for illustration. His language was that of the classical prose authors of the last century. Not only in his writings, but even in his conversation, where men allow them-

selves more latitude, he studiously avoided whatever seemed to him to corrupt the purity of our
language, whether imported from the West or borrowed from the vulgar dialect of our own country.
His favourite authors, ancient and modern, were
those who join simple style to natural sentiment,
and display human nature and human life under
pleasing aspects.   He delighted in pathetic fiction,
if the author, in his delineations of sorrow and
suffering, had not passed the limits beyond which
sympathy becomes torture ; but he was repelled
from those who, in diving into the depths of the
human heart and revealing its misery, seem to aim
at inflicting unmitigated pain on their readers.
Like most men of quick sensibility he relished genial
humour, and thoroughly enjoyed the early works
of Dickens ; not so the hard satire by which other
novelists have acquired reputation.   The same
kindly and candid temper which made him lenient
in his judgment of individual character, and disposed him to think well of those with whom he
had intercourse, and to speak cautiously and mildly
when he disapproved, was irreconcileable with a
taste for pictures of society by writers, whose skill
is shown in analysing human motives, to detect
their impure ingredients, and reducing virtue to
a *caput mortuum* of selfishness.   I do not know that
he ever wrote poetry of the serious class, but when

his mind was at ease, especially in the earlier part of his life, he often amused his friends by sportive verses.

Mr. Wellbeloved has published a sufficient number of sermons to enable a reader of them to judge of his style and manner, as an argumentative and controversial preacher. These more elaborate sermons are not, however, the most characteristic of his mind. In his ordinary pulpit-services he very rarely introduced the disputed points of Christian theology. The truths, the promises, the requirements of the Gospel, in their bearing on the Christian life, were the themes on which he delighted to dwell. In addressing his flock he felt none of that restraint or reserve which ordinarily checked the free expression of his feelings. So much was this the case, that those who knew intimately the course of his life, could often trace, in the sermon of the Sunday, the impression which the events of the week, or the state of his own mind had made upon him, though unrevealed in his intercourse with them. It had thus a freshness of feeling, and a directness of application, which are often wanting in discourses treating upon a theme selected for no special reason, but from the necessity of meeting a weekly demand. After he had surmounted the difficulty of composition which he had felt in early life, the preparation for the Sunday was a pleasure to him, and the duties of the day a

delight.   Often, however, during the busiest period
of his life, the time which could be allotted to this
preparation was short, and the discourse was
finished in haste.   I have no doubt that this circumstance, joined with the severe judgment which
he always passed on his own productions, induced
him to direct the destruction of all his sermons.
The cessation of his College duties allowed him
more time to prepare for the pulpit, and he never
addressed his flock with greater energy and effect,
than during the years which intervened between
this event and the commencement of his decline.

From the specimen of his practical discourses,
afforded by the two entitled " Admonitions to the
Young," published in Dr. Beard's Volume of
Family Sermons, some judgment may be formed
of the wise counsels, the affectionate exhortations,
the appropriate use of scriptural precepts, to which
his hearers had the privilege of listening.   It was
his custom annually to address the young people of
his congregation on a Sunday near the beginning
of the year.   One feature in his sermons could not
escape the notice of any attentive habitual hearer.
His exegesis of the New Testament, as we have
seen, led him to differ widely from readers of the
Bible in general, as to the meaning of many
passages both in the Gospels and the Epistles.
Attributing to them a more limited application
than they are commonly supposed to bear, he would

have considered himself as " handling the word of
God deceitfully," if he had not explained what he
thought their true original meaning, although by
the acknowledgment that they were accommodated
to a sense not originally intended, the force of the
text, as the authoritative enunciation of a truth or
a precept, was somewhat impaired. The practical
reflections which he has subjoined to the portions of
the Old Testament translated by him show, how he
excelled in drawing instruction from the events and
characters of sacred history, enforcing the precepts
of holy men of old, or, if necessary, expanding them,
by an infusion of the more comprehensive spirit of
the Gospel. As biography was always a favourite
study with him, so the biography of Scripture frequently supplied the subject of his sermons. Among
these some of his hearers will, I doubt not, remember a series on the family of Bethany—Lazarus
and his sisters—as peculiarly interesting, from the
skill with which their several characters are delineated and contrasted, and the feeling with
which the writer entered into the friendly relations
subsisting between our Lord and them. One of
the series was preached in Manchester, in 1829,
and Dr. Beard requested a copy of it for publication in his volume; but the application was
declined, on the ground that the author was unwilling to detach it from the rest. Had he published

R

a volume, as he once intended, these discourses I
believe would have been included.

His delivery was, like everything else, unaffected
and natural.   He used no action and practised no
elocutionary arts, but his mode of address was
earnest and animated, at times deeply pathetic.
His ear was correct, his voice melodious, and more
powerful than would be believed by those who
heard him only in the small place in which he
usually spoke.   Had it been as easy to correct what
is faulty as to furnish a good model, his pupils
would have needed nothing but his example for
acquiring a free, distinct, and manly delivery.
Such was the opinion expressed by one of the most
judicious teachers of elocution—the late Mr. Bart-
ley—when he visited York for the purpose of
giving instruction to the students.

To those who are acquainted with his Devotional
Exercises, it will be unnecessary to describe the
manner in which he conducted social worship.
Religious feeling was a part of his inmost nature,
but the expression of it was regulated by the same
sound judgment which characterized him in other
respects.   As there was nothing ascetic in his rule
of life, nothing romantic in his philanthropy,
nothing morbid in his conscientiousness, so there
was nothing mystical or overstrained in his devotion.   His prayers were the expression, from the

Christian point of view, of the feelings, the wants, and the convictions which the condition of human nature, the experience of life, and the suggestions of conscience, make common to all mankind in whom any sense of religion exists. Their language was always simple and scriptural, such as the humblest member of his congregation could understand, and make his own. In his prayers, as in his discourses, he was careful, when freely and appropriately using the language of the Bible, not to pervert it from its true signification, and especially not to fall into the exaggerated strain, which is the result of employing indiscriminately its strongest confessions of moral depravity, or its most fervent effusions of religious emotion, as exponents of the feelings of a body of worshippers.

During the greater part of his ministerial life his engagements were so numerous and urgent, that he had little time for visiting his flock, who regretted that they had not the means of becoming more intimately acquainted with their pastor. They knew, however, that he did not neglect them for the purpose of cultivating the society of others of higher rank; they were proud of the position to which his attainments and his devotion to objects of public utility had raised him among his fellow-citizens; and they were assured that they might reckon upon his presence and sympathy, whenever he could administer consolation to the bereaved, or strength and resignation to the suffering. Probably, in his case, what was at first a necessity grew by degrees into a habit, coinciding as it did with other habits and tastes, the result of a life much devoted to study. From the great length of his life he had survived the friends of his youth and middle age, and, I think, felt the loneliness and want of cheerful society which was the result of this isolation, the place of those whom death had removed not having been supplied.

For many years he mixed little with general society, and almost withdrew from it after his wife's death. It had been otherwise during the earlier part of his residence in York, when he entered freely into it, and had been a welcome guest in its most polished circles. He was full of information and ready to communicate it, but had little relish for the commonplace topics of conversation. He took great pleasure, however, in the friendly meetings of the members of the Yorkshire Philosophical Society, which were held at the Museum on Monday evenings, for the reading of papers on subjects of archæology and science, and their subsequent conversational discussion. For many years he was the chairman of these meetings, and from papers read by him in his turn several of his archæological works had their origin.

The characteristic feature of Mr. Wellbeloved's mind was benevolence. It beamed in his eye;

it spoke in his voice; it diffused itself over his manner, which was kind and courteous to every one, of whatever rank or condition, with whom he had intercourse.   It might be truly said of him that he was "a man made to be loved."   I know from himself that his temper was naturally warm, and that it had cost him considerable efforts of self-discipline to subdue it; but these efforts had been so successful as to have brought it completely under control.   Besides devoting a large portion of his time and thoughts to objects of public benefit, and supporting them by subscription, he gave liberally in private charity, and could with difficulty refrain from complying with an application for relief, till Mendicity Reports and the experience of fraud had taught him to restrain the impulse of his feelings. Entire disinterestedness appeared in all his actions; indeed, it was evident that the work in which he most delighted was that which was to bring no emolument to himself.

His character was altogether a natural one.   No one had ever reason to suspect a covert meaning in his words, or a concealed purpose in his actions. The confidence inspired by his sincerity was an important element in the influence which he exercised.   Through reserve and diffidence he might be misunderstood by a stranger, but affection and esteem always resulted from longer and more intimate knowledge.   There was no affectation in the

humility with which he judged and spoke of himself; it was a genuine sentiment, and while it prevented him from seeking to lead, and induced him
to prefer others in honour before himself, it led
him also to defer to the opinion of those whose
judgment he esteemed, and not to decline the work
which they thought him competent to perform.

Possessing such qualities it is unnecessary to say
that he was the object of his children's reverential
affection.   I believe that after the years of un-
thinking childhood were passed, a purpose of
wilful disobedience to his authority never entered
their minds.   And this authority was maintained
without harshness, even of words; the silent cessation of the usual marks of love was sufficient;
it was indeed the severest rebuke that could have
been given.   The effect of his multiplied engagements was, that he had less time to bestow on the
literary education of his children than he could
have desired.   This, and the limitation of domestic
intercourse with them, arising from the same cause,
were the most costly of all the sacrifices which he
made to the calls of public duty.   The instruction
which he could not himself give them was, however,
carefully provided from other sources, and the life of
their excellent mother was happily prolonged till
they had all attained to maturity.   His biography
has shown by what multiplied bereavements his domestic affections had been tried.   More than half

his family had been removed by death before him, and of the survivors only a daughter remained near him, in the closing years of his life. A testimony more impartial than my own has declared, that by her the duties of filial love were watchfully and tenderly fulfilled.*

Had he anticipated that he should have a biographer, his injunction to him would have been *De me nil nisi verum.* Such a truthful picture, rather than a mere panegyric, it has been my object to give in the preceding pages. I believe that those who knew him will recognize in them the qualities which attracted their esteem and love; and that strangers, if they read them, will understand the veneration in which his memory is held by those to whom he sustained the relations of a parent, a pastor, a tutor, or a friend.

* Christian Reformer, January 1859, p. 31.

APPENDIX.

I.

LIST OF MR. WELLBELOVED'S PUBLICATIONS.

1. The Principles of Roman Catholics and Unitarians contrasted; a Sermon preached Nov. 5, 1799, to a Congregation of Protestant Dissenters, in St. Saviourgate, York. 1799. Second ed. 1800.

2. Devotional Exercises for Young Persons. 12mo. 1801. Eighth ed. 1832.

3. A Sermon preached on Wednesday, Oct. 19, 1803, the Day of National Humiliation. 1803.

·4. A Sermon preached Dec. 26, 1802, on occasion of the death of Robert Cappe, M.D., with a Memoir. 1803.

5. A Guide to the Cathedral Church of St. Peter's, York, commonly called York Minster. 12mo. 1804. Often reprinted.

6. Memoirs of the Life and Writings of the Rev. Wm. Wood, F.L.S., with an Address delivered at his Interment, and a Sermon on Occasion of his Death, preached Sunday, April 10, 1808. 1809.

7. Objects of Pursuit proper for Young Persons who have received a Liberal Education; a Sermon preached in the Chapel in St. Saviourgate, York, Sunday, June 24, 1810. 1811.

8. The Religious and Moral Improvement of Mankind, the constant End of the Divine Government; a Sermon preached at an Annual Meeting of Protestant Dissenting Ministers, Thursday, June 8, 1815. 1815.

9. The Doctrine of Instantaneous Conversion from Sin to Holiness, a Doctrine unsupported by Scripture; a Sermon preached before the Association of Unitarian Christians residing at Gainsbro', Hull, Thorne, and adjacent Places, Wednesday, Sept. 30, 1818. 1818.

10. The Holy Bible, a New Translation, with Introductory Remarks and Notes Explanatory and Critical, and Practical Reflections, designed principally for the Use of Families. 4to. 1819—1838.

11. The Nature and Reward of Christian Watchfulness; a Sermon, preached in the Chapel in St. Saviourgate, York, Aug. 5, 1821, on occasion of the Death of Mrs. Catharine Cappe. 1821.

12. The Charge· at the Ordination of the Rev. J. J. Taylor. 1821.

13. Three Letters to the Ven. and Rev. Francis Wrangham, M.A. 1823. 2nd ed. 1823.

14. Three Additional Letters to the same. 1824.

15. Unitarians not guilty of denying the Lord that bought them; a Sermon preached before the Association of Unitarian Christians, residing at Hull, Thorne, Lincoln, and adjacent Places, at Hull, Sept. 1823. 1824.

16. A Sermon preached Jan. 23, 1825, to a Congregation of Protestant Dissenters, in St. Saviourgate, York, in Aid of a Subscription for the Erection of a Unitarian Chapel in Calcutta. 1825.

17. The Mystery of Godliness; a Sermon preached at Halifax, May 11, 1825, before the Members of the West Riding Tract Society. 1825.

18. Sermons on Various Practical Subjects, by the late Rev. Thomas Watson, to which is prefixed a brief Memoir of his Life and Writings, by C. W. 1826.

19. The large Extent of the Subjects of Knowledge, a Motive for Diffidence and Humility; an Address to the Members of the York Mechanics' Institute. 1828.

20. Account of the ancient and present state of the Abbey of St. Mary, York, by the Rev. C. Wellbeloved, being part of Vol. V. of the *Vetusta Monumenta*, published by the Society of Antiquaries. Fol. 1829.

21. A Letter addressed to the Subscribers to the Restoration of the Choir of York Minster, on the proposed Removal of the Screen. 1830.

22. A Second Letter, addressed to the Subscribers, &c. 1830.

23. Eburacum; or, York under the Romans. 1842.

24. Memoir of Thomas Thrush, Esq., formerly an Officer of Rank in the Royal Navy, who resigned his Commission on the Ground of the Unreasonableness of War. 1845.

25. Descriptive Account of the Antiquities in the Museum of the Yorkshire Philosophical Society. 1852. Third ed. 1858.

The first volume of the Proceedings of the Yorkshire Philosophical Society (1855) contains papers by Mr. Wellbeloved on a hoard of stycas discovered at Bolton Percy ; a discovery of silver coins at Deighton; on a Compotus of St. Mary's Abbey; and on a Roman inscription, of the age of Trajan, recently discovered in York.

II.

The annexed List is taken from the Appendix to a Pamphlet, printed in 1840, and containing a Report of the Proceedings referred to in p. 201.

LIST OF STUDENTS educated at Manchester College, York, under the Rev. CHARLES WELLBELOVED (taken from the College Roll).

NAME.		DATES OF ADMISSION.	
Henry Howson	. D.	September,	1803
John Jones	. D.	,,	1803
—— Lewis	. D.	,,	1803
Daniel Jones	. D.	,,	1803

NAMES.		DATES OF ADMISSION.	
George Stokes	L.	September,	1803
George Nicholson	L.	„	1803
Thomas Henry Robinson	L.	„	1803
Samuel Robinson Philips	L.	„	1803
John Woodhouse Simpson	L.	„	1804
Henry Davies	D.	January,	1805
Griffith Roberts	D.	September,	1805
Thomas Madge	D.	„	1805
John Smethurst	D.	„	1805
John Gooch Robberds	D.	„	1805
Thomas Eyre Lee	L.	„	1805
Sidney Shore	L.	„	1805
George Withington	L.	„	1805
Joseph Hunter	D.	January,	1806
William Turner, jun., M.A.	D.	September,	1806
Richard Astley	D.	„	1806
Arthur Dean	D.	September,	1806
Samuel Marsland	L.	„	1806
Joseph Godman	L.	„	1807
James Darbishire, jun.	L.	„	1807
James Yates, M.A.	D.	„	1808
Miles Fletcher	L.	„	1808
William Scatcherd	L.	„	1808
Henry Lee	L.	„	1808
Abraham Manley	D.	„	1809
Lewis Lewis	D.	„	1809
Richard B. W. Sanderson	L.	„	1809
Jacob Brettell	D.	„	1809
Joseph Ashton	D.	„	1809
Thomas Crompton Holland	D.	„	1809
Hugh Ker	L.	„	1809
John Cooke	L.	„	1809
William Hincks	D.	„	1809
Charles Wellbeloved	L.	„	1809
Joseph Hutton, B.A.	D.	„	1810
Henry Turner	D.	„	1810
Robert Wallace	D.	„	1810
Henry Edward Howse	L.	„	1810
Joseph Douglas Strutt	L.	„	1810
William Johnstone Bakewell	D.	„	1810
Robert Mackay	L.	„	1810

NAME.		DATES OF ADMISSION.
George Kenrick	D.	December, 1810
James Grahame	L.	„ 1810
Benjamin Mardon	D.	September, 1811
John Strutt	L.	„ 1811
Samuel Robinson	L.	„ 1811
Robert Philips	L.	„ 1811
Samuel Smith	L.	„ 1811
Allen Harrison	L.	„ 1811
William Jevons, jun.	D.	„ 1812
William Gurdon Peene	D.	„ 1812
Wharton Crompton	L.	September, 1812
John Bentley	L.	„ 1812
William Andrew Mitchell	L.	„ 1812
Patrick Cannon	D.	„ 1813
John Haslam	D.	„ 1813
John Stratton	L.	„ 1813
Archibald Kenrick	L.	„ 1813
William Houldsworth	L.	„ 1813
John Williams Morris	D.	„ 1814
Offley Shore	L.	„ 1814
John James Tayler, B.A.	D.	„ 1814
James Taylor	D.	„ 1814
Charles Howes	L.	„ 1814
John Bond	L.	December, 1815
Samuel Wood	D.	September, 1815
Charles Thompson	D.	„ 1815
John Wellbeloved	D.	„ 1815
William Needham	L.	„ 1815
Thomas Henry Potter	L.	„ 1815
Peter Heywood	L.	„ 1815
Francis Fletcher	L.	„ 1815
George Crompton	L.	„ 1815
John Charles Langlands	L.	„ 1815
Thomas Benyon	L.	„ 1815
Joshua Stanger	L.	„ 1815
William Burton	D.	February, 1816
William Worsley	D.	September, 1816
George Barker Wawne	D.	„ 1816
Gilbert Wakefield Macmurdo	L.	„ 1816
William Wilson	D.	„ 1816
George Cheetham	D.	„ 1816

NAME.		DATES OF ADMISSION.	
Nicholas Samuel Heincken	. . . .	D.	September, 1816
John Owen	. . . . .	D.	„ 1816
Thomas Sanden Watson	. . .	L.	„ 1816
Andrew Kippis Watson	. . . .	L.	„ 1816
Mark Philips	. . . . .	L.	„ 1816
John Hall	. . . . .	L.	„ 1816
John Yate Lee	. . . .	L.	„ 1816
William Henry Fletcher	. . .	L.	„ 1816
George Huntley Fielding	. . .	L.	„ 1816
Nicholas William Gibson	. . .	L.	„ 1816
Charles Wallace	. . . .	D.	„ 1817
Richard Smith	. . . .	D.	„ 1817
Daniel Lister	. . . .	L.	„ 1817
William Enfield	. . . .	L.	„ 1817
Edward Strutt	. . . .	L.	„ 1817
Nathaniel Lister	. . . .	L.	„ 1817
Robert Lightbody	. . . .	L.	„ 1817
Richard Shawcross	. . . .	D.	„ 1817
John Marshall	. . . .	L.	„ 1817
Evan Evans	. . . . .	D.	„ 1818
Dawson Hamilton Rowan	. . .	L.	„ 1818
John Pemberton Heywood	. . .	L.	„ 1818
James H. Payne	. . . .	D.	October, 1818
William Henry Tayleur	. . .	L.	September, 1819
John Chatfield	. . . .	L.	„ 1819
Henry Enfield	. . . .	L.	„ 1819
John Howard Ryland	. . .	D.	„ 1819
Joseph Benyon	. . . .	L.	„ 1819
Richard Martineau	. . . .	L.	„ 1819
Oliver A. Heywood	. . . .	L.	„ 1819
Edmund Kell, M.A.	. . .	D.	„ 1820
John Relly Beard	. . . .	D.	„ 1820
John Reynell Wreford	. . . .	D.	„ 1820
James Carter	. . . .	L.	„ 1820
Edward Tagart	. . . .	D.	„ 1820
John Kingdon	. . . .	L.	„ 1820
Robert Chatfield	. . . .	L.	„ 1820
John Hugh Worthington	. . .	D.	January, 1821
William Bowen, M.A.	. . . .	D.	September, 1821
John Mitchelson	. . . .	D.	„ 1821
William S. Brown	. . . .	D.	„ 1821

NAME.		DATES OF ADMISSION.
John Woodhouse Crompton	L.	September, 1821
Franklin Howorth	D.	,, 1821
Timothy Hawkes	D.	,, 1821
John Smale	D.	,, 1821
Joseph Busk	L.	October, 1821
George Lee, jun.	D.	September, 1821
Alfred Christie	L.	,, 1821
Robert Brook Aspland	D.	,, 1822
Edward Thomas Busk	L.	,, 1822
Edward Talbot	D.	,, 1822
Brooks Crompton	L.	,, 1822
James Martineau	D.	,, 1822
William Talbot	L.	,, 1822
William Holt	L.	,, 1822
Arthur Tozer Clout	D.	,, 1822
Robert L. Bolton	L.	,, 1822
Stephen Cornish Freeman	L.	,, 1822
Henry William Busk	L.	,, 1823
Francis Rankin	D.	,, 1823
Robert Bayly, jun.	L.	,, 1823
Pilkington Crompton	L.	,, 1823
Edward Higginson, jun.	D.	,, 1823
Francis Darbishire	D.	,, 1823
Joseph Dawson	L.	,, 1823
John Paget	L.	,, 1823
Henry Squire	D.	October, 1823
Nathaniel R. Philipps	D.	November, 1823
Edward Whitfield	D.	,, 1823
Joseph Ketley	D.	September, 1824
Samuel William Cockroft	D.	,, 1824
Henry Robinson Hurst	L.	,, 1824
John Taylor	L.	,, 1824
Richard Taylor	L.	,, 1824
Peter Marsland, jun.	L.	,, 1824
Thomas Davis	D.	,, 1824
William Gaskell, M.A.	D.	,, 1824
Henry W. G. Wreford	D.	,, 1825
Edmund Lonsdale	L.	,, 1825
Charles Fletcher	L.	,, 1825
Samuel Bache	D.	,, 1825
Alfred Paget	L.	,, 1825

NAME.						DATES OF ADMISSION.	
Charles Davidson	.	.	.	.	. L.	September,	1825
Thomas Johnson	.	.	.	.	. L.	„	1825
Charles Danvers Hort	.	.	.	.	. D.	„	1826
Samuel Nicholson	.	.	.	.	. D.	„	1826
- Henry Hunt Piper, jun.		.	.	.	. D.	„	1826
Robert Mitford Taylor	.	.	.	.	. D.	„	1826
George Heaviside	.	.	.	.	. D.	„	1826
Arthur Paget	.	.	.	.	. L.	„	1826
George Paget		.	.	.	. L.	„	1826
Edward Johnson	.	.	.	.	. L.	„	1826
Edward Enfield	.	.	.	.	. L.	„	1826
Thomas Tertius Baker	.	.	.	.	. D.	„	1827
George Whelton Swallow		.	.	.	. D.	„	1827
Edward Worthington		.	.	.	. L.	„	1827
Mortimer Maurice	.	.	.	.	. D.	„	1827
Henry Hawkes		.	.	.	. D.	„	1827
Patrick Corcoran	.	.	.	.	. D.	„	1828
Josephus Rowe Cummins		.	.	.	. D.	„	1828
John Colston	.	.	.	.	. D.	„	1828
John Johns	.	.	.	.	. D.	„	1828
Classon Emmett Porter		.	.	.	. D.	„	1828
Mark Rowntree	.	.	.	.	. D.	„	1829
William Rayner Wood	.	.	.	.	. L.	„	1829
Henry Higginson	.	.	.	.	. D.	„	1829
Charles William Robberds		.	.	.	. D.	„	1829
John Lampray		.	.	.	. D.	„	1830
Cuthbert Relf Greenhow		.	.	.	. L.	„	1830
Samuel Reid	.	.	.	.	. L.	„	1830
Walter Coupland Perry		.	.	.	. D.	„	1831
Evan Evans	.	.	.	.	. D.	„	1831
George Hutton	.	.	.	.	. D.	„	1831
Samuel Fielden	.	.	.	.	. L.	„	1831
Ogden Bolton	.	.	.	.	. L.	„	1831
Robert Needham Philips		.	.	.	. L.	„	1831
Alfred Turner Blyth	.	.		.	. D.{	„	1831
						„	1837
Francis Hart	.	.	.	.	. L.	February,	1832
John Robberds	.	.	.	.	. D.	September,	1832
Marmaduke C. Frankland		.	.	.	. D.	„	1832
John Ebenezer Williams		.	.	.	. D.	„	1832
John Kendall	.	.	.	.	. D.	„	1832

NAME.						DATES OF ADMISSION.	
John Woodhouse Simpson, jun.	.	.	.	.	. L.	. September,	1832
James Milnes Stansfeld	.	.	.	..	. L.	,,	1832
James Nixon Porter	.	.	.	.	. D.	,,	1833
Russell Lant Carpenter	.	.	.	.	. D.	,,	1833
George Winchester Philp	.	.	.	.	. D.	,,	1833
John Harrison	.	.	.	.	. D.	,,	1833
William Mountford	. .	.	.	.	. D.	,,	1833
William Blake	.	.	.	.	. L.	,,	1833
John Dakin Gaskell	.	.	..	..	. L.	,,	1833
Thomas Hincks	.	.	.	.	. D.	,,	1833
Frederick Hornblower	.	.	.	.	. D.	,,	1834
Thomas Houldsworth M'Connel	.	.	.	. L.	,,	1834
Joseph Roberts	.	.	.	.	. D.	,,	1834
Jacob Charles Brettell	.	.	.	.	. D.	,,	· 1834
Arthur Lupton, jun.	.	.	.	.	. L.	,,	1835
William Hargreaves Cowling	.	.	.	. D.	,,	1835
Richard Yale	.	.	.	.	. L.	January,	1835
Alfred Alsop	.	.	.	.	. L.	,,	1836
George Vance Smith	.	.	.	.	. D.	,,	1836
John Briggs	.	.	.	.	. D. .	,,	1836
Philip Pearsall Carpenter	.	.	.	. D.	,,	1837
William Henry Herford	.	.	.	. D.	,,	1837
Richard Shaen	.	.	.	.	. D.	,,	1838
George Heap	.	.·	.	.	. D.	,,	1838
David Davis	.	.	.	.	. D.	,,	1838

Lately Published,

PRICE SIX SHILLINGS,

𝕿𝖍𝖊 𝕳𝖔𝖑𝖞 𝕾𝖈𝖗𝖎𝖕𝖙𝖚𝖗𝖊𝖘 𝖔𝖋 𝖙𝖍𝖊 𝕺𝖑𝖉 𝕮𝖔𝖛𝖊𝖓𝖆𝖓𝖙,

IN A REVISED TRANSLATION.

VOL. I.

Containing the Five Books of Moses, with the Books of Joshua,
Judges, and Ruth.

By the late Rev. CHARLES WELLBELOVED.

Woodfall and Kinder, Printers, Angel Court, Skinner Street, London.